THE VACATIONERS

This Large Print Book carries the
Seal of Approval of N.A.V.H.

THE VACATIONERS

EMMA STRAUB

WHEELER PUBLISHING
A part of Gale, Cengage Learning

GALE
CENGAGE Learning·

Farmington Hills, Mich • San Francisco • New York • Waterville, Maine
Meriden, Conn • Mason, Ohio • Chicago

GALE
CENGAGE Learning®

LIBRARY OF CONGRESS CATALOGING-IN-PUBLICATION DATA

Straub, Emma.
   The vacationers / by Emma Straub. — Large print edition.
     pages ; cm (Wheeler publishing large print hardcover)
     ISBN 978-1-4104-7234-2 (hardcover) — ISBN 1-4104-7234-5 (hardcover)
     1. Young women—Fiction. 2. Majorca (Spain)—Fiction. 3. Family
vacations—Fiction. 4. Large type books. I. Title.
     PS3619.T74259V33 2014b
     813'.6—dc23   2014018153

Published in 2014 by arrangement with Riverhead Books, a member of Penguin Group (USA) LLC, a Penguin Random House Company

Printed in the United States of America
1 2 3 4 5 6 7 18 17 16 15 14

For River,
with a lifetime of
family vacations ahead

It is not so much a matter of traveling as of getting away; which of us has not some pain to dull, or some yoke to cast off?
— GEORGE SAND, *Winter in Majorca*

I'll be the desert island
where you can be free
I'll be the vulture
you can catch and eat
— THE MAGNETIC FIELDS, "Desert Island"

DAY ONE

Leaving always came as a surprise, no matter how long the dates had been looming on the calendar. Jim had packed his suitcase the night before, but now, moments before their scheduled departure, he was wavering. Had he packed enough books? He walked back and forth in front of the bookshelf in his office, pulling novels out by their spines and then sliding them back into place. Had he packed his running shoes? Had he packed his shaving cream? Elsewhere in the house, Jim could hear his wife and their daughter in similar last-minute throes of panic, running up and down the stairs with one last item that had been forgotten in a heap by the door.

There were things that Jim would have taken out of his bags, if it had been possible: the last year of his life, and the five before that, when it came to his knees; the way Franny looked at him across the dinner table at night; the feeling of himself inside a new mouth for the first time in three decades, and how much he wanted to stay there; the emptiness waiting on the other side of the return flight, the blank days he would have to fill and fill and fill. Jim sat down at his desk and waited for someone to tell him that he was needed elsewhere.

Sylvia waited in front of the house, staring down 75th Street, toward Central Park. Both of her parents were the type that believed that a taxi would always present itself at just the right moment, especially on summer weekends, when traffic in the city was lightest. Sylvia thought that was horseshit. The only thing worse than spending two of her last six weeks before leaving for college on vacation with her parents would be missing the flight and having to spend one of those final nights sleeping upright in an airport lounge, a stained seat cushion as her only comfort. She would get the taxi herself.

It wasn't as if she wanted to spend the whole summer in Manhattan, which turned into a melting concrete armpit. The idea of Mallorca was appealing, in theory: it was an island, which promised little waves and nice breezes, and she could practice her Spanish, which she had done well in during high school. Everyone — literally everyone — from her graduating class was doing nothing all summer long, just taking turns hosting parties when their parents went to Wainscott or Woodstock or somewhere else with wood-shingled houses that looked distressed on purpose. Sylvia had looked at their faces enough for the last eighteen years, and couldn't wait to get the hell out. Sure, yes, there were four other kids from her class going to Brown, but she never had to speak to them again if she didn't want to, and that was the plan. Find new friends. Make a new life. Finally be somewhere where the name Sylvia Post came without the ghosts of the girl she'd been at sixteen, at twelve, at five, where she was detached from her parents and her brother and she could just be, like an astronaut floating in space, unencumbered by gravity. Come to think of it, Sylvia wished that they were spending the whole summer abroad. This way, she would still have to suffer through August at home, when the parties were sure to reach their weepy and desperate apex. Sylvia did not plan to weep.

A taxi with its light on rounded the corner and came slowly toward her, bouncing its way over the potholes. Sylvia stuck one arm in the air and dialed her home phone number with her other hand. It rang and rang, and was ringing still when the taxi came to a halt. Her parents were inside, doing god knows what. Sylvia opened the door to the taxi and leaned into the backseat.

"It'll just be a minute," she said. "Sorry. My parents are on their way out." She paused. "They're the worst." This had not always been true, but it was now, and she wasn't shy about saying so.

The taxi driver nodded and clicked the meter on, clearly happy to sit there all day, if need be. The cab would have been blocking traffic, but there was no traffic to block. Sylvia was the only person in the city who seemed to be in a hurry. She hit redial, and this time her father answered after the first ring.

"Let's go," she said, without waiting for him to speak. "Car's here."

"Your mother is taking her time," Jim said. "We'll be out in five."

Sylvia clicked the phone off and scooched her way across the backseat of the taxi.

"They're on their way," she said. Sylvia leaned back and closed her eyes, feeling some of her hair catch on a piece of duct tape that was holding the seat together. It seemed like a genuine possibility that only one of her parents would come out of the house, and that would be it, the whole thing wrapped up like a shitty soap opera, with no satisfying resolution.

The meter ticked away, and they sat in silence, Sylvia and the taxi driver, for ten whole minutes. When Franny and Jim finally came bustling out of the house, the horns of all the cars now stalled behind the cab acted as a processional march, scolding and triumphant. Franny slid in next to her daughter, and Jim sat up front, the knees of his khakis pressing against the dashboard. Sylvia was neither happy nor unhappy to have both of her parents in the taxi, but she did experience a moment of relief, not that she would have admitted it out loud.

"On y va!" Franny said, pulling the door shut behind her.

"That's French," Sylvia said. "We're going to Spain."

"Andale!" Franny was already perspiring, and she fanned at her armpits with their passports. She was wearing her traveling outfit, carefully honed over flights and train rides in all corners of the world: a pair of black leggings, a black cotton tunic that reached her knees, and a gauzy scarf to keep her warm on the airplane. When Sylvia once asked her mother about her immutable

travel habits, her mother spat back, "At least I don't travel with a handle of whiskey like Joan Didion." When people asked what kind of writer her mother was, Sylvia usually said that she was like Joan Didion, only with an appetite, or like Ruth Reichl, but with an attitude problem. She did not say this to her mother.

The taxi pulled forward.

"No, no, no," Franny said, yanking her body toward the plexiglass divider. "Make a left here, then left again on Central Park West. We want to go to the airport, not New Jersey. Thank you." She sank back against the seat. "Some people," she said quietly, and stopped there. No one said anything for the rest of the ride, except to answer which airline they were flying to Madrid.

Sylvia always liked driving to the airport, because it meant traveling through a whole different part of the city, as separate from the corner she knew as Hawaii from the rest of the United States. There were detached houses and chain-link fences and abandoned lots, and kids riding their bikes in the street. It seemed like the kind of place people drove their cars to, which thrilled Sylvia to no end. Having a car sounded like something out of the movies. Her parents had had a car when she was little, but it grew creaky and expensive in the garage, and they'd finally sold it when she was still too young to appreciate what a luxury it was. Now whenever Franny or Jim spoke to someone who kept a car in Manhattan, they reacted with quiet horror, like people who'd been subjected to the rantings of a mentally ill person at a cocktail party.

Jim did his exercise walk around Terminal 7. He walked, or ran, for an hour every morning, and he didn't see why today should be any exception. It was something he and his son had in common, the need to move their bodies, to feel strong. Franny and Sylvia were quite content to sloth themselves into oblivion, to ossify on the sofa with a book or the godforsaken television blasting away. He could hear their muscles beginning to atrophy, but then, miraculously, they could still walk, and did, when properly motivated. Jim's usual route took him into Central Park, up to the reservoir, then across and back down the east side of the park, looping around the boathouse on his way home. The terminal had no such scenery to speak of, and no wildlife, save the few confused birds that had snuck their way in and were now trapped at JFK forever, chirping at one another about airplanes and misery. Jim kept his elbows high and his pace brisk. He was always astonished at how slowly people moved at airports — it was like being held captive in a shopping mall, all wide asses and deranged children. There were a few leashes, which Jim actually appreciated, though in conversation he would agree with Franny that such things were degrading. In practice, parents yanked their children out of Jim's path, and he walked on and on, past the Hudson News and the sports bar, all the way to the Au Bon Pain and back. The moving sidewalks were too crowded with luggage, so Jim walked just beside them, his long legs nearly beating the motorized track.

Jim had previously been to Spain on three occasions: in 1970, when he graduated from high school and spent the summer bumming around Europe with his best friend; in 1977, when he and Franny were newlyweds and could barely afford to go and had nothing but the very best ham sandwiches in the world; and then in 1992, when Bobby was eight, and they'd had to go to bed early every night, which meant they didn't eat a proper dinner for a week, except for what they ordered in from room service, which was about as authentically Spanish as a

16

hamburguesa. Who knew what Spain would be like now, its economic situation almost as tender as the Greeks'. Jim walked past their assigned gate and saw Franny and Sylvia deeply engaged in their books, sitting next to each other but not speaking, as comfortable being silent as only family members can be. Despite the many reasons not to, it was good that they were making this trip, he and Franny agreed. In the fall, Sylvia would be in Providence, smoking clove cigarettes with boys from her French cinema class, as far away from her parents as if she were in another galaxy. Her older brother, Bobby, now waist-deep in swampy Floridian real estate, had done it, too. At first, the separations seemed impossible, like severing a limb, but then it was off, and walking, and running, and now Jim could hardly remember what it was like to have Bobby under his roof. He hoped he would never feel that way about Sylvia, but he guessed that he would, and sooner than he might admit. The greater fear was that when Sylvia was gone, and the whole world began to be dismantled, brick by brick, that the time they had all spent together would seem like a fantasy, someone else's comfortably imperfect life.

It would be all of them in Mallorca: he

and Franny, Sylvia, Bobby and Carmen, his albatross of a girlfriend, and Franny's dear friend Charles and his boyfriend, Lawrence. Husband. They were married now, Jim sometimes forgot. They had all rented a house thirty minutes outside of Palma from Gemma Something-or-other, a British woman Franny knew a bit, an old friend of Charles's. The place looked clean in the photographs Gemma had sent via e-mail, sparsely furnished but with a good eye: white walls, odd rock clusters on the mantel, low leather sofas. The woman was in the art world, like Charles, and relaxed about having strangers in her house in a way that felt distinctly European, which made the whole exchange remarkably easy. All Jim and Fran had had to do was send a check, and it was all settled, the house and garden and swimming pool and a local Spanish tutor for Sylvia. Charles told them that Gemma would have been equally likely to let them have the house for nothing at all, but it was better this way, and a million times simpler than preparing Sylvia for summer camp had been those years ago.

Two weeks was enough time, a good solid chunk. It had been a month since Jim's last day at *Gallant,* and the days had passed so slowly, dripping in molasses, sticking to every possible surface, unwilling to let go. Two weeks away would make Jim feel like he had made a change and chosen this new, free life, like so many people his age did. He was still slim at sixty, pale blond hair still mostly intact, if a bit thin. It had always been thin, though, as Franny sometimes said when she caught Jim patting it in the mirror. He could run as many miles as he could at forty, and he could tie a bow tie in under a minute. All told, he thought he was in pretty good shape. Two weeks away was just what he needed.

Jim circled back around to the gate and let himself drop into the seat next to Franny, which made her shift on her bottom, swiveling her hips slightly so that her crossed legs were pointing toward Sylvia. Franny was reading *Don Quixote* for her book club, a group of women she despised, and she made little clucking noises as she read, perhaps anticipating the mediocre discussion that would follow.

"Have you really not read it before?" Jim asked.

"When I was in college. Who remembers?" Franny flipped the page.

"It's funny, I think," Sylvia said. Her parents turned to look at her. "We read it in the fall. It's funny and pathetic. Sort of like

Waiting for Godot, you know?"

"Mm-hmm," Franny said, looking back to the book.

Jim made eye contact with Sylvia over Franny's head and rolled his eyes. The flight would board soon, and then they'd be suspended in air. Having a daughter whose company he actually enjoyed was one of Jim's favorite accomplishments. The odds were against you, in all matters of family planning. You couldn't choose to have a boy or a girl; you couldn't choose to have a child who favored you over the other parent. You could only accept what came along naturally, and Sylvia had done just that, ten years after her brother. Bobby liked to use the word *accident,* but Jim and Franny preferred the word *surprise,* like a birthday party filled with balloons. They had been surprised, that much was true. The woman at the gate picked up her microphone and announced the pre-boarding call.

Franny closed her book and immediately began to gather her belongings — she liked to be among the first on board, as if she would have to elbow someone else for her assigned seat. It was the principle, Franny said. She wanted to get where she was going as quickly as possible, not like all these other lollygaggers who seemed like they'd be just as happy to stay in the airport forever, buying overpriced bottles of water and magazines they would eventually abandon in a seat pocket.

Jim and Franny sat side by side in reclining pods, seats that lowered almost completely flat, with Franny at the window and Jim on the aisle. Franny traveled enough to accrue the kind of frequent-flier miles that would make lesser women weep with envy, but she would have gladly paid for the larger seats regardless. Sylvia was thirty rows behind them, in coach. Teenagers and younger children did not need to sit in business class, let alone first — that was Franny's philosophy. The extra room was for people who could appreciate it, truly appreciate it, and she did. Sylvia's bones were still pliable — she could easily contort herself into a comfortable enough shape to fall asleep. Franny didn't give it another thought.

The plane was somewhere over the ocean, and the dramatic sunset had already completed its pink-and-orange display. The world was dark, and Jim stared over Franny's shoulder at the vast nothingness. Franny took sleeping pills, so that she could wake up feeling rested and have a leg up on the inevitable jet lag. She'd swallowed the

Ambien earlier than usual, immediately following takeoff, and was now fast asleep, snoring with her parted lips toward the window, her padded silk eye mask tethered to her head with a taut elastic band.

Jim unbuckled his seat belt and stood up to stretch his legs. He walked to the back of the first-class cabin and pulled aside the curtain to peer at the rest of the plane. Sylvia was so far back that he couldn't see her from where he stood, so he walked farther, and farther, until he could make her out. Hers was the only light on in the last several rows of the plane, and Jim found himself climbing over sleeping passengers' socked feet as he made his way to his daughter.

"Hey," he said, putting his hand on the seat in front of Sylvia's. She had her earbuds in, and nodded to the music, creating a shadow on the open pages of her notebook. She was writing, and hadn't noticed him approach.

Jim touched her on the shoulder. Startled, she looked up and yanked the white cord, pulling the headphones out. Tiny streams of music, unrecognizable to him, poured out of her lap. Sylvia hit an invisible button, and the music stopped. She folded her notebook closed and then crossed her wrists on top of it, further blocking her father's vision of her most intimate inner thoughts.

"Hey," she said. "What's up?"

"Not much," Jim said, crouching down to an uncomfortable squat, his back braced against the seat across the aisle. Sylvia didn't like seeing her father's body in unusual positions. She didn't like to think about the fact that her father had a body at all. Not for the first time in the last few months, Sylvia wished that her wonderful father, whom she loved very much, was in an iron lung and able to be moved only when someone else was nice enough to wheel him around.

"Mom asleep?"

"Of course."

"Are we there yet?"

Jim smiled. "Few more hours. Not so bad. Maybe you should try to sleep a little."

"Yeah," Sylvia said. "You, too."

Jim patted her again, his long, squared-off fingers cupping Sylvia's shoulder, which made her flinch. He turned to walk back to his seat, but Sylvia called after him by way of apology, though she wasn't quite sure if she was sorry.

"It's going to be fine, Dad. We'll have a good time."

Jim nodded at her, and began the slow trip back to his seat.

When he was safely gone, Sylvia opened her notebook again and went back to the list she'd been making: Things to Do Before College. So far, there were only four entries: 1. Buy extra-long sheets. 2. Fridge? 3. Get a tan. (Fake?) (Ha, kill me first.) (No, kill my parents.) 4. Lose virginity. Sylvia underlined the last item on the list and then drew some squiggles in the margin. That about covered it.

DAY TWO

Most of the other passengers on the small plane from Madrid to Mallorca were nattily dressed, white-haired Spaniards and Brits in frameless glasses headed to their vacation homes, along with a large clutch of noisy Germans who seemed to think they were headed for spring break. Across the aisle from Franny and Jim were two men in heavy black leather jackets, both of whom kept turning around to shout obscenity-laced slang at their leather-jacketed friend in the row behind. Their jackets were covered with sewn-on patches with acronyms for various associations that Franny gathered had to do with riding motorcycles — one with a picture of a wrench, one with a Triumph logo, several with pictures of Elvis. Franny narrowed her eyes at the men, trying to summon the look that said It Is Too Early for Your Voice to Be So Loud. The most boisterous of the three was sitting by the window, a moon-faced redhead with the complexion of a marathon runner in his twenty-fifth mile.

"Oi, Terry," he said, reaching over the seatback to smack his dozing friend on the head. "Napping's fer babies!"

"Yeah, well, you'd know all about it, then, wouldn't ya?" The sleeping friend picked his face up off his hand, revealing a creased cheek. He turned toward Franny and glowered. "Morning," he said. "Hope you're enjoying your in-flight entertainment."

"Are you an actual motorcycle gang?" Jim asked, leaning across the aisle. Younger editors at *Gallant* were always pitching features that had them test-driving expensive speed machines, but Jim had never ridden one himself.

"You could say that," the sleepy one said.

"I always wanted to have a motorcycle. Never happened."

"Not too late." Then the sleepy one returned his face to his hand and began to snore.

Franny rolled her eyes aggressively, but no one else was paying attention.

The ride was quick, and they landed in sun-drenched Palma in under an hour. Franny put on her sunglasses and shambled from the tarmac to the baggage claim like a

26

movie star who had relaxed into stout-bodied middle age. Commercial airlines were about as glamorous as Greyhound buses, but she could pretend. Franny had taken the Concorde twice, to Paris and back, and mourned the loss of the supersonic speed and the elaborately presented airplane food. Everyone in Palma seemed to be speaking German, and for a moment, Franny worried that they'd gotten off at the wrong place, as if she'd been asleep on the subway and missed her stop. It was a proper Mediterranean morning, bright and warm, with a hint of olive oil in the air. Franny felt pleased with her choice of venue: Mallorca was less cliché than the South of France, and less overrun by Americans than Tuscany. Of course it had an overbuilt shoreline and its share of terrible tourist-infested restaurants, but they would avoid all that. Islands, being harder to get to, naturally separated some of the wheat from the chaff, which was the entire philosophy behind places like Nantucket, where children grew up feeling entitled to private beaches and loud pants. But Franny didn't want too much of that elitist hooey — she wanted to please everyone, including the children, which meant having a big enough town nearby that people could go see movies dubbed into Spanish, if they wanted to fly the coop for a few hours. Jim had grown up in Connecticut and was therefore used to being marooned with his terrible family, but the rest of them were New Yorkers, which meant that having an escape route was necessary for one's sanity.

The house they'd rented was a twenty-minute drive from Palma proper, "straight up a hill," according to Gemma, which made Franny groan, averse as she was to location-mandated forms of cardiovascular exercise. But who needed to walk anywhere when they had so many bedrooms, and a swimming pool, within minutes of the ocean? The idea had been to be together, everyone nicely trapped, with card games and wine and all the fixings of satisfying summers at their fingertips. Things had changed in the last few months, but Franny still wanted it to be true that spending time with her family wasn't punishment, not like it would be with her parents, or with Jim's. Franny thought that the major accomplishment of her life was producing two children who seemed to like each other even when no one else was looking, though with ten years between them, Sylvia and Bobby had had very separate childhoods. Maybe that was the key to all good relationships, having oceans of time apart. It might not even have been true anymore — the children saw each other only on holidays, and on Bobby's infrequent visits home. Franny hoped that it was.

Jim sorted out the rental car while Franny and Sylvia waited for the bags. Even on vacation, Franny didn't see the point in being anything less than efficient — why should they all have to wait to do everything? Jim had to drive, anyway, because all European rental cars were stick, and Franny had only very rarely driven a stick since her high school drivers' education class in 1971. And anyway, there was no reason to spend more time than necessary at the airport. Franny wanted to get a good look at the house, go grocery shopping, pick bedrooms for everyone, find a spot where she could write, know which closet held the extra towels. She wanted to buy shampoo, and toilet paper, and cheese. The vacation wouldn't officially start until she'd taken a shower and eaten some olives.

"Mom," Sylvia said. She pointed to a black suitcase the size of a small coffin. "Is that yours?"

"No," Franny said, watching an even larger bag slide down the luggage chute. "That one."

"I don't know why you packed so much," Sylvia said. "It's only two weeks."

"It's all presents for you and your brother," Franny said, pinching Sylvia's narrow biceps. "All I brought is one extra shroud. Mothers don't need anything else, do they?"

Sylvia fluttered her lips like a horse and went to fetch her mother's bag.

"Oh, those guys," Sylvia said, and gestured with her chin toward the Too-Loud Motorcyclists. "I love them."

"They're overgrown children," Franny said, sighing loudly through her open mouth. "They should have gone to Ibiza."

"No, Mom, they're The Sticky Spokes Rock 'n' Roll Squad, see?"

Sleepy Terry had turned around to pick up his suitcase, a slightly incongruous orange rollie, exposing not only the pale crack of his bottom but also the back of his leather jacket, which read in giant block letters just as Sylvia had dictated.

"That's a terrible name," Franny said. "I bet they'll spend the whole week drunk and killing themselves on tiny little roads."

Sylvia had lost interest and was hurrying over to her own bag, now skidding down to the lip of the conveyer belt with a soft plop.

The Posts hadn't vacationed in years, not

like this. There were the summer rentals in Sag Harbor, the *unhampton,* as Franny liked to call it until it wasn't true anymore, and then the one-month-long stint in Santa Barbara when Sylvia was five and Bobby was fifteen, two entirely different trips happening at once, a nightmare at mealtimes. It was too hard to travel all together, Franny had decided. She took Bobby to Miami by himself when he was sixteen, and granted him mother-free afternoons in South Beach, a trip he would later claim as the inspiration for attending the University of Miami, a dubious honor for his mother, who then wished she'd taken him on a trip to Cambridge instead. Jim and Franny and Sylvia once spent a weekend in Austin, Texas, doing nothing but eating barbecue and waiting for the bats to emerge from under the bridge. And of course Franny was often traveling on her own, covering trends in Southern Californian cuisine for this magazine, or a New Mexican chili festival for that one, or eating her way across France, one flaky croissant after another. Most days of the year, Jim and Sylvia were at home, cobbling together an elaborate meal out of the leftovers in the fridge, or ordering in from one of the restaurants on Columbus Avenue, pretending to argue over the remote control.

31

Franny's own parents, the Golds of 41 Eastern Parkway, Brooklyn, New York, had never once taken her out of the country, and she took it as her duty to provide new experiences for her children. Sylvia's tongue would soften, her Spanish would go from New York Puerto Rican Spanish to Actual Spanish Spanish, and someday, some thirty or forty years down the road, when she was in Madrid or Barcelona and the language came back to her like her first lover, Franny knew that Sylvia would thank her for this trip, even if she was already dead.

The house was in the foothills of the Tramuntana Mountains, on the far side of the town of Puigpunyent, on the winding road that would eventually lead to Valldemossa. No one could pronounce *Puigpunyent* (the car rental agent had said *Pooch-poon-yen,* or something of the sort, unrepeatable with an American tongue), and so when Sylvia insisted on calling it Pigpen, Jim and Franny couldn't correct her, and Pigpen it was. Mallorcan Spanish wasn't the same as proper Spanish, which wasn't the same as Catalan. Franny's plan was to ignore the differences and just plow ahead — it was how she usually got along in foreign countries. Unless you were in France, most people were delighted to hear you try and fail to form the right words. Franny and Sylvia stared out opposite windows, Franny in the front and Sylvia in the back, while Jim drove. It was only twenty-five minutes from the airport, according to Gemma, but that seemed to be true only if you knew where you were going. Gemma was one of Franny's least favorite humans on the planet, for a number of reasons: 1. She was Charles's second-closest female friend. 2. She was tall and thin and blond, three automatic strikes. 3. She'd been shipped off to boarding school outside Paris and spoke perfect French, which Franny found profoundly show-offy, like doing a triple axel at the Rockefeller Center skating rink.

Heading up the mountain, Jim took several wrong turns on roads that looked too narrow to be two-way streets and not just someone's well-paved driveway, but no one particularly minded, because it gave them a better introduction to the island. Mallorca was a layer cake — the gnarled olive trees and spiky palms, the green-gray mountains, the chalky stone walls along either side of the road, the cloudless pale blue sky overhead. Though the day was hot, the mugginess of New York City was gone, replaced by unfiltered sunshine and a breeze that promised you'd never be too warm for long. Mallorca was summer done right, hot enough to swim but not so warm that your clothing stuck to your back.

Franny laughed when they pulled into the gravel drive, so drastically had Gemma undersold her house — another reason to despise her: modesty. In the distance, there were proper mountains, with ancient trees ringing the slopes like Christmas ornaments, and the house itself looked like an actual present: two stories tall and twice as wide as their limestone at home, it was a sturdy-looking stone building, painted a light pink. It glowed in the mid-morning sunlight, the black shutters on the open windows eyelashes on a beautiful face. A good third of the house's front was covered with rich green vines, which crept across from edge to edge, threatening to climb into the windows and consume the house entirely. Tall, narrow pine trees lined the edge of the property, their tippy-tops poking at the wide and empty sky. It was a child's drawing of a house, a large square with an angled roof on top, colored in with some ancient terra-cotta crayon that made the whole thing radiate. Franny clapped.

The back of the house was even better — the swimming pool, which had looked merely serviceable in the single backyard photograph, was in fact divine, a wide blue rectangle tucked into the hillside. A cluster of wooden chaise longues sat at one end, as if the Posts had walked in on a conversation already in progress. Sylvia hurried behind her mother, holding on to the sides of her tunic like a horse's reins. From the lip of the pool, they could see other houses tucked into the side of the mountain, as small and perfectly shaped as Monopoly pieces, their gleaming faces poking out from a blanket of shifting green trees and craggy rocks. The ocean was somewhere on the other side of the mountains, another ten minutes west, and Sylvia huffed in the fresh air, sniffing for salt particles. There was probably a university in Mallorca — at the very least, a swimming and tennis academy. Maybe she would just stay and let her parents go home alone and do whatever had to be done. If she was on the other side of the world, what difference would it make? For the first time in her life, Sylvia envied her brother's distance. It was harder to mourn something you weren't used to seeing on a daily basis.

Jim left the bags in the car and found the front door, which was oversized, heavy, and unlocked. It took a moment for his eyes to adjust to the relative dark. The house's foyer was empty except for a console table on the left-hand side, a large mirror hanging on the wall, and a ceramic pot the size of a small child on the right.

"Hello?" Jim called out, even though the house was supposed to be empty, and he wasn't expecting an answer. In front of him, a narrow hall led straight to a door to the garden, and he could see a sliver of the swimming pool, backed by the mountains. The room smelled of flowers and earth, with a soupçon of cleaning products. Bobby would like that, when he arrived — ever since he was a child, when Jim and Franny would drag him along on their trips to Maine or New Orleans or wherever, staying in crumbling vacation houses with mismatched forks, Bobby made his disgust for the unclean known. He detested antique furniture and vintage clothing, anything that had had a previous life. It was why he liked Florida real estate so much, Jim thought — everything was always brand-new. Even the gigantic piles in Palm Beach were gutted every few years, their insides replaced with shinier parts. Florida suited Bobby in a way that New York never had, but he wouldn't mind this, either. At least not for two weeks.

Jim walked through the archway on his left, into the living room. As in the photos, it was stylishly underfurnished, with only two low sofas and a nice rug, with paintings on the walls in places where the sun wouldn't hit them directly. Gemma was an art dealer, or a gallerist, or something. Jim's vague understanding was that she had so much money that a strict job description was superfluous. The living room led into a dining room, with a long wooden farm table and two rustic-looking benches, which in turn led into the large kitchen. The windows above the sink looked out onto the pool, and Jim paused there. Sylvia and Franny were lying on neighboring chaises. Franny had unwrapped her shawl from her shoulders and placed it over her face. Her sleeves were rolled up, and her legs splayed out to the sides — she was sunbathing, albeit with most of her clothes on. Jim exhaled with satisfaction — Franny was already having a good time.

To say that Franny had been uptight in the preceding month would be too delicate, too demure. She had been ruling the Post house with an iron sphincter. Though the trip had been meticulously planned in February, months before Jim's job at the magazine had slid out from under him, the timing was such that Fran could be counted on to have at least one red-faced scream per day. The zipper on the suitcase was broken, Bobby and Carmen's flights (booked on Post frequent-flier points) were costing them hundreds of dollars in fees because they had to shift the flights back a day. Jim was always in the way and in the wrong. Franny was expert in showing the public her good face, and once Charles arrived, it would be nothing but petting and cooing, but when she and Jim were alone, Franny could be a demon. Jim was grateful that, at least for the time being, Franny's horns seemed to have vanished back inside her skull.

The far end of the kitchen spat Jim out into the narrow hall opposite the entrance. On the other side of the foyer were a small bathroom with only a toilet and a shower stall, a laundry room, a study, and a single bedroom with its own bathroom attached, what Americans called mother-in-law suites, a place where you could stash the person everyone wanted to see the least. Normally, Jim would have claimed the study for his own, or at least fought Franny hard for it, but then he realized that he wouldn't have anything to do there — there were no deadlines looming, no pieces to edit, no writing to do, no queries to be made, no books to read for any purpose other than his own pleasure and edification. He needed a desk like a fish needed a bicycle, that's what the bumper sticker would have read. *Gallant* would soldier on without him, telling the intelligent American man which books to buy, which soap to use, and how to tell the difference between Scotch and Irish whiskey. Jim tried to shake off his discomfort with this, but it lingered as he made his way into the bedroom.

The room was cozy, with a quilt covering the double bed, a large dresser, and a writing desk in front of the window that faced the far side of the house. Uncharitably, Jim thought about whether they could put Bobby and Carmen in that room, and not upstairs, where the rest of the bedrooms must be, but no, of course they would give Charles and Lawrence the most privacy. There was an old-fashioned key sitting in the lock on the inside of the bedroom door, which made Jim happy. If they were all going to be in this house together, at least they could lock the doors. Jim briefly fantasized about locking himself in and playing possum for the rest of the day, a lazy man's Walter Mitty.

Sylvia and Franny banged in from the outside just as Jim was pulling the door closed.

"The pool is *great,*" Sylvia said, though she hadn't been in. "What time is it?" She had the wild look of someone who hadn't slept in twenty-four hours, with purplish semicircles underneath both her eyes. Being eighteen was like being made out of rubber and cocaine. Sylvia could have stayed up for three more days, easy.

"Want to sort out the bedrooms?" he said, knowing that Franny would want to choose theirs. "I thought Charles and Lawrence . . ." Jim started, but Franny was already halfway up the stairs.

Predictably, both Jim and Sylvia fell asleep as soon as they were given a bed in which to do so. Franny dragged her bag from the trunk of the car into the foyer. Gemma had left a small dossier on the house, pool, and surrounding towns in a red folder on the kitchen counter, and Franny leafed through it quickly. There were a few restaurants at the bottom of the hill — some tapas, some sandwiches, some pizza — and a serviceable grocery store and vegetable market. Palma, the largest city on the island, which they had just circumnavigated on their way from the airport, had everything else they could need — department stores for forgotten bathing suits and such, Camper shoes

40

made on Mallorca. Gemma herself was fully stocked with beach towels and suntan lotion, pool floats and goggles. There were clean sheets on the beds and more in the linen closet. Someone would come the following weekend to service the pool and take care of the garden. They weren't to lift a finger. Franny closed the folder and knocked her knuckles against the stone countertop.

It wasn't fair, the way women had to do absolutely everything. Franny knew that Gemma had been married a handful of times, twice to an Italian with a job in global finance, once to an heir to a Saudi oil company, but there was no way that any man would ever have typed up a list of instructions and usual information for his home, unless of course he were being paid to do so. It was the kind of thoughtful touch that only women were intrinsically capable of, no matter what any quack therapist on television said. Franny heard a rumble upstairs — Jim's nasal passages had never taken well to transatlantic flights — and shook her head. She did some yogic breathing, the kind that Jim thought sounded like a sweaty Russian in a bathhouse, as if he were in a position to judge, and tried to clear her mind, to no avail.

Just because no one else had slept on the

plane and the rest of her family seemed perfectly content to slip into a vampiric schedule out of laziness didn't mean that Franny had to, too. She fished her sunglasses out of her purse and set out into the world, leaving her slumbering family members unprotected from the local evils, whatever they might be. She pulled the heavy front door shut behind her and began to walk down the hill in the direction of the local market, as directed by Gemma's careful instructions. Someone needed to buy food for dinner, after all, and Sylvia's Spanish tutor was scheduled to come over at three-thirty, after he was done with church, Franny guessed, seeing as they were in a Catholic country. She didn't care one way or the other, only that he arrived more or less on time and didn't make Sylvia's Spanish any worse. Kids needed to be occupied, after all, whether they grew up in Manhattan or Mallorca, or, God bless them, on the mainland.

They would drive to a larger supermarket later, maybe tomorrow, but for now all they needed were a few things to make for dinner. Franny was the mom, which meant that all the planning fell to her, even if anyone else had been awake. No matter that Jim no longer had a job — some retirees took up cooking as a hobby, turning their kitchens into miniature Cordons Bleus, filling drawers with brûlée torches and abandoned parts of ice cream makers, but Franny couldn't quite imagine that happening. Most retirees had chosen to leave their jobs, after decades of service and repetitive-stress disorders, and that wasn't what had happened to Jim. What had happened to Jim. Franny kicked a loose rock. They'd always enjoyed vacations, the Posts, and this seemed like as good a send-off as any, complete with days at the beach and views to kill. Franny wished she had something to break. She bent over to pick up a stick and flung it over the cliff.

The road to the small town — really just an intersection with a few restaurants and shops on either side — was narrow, as they'd noticed driving up the mountain, but walking along the side of the road, Franny felt as though it had shrunk even further. There was hardly room enough for a fleet of bicycles to whiz by her, let alone a car, or, God forbid, two, going in opposite directions, but whiz they did. She clung to the left side of the road, wishing that she'd thought to pack some sort of reflective clothing, even though it was still the middle of the day and anyone driving could see her plainly enough. Franny was not a tall woman, but she wasn't as short as her mother and sister. She liked to think of herself as average size, though the averages had of course changed over time, Marilyn Monroe's size twelve being something like a modern size six, and so on. Yes, it was true that Franny had gotten thicker in the last decade, but that was what happened unless you were a high-functioning psychotic, and she had other things to think about. Franny knew plenty of women who had chosen to prioritize the eternal youth of their bodies, and they were all miserable creatures, their taut triceps unable to conceal their dissatisfaction with their empty stomachs and unfulfilling lives. Franny liked to eat, and to feed people, and she wasn't embarrassed that her body displayed such proclivities. She'd gone to one horrible Overeaters Anonymous meeting in her early forties, in a stuffy room in the basement of a church, and the degree to which she recognized herself in the other men and women sitting on the folding chairs had scared her away for good. It might be a problem, but it was her problem, thank you very much. Some people smoked crack in alleyways. Franny ate chocolate. On the scale of things, it seemed entirely reasonable.

The grocery store was a modified farm stand with three walls and two short rows of open shelving with canned food and other staples. A handful of people were on their way in or out, some on bicycles, and some pulling their cars off to the non-existent shoulder of the road. Franny wiped the sweat off her cheeks and started to pull things off the small shelves. There was a cooler in one corner with some sheep's milk cheese wrapped in paper, and dried sausages hung from the rafters at the other end of the room. A woman in an apron was weighing the produce and charging the customers. If Franny could have chosen another life, one far from New York City, this is what she would have chosen: to be surrounded by olives and lemons and sunlight, with clean beaches nearby. She assumed the Mallorcan beaches were clean, not at all like the filthy Coney Island of her youth. Franny bought some anchovies, a box of dried pasta, two fat links of sausage, and cheese. She bought a small bag of almonds, and three oranges. That would do for now. She could already taste the salty cheese melting into the pasta, the tang of the anchovies. Surely there was olive oil at the house — she hadn't checked. That didn't seem like something Gemma would overlook. She probably had her own oil pressed from the trees on her property.

"Buenos días," Franny said to the woman in the apron. If she was being truly honest, Franny was slightly disappointed that the women in the market were all wearing perfectly normal clothing, with mobile phones sticking out of their pockets, just like women in New York. It was even true in Mumbai, that a woman in a sari would whip a cell phone out of her pocket and start talking. When Franny was young, everywhere she went felt like another planet, like some glorious wonderland on the other side of the looking glass. Now the rest of the world felt about as foreign as a shopping mall in Westchester County.

"Buenas tardes," the woman said back, quickly weighing and bagging all of Franny's items. *"Dieciséis.* Sixteen."

"Sixteen?" Franny plunged a hand into her purse and felt around for her wallet.

All of Franny's friends with children were so excited for her, to have Sylvia finally heading off to school. *It'll be like a vacation,* they said to her, *a vacation from being a full-time parent.* What they meant was, *You aren't getting any younger, and neither are your children.* Some of her friends had children who weren't even in high school yet, and

46

their lives revolved around piano lessons and ballet class, like Franny's had so many years ago. Or like it might have, if she'd worked less. They all complained about not having any free time, about never having sex with their husbands, but really they were bragging. *My life is too full,* that's what they were saying. *I have so much left to do. Enjoy menopause.* While it was true that Franny was going to have her life back in some way, it wasn't going to be the life of a twenty-year-old, all late nights and hangovers. It was going to be the life of an older person. She was six years away from a senior discount at movie theaters. Six years of looking at Jim in the kitchen and wanting to plunge an ice pick in between his eyes.

"*Gracias,*" Franny said, when the woman handed her the change.

Sylvia had passed out immediately in the smallest bedroom, which looked like it had been built for a nun: a bed hardly wider than her slim teenaged body, white walls, white sheets, painted white floor. The only thing un-nunlike about the room was a painting of a naked woman in repose. It looked like one of Charles's, and she was used to those. He loved to paint those tender triangles of pubic hair, often of her

47

mother in her youth. It was what it was. Other people had the luxury of never seeing their mother naked, but not Sylvia. She stretched lazily, her pointed toes hanging over the end of the bed. The house smelled weird, like wet rocks and frogs, and it took Sylvia several minutes to remember where she was.

"Me llamo Sylvia Post," she said. *"Dónde está el baño?"*

Sylvia rolled onto her side and pulled her knees up to her chest. The single window in the room was open, and a nice breeze came in. Sylvia had few thoughts about Spain: it wasn't like France, which made her think of baguettes and bicycles, or Italy, which made her think of gondolas and pizza. Picasso was Spanish but looked French and sounded Italian. There was the one Woody Allen movie that took place in Spain, but Sylvia hadn't actually seen it. Matadors fighting bulls? That was Spain, wasn't it? She might as well have woken up in a sunny bedroom somewhere on the island of Peoria, Illinois.

The bathroom was down the hall, and it looked like it hadn't been renovated since 1973. The tiles on the wall above the bathtub and behind the sink were the color of split-pea soup, a food group that Sylvia planned to happily avoid for the rest of her life. There was no proper shower, just a handheld nozzle on a long silver neck that began at the hot and cold knobs. Sylvia turned the hot one and waited for a minute, running the water over her hand to feel when it got warm. She waited for a few minutes, and when the warmth didn't arrive, she turned the other knob, stripped off her clothes, and climbed in. She had to stoop in order to get the nozzle to reach her head and was able to really dampen only one body part at a time. There was a bar of soap in the dish, but Sylvia couldn't quite work out how to wash her body with one hand and douse herself with freezing-cold water with the other.

All the towels in the bathroom seemed to have been made for little people — Thumbelina-sized people, people even shorter than her mother. Sylvia tried to wrap her upper and lower parts with two of the glorified washcloths. She combed her hair with her fingers and looked at herself in the mirror. Sylvia knew she wasn't bad-looking, she wasn't deformed, but she also knew that there was a vast chasm between her and the girls at her school who were beautiful. Her face was a little bit long, and her hair hung limply to her shoulders, neither short nor long, neither blond nor brown, but somewhere in the middle. That was Sylvia's whole problem: she was the middle. Sylvia couldn't imagine how she would explain herself to someone else, to a stranger: she was average, with blue eyes that weren't particularly large or shapely. Nothing anyone would write a poem about. Sylvia thought about that a lot: so many of the world's best poems were written before their authors were really adults — Keats, Rimbaud, Plath — and yet they had packed so much beauty and agony into their lives, enough to sustain their memory for centuries. Sylvia stuck out her tongue and carefully opened the bathroom door with the hand holding the towel around her waist.

"Perdón!"

There was a boy attached to the voice. Sylvia shut her eyes, hoping that she was hallucinating, but when she opened them again, he was still there. Maybe *boy* wasn't the right word — there was a young man standing in front of her, maybe Bobby's age, maybe younger, but definitely older than she was.

"Oh my God," Sylvia said. She didn't want to notice that the complete stranger who was staring at her while she was wearing very tiny towels was handsome, with dark wavy hair like someone on the cover of a romance novel, but she couldn't help it. "Oh my God," she said again, and hurried around him, taking the smallest steps possible, so that her legs were never more than two inches apart. When she was safely on the other side of her bedroom door, Sylvia let the towels drop to the floor so that she could use both of her hands to cover her face and scream without making any noise at all.

"A *doctor,* that's so wonderful," Franny said. She was fawning, she could feel herself fawning, but it was out of her hands. There was no stopping the flirtation once it was in motion; she could sooner have stopped a speeding train. There was a twenty-year-old Mallorcan in her dining room, and she wanted to cover his body with local olive oil and wrestle until dark.

"Probably, yes," he said. The boy's name was Joan, pronounced Joe-*ahhhn,* and he was to be Sylvia's Spanish tutor for the next two weeks, coming over for an hour every weekday during their stay. Joan's parents lived nearby and were friendly with Gemma. (She'd mentioned some gardening club they had in common — Franny had stopped reading the e-mail. Training succulents, maybe.) He'd tutored before, and charged only twenty dollars per hour, which was absurdly inexpensive, even before Franny knew what he looked like, but now seemed like a crime against beauty. The boy was in his second year at the university in Barcelona, home for the summer, living with his parents. He probably ate dinner with them, too! Bobby had never once come home for an entire summer. As far as Franny knew, he'd never even considered it. Once he'd left for Miami, New York was no more home to him than LaGuardia Airport was. Franny felt her cheeks begin to flush, and she was glad to see Sylvia lurking in the hall when she looked up.

"Oh, good, here's my daughter now. Sylvia, come meet Joan. Joe — *ahhhn*!" Franny waved her over. Sylvia shook her head and stayed put in the shadows. "Sylvia, what's the matter with you?" Franny felt her soft, melty feelings about Joan begin to move toward embarrassment at her daughter's childish behavior.

Sylvia dragged herself into the dining room, moving as if her bare feet were made of glue. Glue that very recently had been seen almost entirely naked.

"This is Joan, he's going to be your Spanish tutor," Franny said, gesturing to the man, who Sylvia now was forced to shake hands with.

"Hi," Sylvia said. Joan's grip was a little bit soft, which made it easier to keep breathing. She might have died if he had a handshake as good as his hair.

"Very nice to meet you," Joan said back. There was no wink, no acknowledgment of the run-in at the bathroom door. Sylvia slid into the chair next to her mother without taking her eyes off him, just in case he did make a gesture that indicated he had seen parts of her body that he shouldn't have.

Franny had slept with a Spaniard once, when she was at Barnard. He was visiting for the year, and lived in the dormitory on 116th Street, just across the street. His name was Pedro — or was it Paulo? — and he had not been an expert lover, but then again, neither was she, yet. Like most things, sex got better with age until one hit a certain plateau, and then it was like breakfast, unlikely to change unless one ran out of milk and was forced to improvise. All Franny could remember was the way he murmured at her in Spanish, a language she didn't speak, and the sound of those *r*'s rolling off his soft, persistent tongue. Franny had hoped for some love letters in Spanish when he returned home, but by the time he left New York, they weren't even seeing each other anymore, and so she hadn't gotten any. Pedro-Paulo hadn't been nearly as good-looking as Joan, anyway. The boy at her dining room table was built like an athlete and wanted to be a doctor; he had a strong chin with the slightest hint of a cleft at the center. He hadn't come from church — he'd come from playing tennis with his father. They played at a tennis center about fifteen minutes away, the home turf for Mallorca's most famous son, Nando Filani, who had won two grand slams already this season. Now all Franny could do was picture Joan in a sweat-drenched T-shirt, the muscles in his arms flexing as he ran for a shot. If Sylvia had been a different kind of girl, Franny might have been worried about leaving her alone with Joan for so many hours over the next two weeks, but things being as they were, she wasn't.

"Mom?"

"Sorry, sweetie. Did you say something?"

"We're going to start tomorrow at eleven. Is that okay?"

"*Perfecto!*" Franny clapped twice. "I think this is going to be so much fun."

They all stood up to walk Joan to the door, and Franny grabbed Sylvia by the hand as he climbed into his car and did a three-point turn to drive back down the hill.

"Wasn't he *gorgeous*?"

Sylvia shrugged. "I guess. I don't know. I didn't really notice." She spun on her heels and ran up the stairs to her bedroom, shutting the door with a loud clunk. As Franny suspected, she had nothing to worry about. It was only after Joan had gone home and Sylvia had gone upstairs that Franny realized that the age difference between her and the tutor was as wide as the difference between Jim and that girl, which made her audibly gulp, as if she could swallow her sickened feeling like a bit of traveler's indigestion.

Everyone agreed that an early dinner was best. While she was boiling the water for the pasta, Franny put some olives out in a shallow bowl, with a second small bowl for the pits. She sliced the dried sausage and ate a few pieces before returning her attention to the capers and cheese. The sausage was a little bit spicy, with flecks of fat that melted on her tongue. Franny loved cooking in the summertime, the ease of almost every ingredient being at room temperature. She opened the jar of capers and let a dozen or so fall into a large bowl, into which she then grated some of the cheese. That was all they needed — oil and starch, fat and salt.

Tomorrow they would eat vegetables, but tonight they were truly on vacation, and eating only for pleasure. She should have tried to find some ice cream for dessert, but they could do that tomorrow, when everyone was there. Charles loved to buy the crazy local flavors, always: the dulce de leche, the Brazil nut, the tamarind. She opened and closed the kitchen cabinets, looking for a colander, and found it on the third try. The water was still only at a simmer, and so Franny kept opening and closing cabinet doors, just to see what else was on hand: a mandoline, pots large enough to boil lobsters, lost attachments to a stand mixer long forgotten in a dusty corner. The last cabinet she opened had two pull-out drawers stocked with pantry items. An extra box of dried pasta had been in here, and the olive oil. Franny pawed through, seeing what else she could add to their supper, what else was hiding. A jar of Nutella was in the back row, next to a crusty-looking jar of peanut butter. Franny looked out the window over the sink: Jim and Sylvia were still swimming, already cultivating the healthy glow they got every summer, no matter the weather or the location. Some people were just built that way, as though they could happen upon a triathlon and complete it without any training whatsoever. Even though Sylvia was bookish and wan for most of the year, eschewing organized sports of any and all kinds, she was her father's daughter, competitive and built for physical exertion, whether she liked it or not.

Franny plucked the jar of Nutella out of the drawer and unscrewed the cap. It wasn't even half full — hardly enough for the three of them to spread on toast in the morning, if they'd had a loaf of bread. She was almost impressed with Gemma for entertaining such base pleasures, but it had probably been bought by some other guest, or for a small child's sophomoric palate. Franny plunged her pointer finger into the wide mouth of the jar and dragged it around the edges, until there was a large crashing wave of the creamy stuff in between her knuckles. She put the whole thing in her mouth and pulled her finger out slowly, with a low moan. Franny screwed the top back on the jar and hid it in a different cabinet, one where no one else would look, just in case.

The setting sun had shifted over the mountain, and now Jim and Sylvia swam through the shade on their laps back and forth in the swimming pool. From *Gallant*'s current issue: "Why Doing Laps Will Make You Live to 100," written by a novelist with a weak breaststroke and a spare tire, a piece Jim had commissioned because he thought it sounded like something Franny would like. *Gallant* was always looking for more female eyes. Jim's fingers began to prune, but he didn't mind. From the deep end of the pool, he could see mountains and trees and the back face of their little pink house. An airplane flew overhead, and both Sylvia and Jim were grateful not to be on it, not to be leaving anytime soon. A good swimming pool could do that — make the rest of the world seem impossibly insignificant, as far away as the surface of the moon.

"It's not bad, huh?"

Sylvia swam over to the far lip of the pool and hoisted herself up on her elbows.

"It'll do." She wiped the water out of her eyes. "What time do Bobby and whatsherface get here? And Charles?"

"In the morning, like we did. They'll be here early." If they'd been in New York, standing on opposite sides of 75th Street, they wouldn't have been able to hear each other: the cars, the people, the airplanes, the bikes, the noise of everyday life in the city. They hadn't been talking as much as usual, anyway, not lately. Now they were twenty feet apart and could hear each other perfectly. If they'd shouted, their voices would have bounced off the trees lining the mountain and echoed into the valley below, into Pigpen proper, maybe all the way to the ocean.

"I wish he was coming by himself," Sylvia said.

"Who, Bobby? Or Charles?" Jim swam slowly over to Sylvia's side of the pool.

"Both of them."

"I thought you liked Lawrence," Jim said. He extended his arms and grabbed the lip next to Sylvia. She let go and floated onto her back.

"I do, I do, it's just . . . I'd rather have him alone, you know? When Lawrence is around, Charles has to pay attention to him, like he's a little dog. They're not like you and Mom, who are, like, just people who happen to be married to each other, you know? They're always fixing each other's clothes and reading over each other's shoulders. It's gross." Sylvia shuddered, her wet hair sending droplets of water flying into the pool. "It's like, at a certain age, people should get over the idea of being in love. It's gross," she said again.

"That's not true," Jim said. He wanted to say more, to tell his daughter that she was wrong, but couldn't find the words.

Franny opened the back door and poked her head out. "Dinner! No bathing suits at the table."

Jim had found a stack of beach towels in the laundry room, and Sylvia grabbed one after she hoisted herself out of the pool. Her father stayed bobbing in the pool, his hands cupping the concrete rim.

"You'll be happy to see Bobby, though, won't you?" Jim asked, staring up at Sylvia. He wanted the children to remain uncomplicated with each other, though he knew it was futile. Parenting adults wasn't at all like parenting kids, when the whole merry band was inclined to believe you, just because. Sylvia knew what had happened because she lived in the same house as the two of them, and it was impossible to keep it from her. It would have been hard to keep it from a child, but teenagers had ears like suction cups, soaking up everything around them. Bobby didn't know anything. Jim almost wished that he was staying at home, staying far, far away from the implosion of his nuclear family.

Sylvia had wound one gigantic towel around her body and another around her hair. "Sure," she said. "I guess." She waited for Jim to pull himself out of the pool before going inside, but she didn't say anything else, challenging him to complete his own thought.

The master bedroom was over the study, and had its own en suite bathroom. There was a closet on the left-hand side of the bed and a dresser on the right. Jim had unpacked his things in five minutes flat, and was sitting on the edge of the bed, watching Franny transport armfuls of tunics and airy, light dresses from her suitcase into the closet. She went back and forth, back and forth.

"How much clothing did you bring?" Jim took off his glasses and placed them, folded, into his shirt pocket. "I'm exhausted."

Franny spoke as if she hadn't heard him. "Well, Bobby and Carmen and Charles and Lawrence all get in at the same time, roughly, so we could either drive down to meet them or they could all drive together, what do you think?"

"Wouldn't it make more sense for them to all drive together and save us the trip?" Jim knew it wasn't the answer she wanted. He stood up and cracked his knuckles.

Franny pushed past him, carrying another load. "I suppose so, yes, but if I go pick them up, then maybe one car can go to the grocery store while the other one comes right back," she said. "Sylvia's tutor is coming at eleven, so why don't the two of you stay home? I'll go pick up Bobby and Carmen, since Charles is renting the car, and then maybe we'll swap cars so that Bobby and Carmen and Lawrence come right home, and Charles and I will go food shopping. That makes the most sense, really. Why don't we do that?"

It didn't make any sense, not to Jim, but he wasn't going to argue with her. This was the problem with including Charles and Lawrence: Franny would do anything to rearrange plans in order to be with Charles twenty-four hours a day for as many days as possible. It didn't matter that Charles was married now, or that the rest of her family was here, and the vacation was ostensibly about spending time with Sylvia. The plan had been to use the trip as a celebration for their thirty-fifth wedding anniversary, too, but that idea, that it was to be in some way a celebration of their marriage, now seemed like a joke with a terrible punch line. Once Charles arrived, Franny would start laughing the way she had when she was twenty-four, and the rest of them could start setting one another on fire for all she cared. That's what best friends did: ruin people for everyone else. Of course, Franny would have said that Jim had already ruined every-thing.

Jim ambled into the bathroom and dug his toothbrush out of the dopp kit. The tap water tasted like old metal, but it still felt good to brush his teeth and wash his face. He purposefully took longer than usual, in part because he wasn't sure how the night would go. How the night went, so went the vacation. If Franny had softened on the airplane, or in the beautiful house, or while unpacking, that would be a welcome sight. When he came back into the bedroom, Franny was sitting up in bed with *Don Quixote* on her lap. Jim pulled back the thin coverlet and started to slide in, but Franny put out a hand, flat.

"I would prefer if you slept in Bobby's room. For the night," she said. "Obviously not once they get here."

"I see," Jim said, but he didn't move.

"Sylvia sleeps like a hibernating bear, she's not going to hear you," Franny said, opening her book.

"Fine," Jim said. "But we'll have to deal with this tomorrow, you know." He picked up the novel he was reading from his night-stand and made his way to the door.

"Yes, we'll have to deal with this, won't we?" Franny said. "I love that you make this seem like it's my choice." She opened her book and turned her attention to somewhere far, far away.

Jim pulled the door closed behind him and waited for his eyes to adjust to the dark.

DAY THREE

When Lawrence ducked into the men's room, Charles leaned against the terminal wall, pulled his wheeled suitcase so that it rested against his feet, and shut his eyes. They'd left their house in Provincetown at three o'clock the previous afternoon in order to get to Boston Logan for their evening flight, and flying coach was more exhausting than he remembered. Lawrence was the thrifty one — if Charles had come alone, he would have sprung for business class, at the very least. He was fifty-five years old. What was he saving the money for, if not for transatlantic flights? Lawrence would have scolded him, had he been able to hear Charles's thoughts. This was a conversation they had on an extremely regular basis. Just because a baby hadn't come along yet didn't mean that one wouldn't, and then wouldn't he feel guilty about those thousands of wasted dollars floating somewhere over an ocean? Weren't organic apples/private school/tennis lessons worth it? They were, Charles would always agree, even though he had lately come to believe that their shared dreams of having a family would soon go the way of the dodo, at which point they could resume their happily selfish lives. Almost all of the other couples they'd met at the adoption agency already had their babies — one, if not two — and Charles thought there might be something written in invisible ink in their letter to the birth mothers. *I'm conflicted,* maybe, or *I don't know, do we look like good parents to you?*

The terminal smelled like disinfectant and heavy perfume, a mixture that gave Charles a headache on the spot. He shifted his body to the right, so that he was facing the stream of disembarking travelers. The Spanish ones had better faces than the tourists — better cheekbones, better lips, better hair. When he was younger, Charles would paint from life, but now he just snapped photos with his digital camera and painted from those. He loved that freedom, being able to have anyone's face in his pocket.

"Hey," Lawrence said. He wiped his wet hands on his pants.

"Welcome back," Charles said. He leaned

his head against Lawrence's shoulder. "I'm tired."

"I know you are. But hey, at least you're not wearing an adult-sized playsuit," he said, gesturing to a woman walking out of the jet bridge at the gate opposite the bathroom. She was small, probably not much over five feet tall, with soft pink terry-cloth sweatpants and matching sweatshirt, both of which were snug enough to show off her round bottom and otherwise compact figure. "Weren't those outlawed a decade ago?" The woman stepped out of the line of traffic and turned around, waiting for someone. A tall man with a moppish head of brown curly hair emerged, nodding at the waiting woman in pink.

Charles spun around so that he was facing the wall. "Oh, shit," he said. "It's Bobby's girlfriend."

"Not the one in the playsuit," Lawrence said, turning his body so that they were both facing the wall.

"We can't both be pointing this way," Charles said. "Shit."

"Charles?"

Charles and Lawrence both turned around, arms open wide. "Hiiiiiiii," they said in unison. Bobby and his girlfriend had shortened the gap between them, and were

67

now no more than four feet away.

"Hello, handsome," Charles said, pulling Bobby close for a hug. They patted each other on the back affectionately, and when he pulled out of the embrace, Bobby kept one arm slung around Charles's shoulder as if they were posing for a team photo.

"How was your flight? Hi, Lawrence." Bobby smiled widely. He had the easy tan of a person who spent most of his days outdoors, though that wasn't the case. Lawrence thought Bobby might in fact look too tan, as driving around real estate properties in Miami wouldn't afford so much sunlight unless he drove a convertible, which seemed unlikely. Maybe he spent every weekend on the beach, his face and arms and chest slathered in tanning lotion, like some 1975 bodybuilder. That seemed unlikely, too. Lawrence wasn't quite sure how to reconcile himself to the fact that Bobby's golden-brown suntan was almost certainly fake. The rules were different in Florida.

"Fine. How about yours?" Charles said. No one had spoken to Bobby's girlfriend, nor had there been any effort to introduce her. Charles knew that they'd met once or twice at a Christmas dinner, or at one of Franny and Jim's large anniversary parties

— maybe it was their thirtieth, five years ago now? Charles had a dim recollection of seeing this woman standing next to Franny's literary agent, assiduously avoiding conversation by performing an extremely thorough investigation of the ceiling. The girlfriend was at least a decade older than Bobby, which was what had made her sweatsuit so absurd. She was almost Lawrence's age, young only as viewed from the other side of sixty. Franny had a lot to say on the matter, but only after half a bottle of wine. Until then, she remained coldly impartial. They'd been together for years, off and on, but none of the Posts seemed to care one way or the other, at least in polite company, the way one might ignore the flatulence of an otherwise friendly dog. Charles couldn't believe that he didn't remember her name. She was native to Miami, with Cuban parents. Was it Carrie? It wasn't Mary. Miranda?

"Carmen was so excited, we didn't sleep at all," Bobby said, finally looking over his shoulder to find her. "You remember Charles and Lawrence, right?"

"Hello," she said, reaching out her hand. Lawrence shook it first, then Charles. Carmen had a firm grip, a handshake that surprised them both. She had olive-colored,

69

creaseless skin that belied her age, and a ponytail that looked mussed from the airplane, an off-center whale spout. Lawrence thought she looked like one of the Spice Girls after a decade out of the spotlight, slightly worse for wear.

"Of course," Charles said. "How could we forget?"

Franny was waiting at the baggage claim, rubbing her hands together. When Bobby and Carmen rounded the corner and came into view, she squealed and jumped awkwardly in her slip-ons, one of which slid off her foot and skidded a few inches across the slick polished floor. She hurried back into it and ran across the room, as slowly as if through molasses. Bobby stooped down to let himself be folded into his mother's arms.

"Oh, yes, yes, yes," she said, rubbing his back. Franny felt terrible about keeping Bobby in the dark about Jim, but it wasn't the sort of thing you explained over the telephone. Now that he was in her clutches, she thought it would be so much easier if information could be passed telepathically, like on a science-fiction television program, just *zzzzzzpppp* from one brain to the next. "Oh, yes."

"Hi, Mom," Bobby said, blinking his eyes at Carmen over his mother's shoulder. "You can let go, really, I'll be here for weeks."

"Oh, fine," Franny said, and reluctantly pulled back. "Carmen, hello," she said, and quickly gave her a kiss on the cheek. "The flight was okay?"

"Fine," Carmen said, smiling. "We watched movies." She shifted her weight from one leg to the other, stretching out her calves.

"Great," Franny said. "Did you happen to run into Charles? He should be around here somewhere." She looked past Carmen, back down the hall they'd come from. Sure enough, Charles and Lawrence were pulling their suitcases behind them, laughing. Franny's eyes misted over, as if she thought he wouldn't really have come. She took a few steps past Bobby and Carmen so that they wouldn't be able to see her start to cry. Charles finally saw her and began to walk more quickly, scooping her up like a long-lost lover after a war.

Franny's Chinese fire drill went off without a hitch: Bobby and Carmen and Lawrence got in Charles's rental car, and Charles got into Franny's car, and off they went. Carmen could drive stick, and so she drove the

71

first car, while Charles drove the second. Lawrence was too tired to complain, and if Charles had perked up enough to go grocery shopping, that was better for everyone, wasn't it? Charles waved limply from the passenger-side window as the car drove away, Lawrence now the captive of the two strangers he wanted to come on vacation with the least.

"It's so good to see you, Lawrence," Bobby said. "I haven't seen you since before you guys got married. When was that, a year ago? Two years ago? I know it was in the summer." Carmen jerked the car forward and merged into the airport traffic.

"It'll be three years next month," Lawrence said, closing his eyes and briefly thanking a godlike figure that the Spanish drove on the right side of the road. "You know what they say about time."

"What's that?" Bobby said, lowering his window shade to take a peek in the mirror. For a moment, he caught Lawrence's eyes and smiled. Bobby was sweeter than his sister; in fact, he was sweeter than the entire rest of the family. As far as Lawrence could tell, Bobby had no hard edges whatsoever, a quality one didn't often come across in people who had grown up in Manhattan. Lawrence felt his shoulders relax a bit.

"Oh, you know. It flies." Lawrence crossed his arms and stared out the window. His own family had never been on vacation together, not since he was a child. Even then, he didn't think they'd done more than one or two trips to a smoky campsite, where they'd all slept in the same dank, mildewing tent. It seemed like folly to imagine that one could fill a house (or a tent) with relatives and still expect to have a pleasant vacation. He and Charles had already discussed this: after Mallorca, they were going to go somewhere else for a few days, just the two of them, where they would be mercifully free from small talk and other people's emotional baggage. Lawrence was thinking about Hudson, or maybe Woodstock, but Charles found upstate New York too buggy. They could wait until the weather shifted and then fly to Palm Springs. All Lawrence wanted to talk about was who had a baby, who was still waiting, about wallpaper for the nursery, about names and strollers and where they could buy some nice lesbian's breast milk.

"That's so true," Carmen said. She pulled her purse onto her lap and took out a large plastic bag full of makeup, all of it miniature, as if made for dolls. "Samples," she said over her shoulder, by way of an explanation. "This way I can fit everything I need. Three ounces or less." She unscrewed a cap the size of a baby's thumbnail and squeezed out a drop of cream onto the pad of her index finger. Lawrence watched as she rubbed it vigorously onto her face and neck with one hand while driving with the other, and then tightened his seat belt. Other people's families were as mysterious as an alien species, full of secret codes and shared histories. Lawrence watched Carmen repeat the process a few more times with different potions. The car rocked to the side as she took a turn too quickly, and Bobby yelped, not without a sense of humor.

"She's a terrible driver," he said, and then braced himself against Carmen's retaliation.

Bobby's sweetness didn't matter, not really, not any more than Franny's bossiness or Jim's reserve, or Sylvia's precociousness. The problem was that Charles had abandoned him before they'd even left the airport. How much could two weeks undo?

"I'm a bit tired," Lawrence said. "I think I'll just shut my eyes, if you two don't mind."

"Of course," Bobby said. "Knock yourself out."

Lawrence closed his eyes. He'd begun to sweat, and the car's air-conditioning seemed inadequate to the task at hand. He wondered briefly if Bobby and Carmen would chat in the way that couples do, about nothing of importance, but they remained silent.

The grocery store in Palma was heavenly. Franny and Charles clutched each other at the head of every aisle. The packaging was sublime, even on canned sardines and tubes of tomato paste. Being in a foreign country made even the smallest differences seem like art. Charles had once painted Franny from a photo in a Tokyo supermarket, her wide face beatific. It was one of their very favorite things to do together.

"Look," Charles said, holding up a package of flan pudding.

"Look," Franny said, holding up a bag of *jamón*-flavored potato chips.

The ham aisle was magnificent: chopped ham, bacon, chorizo, mortadella, sobrassada, salami, *ibérico,* hot dogs, ham pizza, sausages, ham jerky. They filled a shopping cart with jars of peanut butter and jam and toilet paper and juice — *zumo* — and lettuce and oranges and manchego and loaves of sliced bread. "What time is it?" Charles asked, as they stood on line at the cashier. "It feels like three in the morning."

"Poor little duck," Franny said, and

wrapped her arms around his shoulders. When they'd met, both Franny and Charles had been young and beautiful-ish, with enough style to fudge the rest. Her waist had nipped in with a good strong belt, and his hairline was only just starting to announce itself. They could live to be a hundred years old, and that would still be how Franny saw him — like a shorter James Dean, with curious eyebrows and curvy lips, just as gorgeous as possible. It didn't matter that Charles was now completely bald, with only a laurel of stubble clinging to his skull — to Franny, he would always be the one she loved the most, the most handsome boy she could never have, except in all the ways she did have him, forever.

"How's it going? With Jim, I mean."

"Oh, you know," Franny started, but didn't know how to finish the sentence. "Bad. Bad, bad, bad. I can't look at him without wanting to cut off his penis."

"Sylvia seems like she's taking it all well, though," Charles said, nodding at the cashier. He spoke even less Spanish than Franny did, which wasn't saying much.

"But you haven't even seen her yet," Franny said, confused.

"Facebook."

"You're on Facebook?"

Charles rolled his eyes. "*Sí*. And why aren't you? Oh, lovey, you are really missing out. But yes, Sylvia and I do the Facebook chatting all the time. I think she probably does it at the dining room table, sitting right across from you." He lowered his voice. "She tells me all her secrets."

Franny let go of Charles's shoulder and knocked her body against his, threatening a stack of chocolate bars behind him. "She does not," Franny said, jealous of both the fact that Charles knew things about her daughter that she didn't and that Sylvia had found a way to communicate with Charles that she didn't even know existed. "Sylvia doesn't have any secrets. That's what's so wonderful about her. She's the first teenager on the planet to just be happy."

"Of course she is," Charles said. He bowed his head. So much of being a good friend was knowing when to keep your mouth shut. "And that's the good part, after all. No matter what happens with Jim, you'll always have Syl and Bobby. Kids are forever, even if love isn't, right?"

"I'll love *you* forever," Franny said, sliding her credit card out of her wallet. "Kids, too, I suppose."

Bobby knocked on the front door, though

the house was as much his as anyone else's. When no one answered, he tried the knob and found that it was unlocked. He turned to Carmen and Lawrence behind him, who both nodded. He pushed open the door. "Hello?" The house was completely silent except for the sounds of the trees swishing in the breeze and the occasional car on the road. "Hello?" Bobby said again, taking a few tentative steps into the foyer.

There was a thump from upstairs, and then the creak of a door slowly opening. Sylvia appeared at the top of the stairs, on her hands and knees.

"I'm jet-lagged," she said.

"Come and help us with our bags!" Bobby said, his voice booming.

"Yessir, I'll get right on that," Sylvia said, before turning around and crawling back into her bedroom. The door closed with a thunk.

Joan wanted to get a sense of where Sylvia stood, and came over brandishing a workbook like one she hadn't seen since middle school, with pictures of cows and broomsticks and other objects to identify. *How does Mariella tell her friend that she MIGHT come over for dinner? How would she say that she WILL come over for dinner?* Sylvia dutifully filled out a few pages before Joan, reading over her shoulder, stopped her. He was sitting close enough that Sylvia could smell his cologne. When guys at her school wore cologne it was obviously disgusting, but Joan made it seem sophisticated, like a Mallorcan James Bond. Sylvia imagined Joan's medicine cabinet, each shelf crowded with male grooming products. His hair alone no doubt required half a dozen potions to move the way it did. Sylvia breathed as shallowly as possible while Joan checked her work. He clicked his pen against the table, *open, closed, open, closed.*

"Sylvia," he said, "your written Spanish is good." Joan stretched her name out to four syllables, like it was made of honey. *See-ill-vee-ah.*

"It's okay," she said. She wanted him to say her name again.

Joan backed his chair a few inches farther away. "We should spend our time just talking, you know, conversational." He was wearing a polo shirt with the buttons undone at his neck. Outside, someone laughed, and Sylvia turned to look behind her, out the dining room window. Bobby and his girlfriend were in the pool, and she was riding around on his shoulders in a one-team chicken fight. Carmen was old, over forty. Bobby was an entire decade older than Sylvia, so he already seemed ancient, and that Carmen was more than ten years older than *him* made her seem like she was trying to drink his blood. They'd met six or seven years ago at the gym where Carmen was a personal trainer. Bobby'd been working out there, and then he'd brought her home. Sylvia found the entire thing very tacky, about as tacky as she found Carmen herself, who wore eyeliner every day and the kind of sneakers that were supposed to make your butt better, even though she was a personal trainer and had a fine butt and should know better, anyway.

"It's weird to go on vacation with your whole family," Sylvia said, in Spanish. *"Really weird."*

"Tell me about them," Joan said. He swiveled in his chair so that he was looking out the window, too. *"That's your brother?"*

"That's what they say," Sylvia said.

There were footsteps in the hall, and both Joan and Sylvia turned to look. Lawrence had changed into his bathing suit and was holding a sweating glass of water. He walked up to the door to the garden and watched as Carmen and Bobby took turns doing handstands in the shallow end.

"Maybe I'll just take a nap," Lawrence

said, and turned back around.

"And who's that?" Joan asked.

"My mother's best friend's husband. They're gay. I don't think he wanted to come." Sylvia paused. She wanted Joan to laugh, but only because of Lawrence's reluctance. This was important.

"And now he's stuck with you for how long?" Joan asked, the right question.

"Two weeks," Sylvia said, smiling so hard that she had to lean forward and pretend to take a sip out of her empty water glass. If she didn't interact with anyone else for the entire two weeks, Sylvia thought, that was okay. Joan looked like an excellent candidate for sex. In fact, if sex had made a poster advertising its virtues, they might have put his face on it. Sylvia let her lips linger around the rim of the glass. Wasn't that what one was supposed to do, draw attention to one's mouth? She gave the glass one little lick, decided that she felt like a camel at a zoo, and put it down, hoping he hadn't noticed at all.

It was too hot to walk during the middle of the day, and so Jim waited the sun out. He switched into his running clothes (Lycra, windbreaker) and sneakers and headed out with just a quick wave to Sylvia, who was

81

curled into one of the living room sofas with a book three inches from her face. She was on *Villette,* working her way through the Brontës. She'd read all of Jane Austen that year — Austen was good, but when you told people you liked *Pride and Prejudice,* they expected you to be all sunshine and wedding veils, and Sylvia preferred the rainy moors. The Brontës weren't afraid to let someone die of consumption, which Sylvia respected.

"Be back soon," he said.

Sylvia grunted a response.

"Tell your mom I went for a walk."

"Where else would you have gone?" Sylvia asked, still without looking up from her book.

Jim headed up the hill. Mallorca was dustier than he'd anticipated, less rolling and green than Tuscany or Provence, more rocky and sun-bleached, like Greece. There was supposedly a plateau of some kind a few hundred feet up the road, from which one could see the ocean, and Jim liked the idea of a vista.

Weekends were fairly easy — he wouldn't have been at the office, anyway, and so running his normal errands felt good, natural. He would watch a movie with Sylvia if she'd let him, he would debate about which restaurant to order dinner from, he would run around the park a couple of times. The weekdays were the challenge — Monday mornings, in particular. Being in Mallorca would make that easier. He still woke up at seven a.m., popping out of bed and into the shower. Jim was not a foot-dragger or a lay-about, not like all these young people who were living with their parents until they were thirty and spending their time playing video games. Jim liked to work. The weekend hadn't been bad, but today was worse, though not as bad as when they were at home, when his chest seized just at the moment the alarm was to go off, his body panicked at its lack of forward momentum.

For the past forty years, every day at work had been spent moving ahead, trying to be the smartest he could, trying to be the best he could, trying to open as many doors as possible, and now, just like that, the doors had closed, and he had nothing to do but sit at home and wait for the phone to ring. Which it wouldn't. The board had made that clear: it wasn't a threat, it was a prom-ise. Jim was finished, professionally. As long as he wanted them to keep their mouths shut, he would stay home and take up bird-watching. This was presented as a courtesy. The gaping maw on the other side of the silence was that every magazine in New York and every website with a gossip column would be delighted to list the salacious details at length. Jim would have balked at the threat if he hadn't recognized it as the truth. *Gallant*'s new editor would be a clear-eyed man of thirty-five — even if no tragedy had taken place, Jim's tenure had an expiration date. No one wanted advice from their father.

The road was steep, and even though the most intense heat of the day had passed, there was no cover over Jim's head, and the sun felt strong on the back of his neck. If this house had come along three months later, Franny wouldn't have taken it. If Sylvia hadn't graduated, if the whole vacation hadn't been pitched as a gift to her, Franny would have canceled it. Jim didn't know if he should feel grateful that the wheels had already been in motion, or stuck, as though he'd been caught in a bear trap. At home, there were always other quiet rooms, places to hide. Their house had been the right size, once, when there were two kids and a babysitter and visiting grandparents, but now it was far too big. The three of them not only had their own rooms, but had multiples: Jim had his office, and a den that Franny avoided, Sylvia had her room and

Bobby's, which she had turned into a holding pen for local disaffected youth, and Franny had everything else: the kitchen, the garden, the bedroom, her office. They never had to see one another if they didn't want to, could spend days walking in their own loops, like the figurines above the entrance to the Central Park Zoo.

Gallant's board had been unanimous in their decision. That's what surprised Jim the most — he expected censure, yes, but not outright vitriol. The girl — he hated to remember the excitement he felt just hearing her name, Madison, a name he would have ridiculed otherwise — had been twenty-three, the age that Franny was when they got married, so many thousands of years ago. Twenty-three meant that she was an adult, out of college and ready to enter the workforce. An editorial assistant. Franny had pointed out that Madison was only five years older than Sylvia, but twenty-three was an adult, a full-grown woman. Capable of making her own decisions, even if they were bad ones. When the board mentioned Madison, they used the word *girl,* and, once, *child,* which Jim's lawyer had objected to, rightly. It wasn't a courtroom, though, and such language held no weight. They were all sitting around the table in the conference room, as they had so many times before, discussing tedious matters. All ten board members had shown up for the meeting, which was unusual, and Jim knew the moment they walked in that things weren't going to go his way. Not one of the three women on the board looked Jim in the eye.

Jim rounded a corner. There was a long stone wall a few yards ahead, on the ocean side of the road. The mountains seemed to have shifted color with his elevation, and now were tinged with blue. He brushed off the stones and sat down, swinging his legs over so that they dangled a few inches off the ground on the other side. Before him, sheep grazed and strolled, their heads low and content. They wore bells around their neck, which clanged pleasantly as the sheep snuffled in the grass. He didn't know how much Franny had told Charles about the situation at the magazine. The children didn't know much — Bobby didn't know *anything* — and he wanted to keep it that way. According to Jim's resignation, he was leaving his position as editor in order to pursue other passions, to spend more time with his family, and to travel more. Though of course that's exactly what Jim was doing, the implied motives were completely false. If Jim could have, he would have returned from Mallorca and gone straight back to work, gone straight back to work every single day until he dropped dead at his desk, horrifying the young staff, now all trying to be so adult with their natty tie-clips and shiny shoes.

The sun wouldn't set for a few more hours, but it had dipped behind the mountains, and the blue was darker now, as if a watercolor brush had swabbed over the trees and rocks and hillside. Jim could have walked farther, but the road was steep, and more than exercising, he just wanted a few minutes away. Jim sat and watched the sheep until they all stopped moving and just stood, staring off into the distance or at one another or at the grass underneath their bodies, as if they'd all coordinated it beforehand, this moment of silence. It was the sort of thing you might remark on to the person sitting next to you, a tiny and unimportant but nonetheless noteworthy part of the day. If he had been a different kind of man, he might have written a poem. Instead, Jim swung his legs back over the wall and started his way down the hill. Behind him, the sheeps' bells began to ring again, without hurry. It was all up to Franny, in the end. She wanted to take these two weeks, she'd said. These two weeks to make her decision, with all of them together like a real family. He'd already started to mentally mark things as the last time — the last time he'd do this with his daughter, the last time he'd do that in his house. It had taken thirty-five years to build, and would take only two weeks to fall apart. Jim couldn't take back what he'd done. He had apologized, to Franny and to the magazine, and now it was up to them to decide what his punishment would be. He only hoped that his wife would be less harsh than the stony tribunal of board members, though she (Jim knew, he knew) was entitled to the most ire of all.

It didn't matter that most of the party had flown in that morning, and that they would need to have a third wind in order to stay awake through dessert. Franny had cooked, and everyone was going to sit at the table together. She'd bought fish at the market, and lemons, and Israeli couscous, and fruit for a tart, and enough wine to make the whole thing float. Her hands smelled like rosemary and garlic, which was better than soap. She'd found the rosemary growing in the yard, a great big bush of it, well tended and right by the kitchen door. Carmen was in the shower, and Bobby was changing out of his swimsuit, but everyone else was already dressed and in the dining room. Franny liked this moment most of all: being alone in the kitchen after almost everything was finished, and listening to the assembled guests chatting happily, knowing they were soon to be fed. Charles hadn't come with them on vacation since Bobby was a baby, not for longer than a weekend, and Franny's pulse quickened happily at the sound of his voice and Sylvia's together. They were friends. How had that happened? It felt impossible that Sylvia was already eighteen, and that she would be leaving so soon. *Leaving.* That was the word she liked to use. Not *going away*, which implied a return, but *leaving,* which implied a jet plane. Franny would never have been so cruel to her own mother, who had insisted on weekly dinners throughout her first year at Barnard, as if Brooklyn and Manhattan had anything to do with each other, as if she hadn't just moved to another hemisphere. If she and Jim were really over, Sylvia would have it even worse. When she came home to visit, where would she go? To her mother in an otherwise empty house? To her father in a bachelor apartment, slick and sad with all new furniture? Franny stared into space, her hands still on the corkscrew.

"Can I help with anything?" Carmen appeared just behind Franny's right shoulder, startling her.

"No, no, all done," Franny said. "Well, you can carry this to the table." She put down the bottle of wine and handed Carmen a bowl. "No, wait," she said, and handed her a different one. Franny always wanted to carry in the most impressive-looking dish, no matter that everyone knew she'd cooked everything on the table.

Carmen's dark hair was wet, and her curls hung heavily over her shoulders. It was what Franny's hair had looked like before she'd had the Brazilians zap it with lasers, or whatever they did at the salon. It was the first beauty treatment she felt was truly life-altering, after discovering mustache bleach when she was a teenager.

"Thank you for having us here," Carmen said. She had put on makeup, which Franny found distasteful. After all, it was only the family, and they were only having dinner. She would just have to wash it off in a few hours. Putting on makeup for this crowd, at this hour, smacked of deep-seated insecurity, which Franny had little patience for, both as a host and as Carmen's boyfriend's mother, on his behalf. Of course, Franny didn't trust anyone whose life's work was shaping other people's altoids, anyway. No, Altoids were the mints. Deltoids. Still, it was nice that she was making an effort.

"Of course," Franny said. "We're so glad you could join us. And how is everything going, at the gym?"

"It's good! It's busy. Really good. Yeah." Carmen nodded several times.

"Well, shall we?" Franny asked, gesturing toward the dining room. She waited until Carmen had passed in front of her to roll her eyes. Life would be so much easier, Franny often thought, if one were permitted to select romantic partners for one's children. There was nothing physically wrong with Carmen, save for the lack of egg production in her forty-year-old ovaries, but that wasn't even the worst of it. She was a deadly bore, and that problem couldn't be solved with in vitro. Still, she had shown up, and offered to help, which was more than Franny could say for either of her children.

DAY FOUR

Bobby and Carmen's room was between
Sylvia's room and the bathroom and overlooked the pool, which meant that any noise
louder than a whisper could potentially be
heard by everyone in the entire house.
Bobby was awake but hadn't moved yet, not
even wiggled his toes — Carmen was still
snoring softly next to him, and he didn't
want to disturb her.

At their apartment in Miami, Carmen was
up before dawn. Her clients liked to get in a
workout before heading to the office, and so
she started seeing people at five-thirty a.m.,
straight through until ten a.m. Then there
was a break until the lunchtime crowd, and
then she was booked again from eleven a.m.
until two p.m. She saw up to eight clients a
day, sometimes more. Everyone at Total
Body Power knew that Carmen got results,
and that she worked you harder than the
other trainers. She'd been seeing some of

her clients for more than a decade, back from when she was fresh out of kinesiology school and working at the YMCA. Bobby'd come to the gym looking for some help with his lats and traps, and that was that. Of course, that was when Bobby had the money to spend on a personal trainer twice a week.

His mother was up — Bobby could hear the pans banging onto and off the stove, the sound of pancakes being distributed or eggs being cracked. Maybe both. Franny liked to show off for a crowd, to separate whites from yolks with a single hand, to warm the syrup on the stove. His mother's favorite currency was food. When Sylvia was small and Bobby was still at home, Franny would pour pancakes into the shapes of animals, which thrilled them both, even though Bobby had always felt that it was his duty as the older child to pretend not to care.

Carmen grumbled and turned onto her side, taking the sheet with her.

"Good morning," Bobby said, using his best newscaster voice. Carmen thumped him in the chest without opening her eyes. "It's late."

"How late?" she said, eyes still closed.

"After eight."

"Jesus." Carmen shimmied her body

93

backward until she was sitting up against the wrought-iron headboard. She was wearing her pajamas: a pair of faded boxer shorts that preceded her relationship with Bobby, now going on six years, and a pale pink camisole that clung to her rib cage and small breasts, her dark bull's-eye nipples showing through. If you asked the Posts, they would all tell you exactly what kind of body Bobby found attractive: a thickened teenage gymnast, women who looked like they couldn't ovulate if you gave them a million dollars. He didn't care. Bobby loved how hard Carmen worked on her body. Her thighs were her calling cards; her biceps were her advertisements. She looked strong and serious, which she was. Bobby respected that she always knew what she wanted, from herself and from her clients. If she told him to drop to the ground and give her twenty push-ups, he'd do it. She had a strong sense of the human body, and of what people could do, if encouraged. It was one of the things Bobby liked most about her.

"When are you going to talk to them about the money?"

Bobby had been putting off a real conversation with his parents for months — every time his mother called, he got off the phone as quickly as possible, or else turned the chat around and asked Franny about whatever she was doing, which would get her going for at least twenty minutes, a respectable period of time. He hated to ask for money, and even more than that, he hated the reason he needed it. At first he'd just needed a little sideline business, something to tide his bank account over until the real estate market picked back up. He hadn't planned to stay at the gym for longer than a few months. When the best membership salesman at Total Body Power approached Bobby about selling the supplement powders, it sounded like a no-lose scenario. Those were his exact words: "no lose." So far, Bobby had lost every penny he'd ever saved, plus about a million pennies he'd never had in the first place.

"Soon. I just need to find the right moment. You don't know them," Bobby said. "It has to be at the right time." He leaned back against the wall.

"Fine. Just remember that you said you were going to do it, and so you actually have to open your mouth, okay?" She got out of bed and stretched. "I think we should go to the beach, don't you? Or do you need to think about that, too?"

"I'm coming, I'm coming, yes," Bobby said, even though the idea of staying in bed,

95

alone, sounded suddenly blissful. He swung his legs over to his side and touched his toes to the cool stone floor. Charles and Lawrence were in the kitchen now — he could hear their voices, and then his mother's laugh. There would be plenty of time spent sitting around, listening to them all tell the same stories over and over again, Sylvia somehow laughing inside it all. Bobby knew that the conventional thought was that she had been the accidental child, that she was the one born too late, but he couldn't help feeling that it was the other way around, that he'd been born too early, before his parents got their act together. He'd had to figure out so many things on his own, not that they'd ever acknowledge that. The Posts were masters of self-delusion, all of them. "Yeah, let's go."

Gemma had promised Wi-Fi (password: MALLORCA!), but she hadn't mentioned details: the network was slower than dial-up and worked only when the laptop or telephone in question was held over the kitchen sink. Lawrence hadn't technically taken a vacation, but since he worked from home, what was the difference? Spain was the same as New York, which was the same as Provincetown, not counting time zones. Charles liked to make fun of Lawrence by saying that he had the least glamorous job in the most glamorous field — he did accounting for the movies, keeping track of the budget and the salaries and the deductions. The trailer rentals, the lights, the gluten-free wraps with hummus and bean sprouts. He was working on a movie that was filming in Toronto, a Christmas-themed werewolf comedy called *Santa Claws.* A lot of the money went to fake fur and soap flakes to be used as snow.

"Oops, sorry, Lawrence," Franny said, bumping her bottom into his hip as she bent down to reach into the oven to check on a quiche. "Close quarters!"

"No, no, I'm sorry, I'm just completely in the way," he said, and then flapped his free hand in frustration. "I just need to send this one spreadsheet, and then I'm really done." Lawrence held the computer up toward the ceiling and waved it a bit from side to side until he heard the telltale *whoosh* that meant the e-mail had been sent. There was a noise that some more e-mails had come in, but he didn't even scan through them before bringing the laptop back down to his chest and closing it. "All yours."

It was just the three of them — Sylvia was still in bed, Bobby and his girlfriend had gone off to the beach, both of them entirely clothed in high-tech fabrics as if they were about to run a triathlon, and Jim was swimming laps in the pool, visible through the kitchen windows. Charles sat at the head of the table, a cup of coffee held daintily in his hands, as if he were expecting the queen of Spain to walk through the door. Lawrence loved so many things about his husband: the way his white and gray stubble looked on his face and head, all more or less the same length and prickliness; the expression on his face when he was looking at something he wanted to keep, something he wanted to paint. But Lawrence did not love that he felt invisible whenever Franny Post was in the room.

"Darling, do you remember that woman who used to be married to George, what was her name, Mary someone?" Franny asked, poking a finger into the eggy surface of her quiche, which would sit out on the counter all day, everyone nicking a slim piece when they felt like it. Franny was good at producing massive quantities of the sort of food no one notices — the dense, dark muffins that were equally good at four p.m. as they were for breakfast; the cut-up fruit in a large bowl on the center rack of the refrigerator. She liked a house full of grazers, thinking that satisfied stomachs led to satisfied guests.

"Rich Mary? The one with the limp?" Charles didn't take his eyes off Franny as Lawrence scooted around to the far side of the table, to the seat next to him. Lawrence opened his computer again to look at the e-mails, hoping that the stupid werewolves would leave him alone for a few hours. There were a bunch of junky e-mails — sample sales in Chelsea at the place where he liked to buy their sheets; J.Crew; a forwarded series of political cartoons sent by his mother; the New York Public Library; MoveOn.org. Lawrence deleted them all quickly. Then, left at the very top, was an e-mail from their social worker at the adoption agency. Lawrence felt suddenly out of breath. Charles and Franny kept talking, but he could no longer hear them. He read the e-mail once, and then again. The words jumbled together on his screen. *I know you're on vacation, but there is a baby boy. Please call me as soon as you can.* He tried to tune back in to the conversation so he could extricate his husband as quickly as possible. He didn't care how much it cost to call New York, or what time it was. They were getting on the phone.

"Rich Mary! You should see her now! Her

face is like the surface of a balloon. It used to have angles and now it's all" — here Franny made a sucking noise — "*smooth*. And they're not even married anymore. I think she used all of her divorce money to get someone to put a vacuum cleaner on her face." Franny turned off the oven, satisfied.

"Some people," Charles said, shaking his head and laughing, though Lawrence knew that both Franny and Charles had had needles injected into their foreheads in order to make wrinkles disappear. They'd gone to the same dermatologist. Vanity was a problem only when it was someone else's. Lawrence wondered what the cutoff was: knives, maybe, or general anesthesia.

"Honey," Lawrence said, standing up, "can I talk to you for a second?"

Before Charles could respond, Jim hurried in through the back door, his hair plastered to the side of his head like a Ken doll's. He hunched over, his towel wrapped around his wet shoulders.

"How's the water?" Charles asked. Franny crossed her arms and leaned back against the fridge.

"Fine," Jim said. He shook his head to one side, clearing out a clogged ear.

"How's life at *Gallant*?" Lawrence asked

out of habit, wanting to be polite but really just trying to get out of the room as quickly as possible, but as soon as the syllables were out of his mouth, he remembered. Lawrence felt Charles grab his knee and give it a hard squeeze, too tight to be flirty. "I mean, how is it being at home?" Lawrence felt his face begin to flush. All he knew was that Jim had been "let go"; Charles hadn't wanted to say more.

"Well," Jim said, standing up straight again. He looked toward Franny, who hadn't moved or smiled. "It's a change, that's for sure." He narrowed his eyes at a spot on the ceiling, and Lawrence followed his gaze, finding nothing but a tiny crack in the white paint. "Think I'll go shower off."

Lawrence, Charles, and Franny all stayed exactly where they were, like actors in a play the moment before the lights came on, until they heard the bathroom door click shut. Charles was out of his chair and across the room before Lawrence could speak again. Lawrence watched as his husband drew Franny into his arms. Her arms wrapped all the way around Charles's back, where she clasped her own wrist, the way sixth-grade boys knotted their arms around their dance partners. Franny's thick shoulders began to jerk up and down, though her crying didn't make a sound. Lawrence wished he could see Charles's face, but it was pointing in the other direction.

"I'm really sorry," Lawrence said. "I don't know what happened," meaning both that he didn't know what had gone down at the magazine and that he didn't know what had occurred in the three previous minutes. Neither Franny nor Charles made any sign that they had heard him. The kitchen smelled like warm food and tenderness. Lawrence knit his fingers together in his lap and waited for the moment to pass, which it did. Franny gave her head a shake and patted her damp cheeks with her fingers. Charles kissed her on the forehead and then returned to his chair. No one would have cried if they'd gone to Palm Springs and done nothing but had sex and read books for two weeks. Lawrence said a little prayer for the vacation he'd actually wanted, and then watched it — *poof* — float away. He needed Franny to stop crying, and then he needed his husband's full attention, before someone else called the agency and claimed the child, before the open door was closed and their baby wasn't their baby, before they were old and creaky and alone forever and ever, just the two of them and Charles's paintings of other people's children. He waited patiently, counting his breaths until he got to ten, and then starting over.

Sylvia woke up with a dry, open mouth. She'd had four glasses of wine at dinner, and the jet lag made her feel like she had cinder blocks tied to her ankles. She rolled onto her stomach and reached for the clock — her own clock, also known as her watch, also known as her iPhone, was on permanent airplane mode, lacking all of its usual distractions and conveniences, and she found the separation from the object jarring, as if she'd woken up and found that she was missing a finger. A good finger. It was something she hadn't considered when her parents presented her with the notion of a trip to Spain. Of course the Internet was still there, whoring away at all hours, and she could get access to everything on her laptop. If the sensation of loss hadn't been so great, Sylvia might have liked having a little distance from the rest of the world. The problem was you never knew what people were saying about you when you were gone. It was an even bigger problem than knowing what people were saying about you when you were within earshot.

The photos were taken at a party, one of the first "last parties" of the year. There was

the last party at the park the cops never
checked, there was the last party at someone's free house, then the last party at
someone *else's* free house. The party in
question had taken place at an apartment
on the sixth floor of the Apthorp, a giant
building on 79th Street, only five blocks
from the Post family manse. Sylvia hadn't
wanted to go, but she had, because she did
like *some* of the people she was graduating
with, if not very many of them. When the
photos surfaced on Facebook the next day,
her skin slick with sweat, her eyes blurry
from too many plastic cups full of cheap
beer, her tongue in one boy's mouth and
then another and another, boys she didn't
even remember speaking to, she vowed to
herself that she would never go to a party
ever again. Or on the Internet. Moving to
Spain was sounding better and better.

"Shit!" she said, looking at the time. She
had three minutes to get dressed and downstairs before Joan would arrive. Sylvia pulled
on her jeans and a black T-shirt from the
pile on the floor. She leaned against the mirror and looked at her pores. There were girls
at school who spent hours in the ladies'
room putting on makeup expertly, as though
they were each teaching their own YouTube
tutorial, but Sylvia didn't know how, nor

did she want to learn. It was almost impossible to change anything about yourself at a school you'd been attending since you were five — with every tiny step away from your former shell, someone was bound to say, "Hey! That's not you! You're faking!" Sylvia lived in fear of such fakery. Going to college was going to be amazing for many reasons, the first of which being the simple fact that Sylvia planned to be a completely different person the moment she arrived, even before she made her bed and pushpinned stupid posters on the walls. This new person was going to know how to put on makeup, even eyeliner. She stretched her mouth open and peered into her throat, thinking, not for the first time, that it was all completely and utterly hopeless and that she was almost certainly going to die a sad, lonely virgin who had accidentally gotten drunk and made out with every single boy at a party her senior year of high school, a slattern without the added benefit of actual sex. She dug through the plastic baggie she used for makeup until she found a tube of strawberry ChapStick and slathered it across her lips. She'd try harder tomorrow.

Lawrence pulled Charles into their bedroom as quickly as he could.

"What are you doing, my strange little munchkin?" Charles was amused, despite having just left Franny's soggy embrace.

In lieu of an answer, Lawrence opened his laptop and spun it in Charles's direction.

"Give me the phone," Charles said. "What time is it in New York?"

It was just before five p.m. in New York, and they managed to catch the social worker before she was out the door. Deborah read them the details off a form: the baby weighed five pounds, ten ounces and was seventeen inches long, born to a twenty-year-old African-American mother. The father was Puerto Rican, but he was out of the picture. The birth mother had chosen their letter out of the book at the agency. The baby's name, which they would of course be welcome to change, was Alphonse.

"Are you interested in proceeding?" Deborah waited.

Charles and Lawrence held the phone between their faces, both leaning forward, so that together their bodies formed a steeple. They looked at each other, eyes wide. Lawrence spoke first.

"Yes," he said. "Yes, we are."

Deborah explained what would happen next — they'd heard it before, but like everything important, the minute that it became a reality, they'd forgotten all the details. The birth mother could choose any number of families, and the agency would approach them all on her behalf. Once those families had said yes, the agency would go back to her with the list. The birth mother would then pick the winners, as it were. The choice was out of their hands.

"We're in Spain," Lawrence said. "Should we come home? Should we come home right now?" He glanced around their bedroom, calculating how long it would take them to pack and drive to the airport.

"Stay on vacation," Deborah said. "Even if the birth mother does choose you, we're looking at a couple of weeks before you'd be able to bring Alphonse home. If you can stay, stay. I'll be in touch whenever I hear something, probably next week." She hung up the phone, leaving Charles and Lawrence standing there, the precious object now silent between them.

"Do you want to go home?" Charles asked.

Flying back to New York and furiously buying cribs and bouncy seats and high chairs and then not being chosen would be even worse than staying where they were, Lawrence knew. Let Mallorca be a distraction. Let the Posts try to get him to think about anything else, when there was Alphonse, sweet Alphonse, a baby in a hospital somewhere in New York City, a boy who needed his fathers. Staying was better than rushing back and not being picked. Lawrence didn't want to let himself get too excited or take anything for granted. He wished he knew if the birth mother had picked all gay couples, who else they were up against. He wanted to see photographs of smiling families, and then to strangle the competition.

"We can stay," Lawrence said. "Let's stay."

Joan was waiting at the door. It took such self-confidence to just stand there, knowing that someone would let him in. Sylvia was sure that Joan had never worried about anything in his entire life. He probably wouldn't have rung the bell for another ten minutes, content to breathe in the clear air, to watch packs of bicyclists zoom by, their spandex clothes blurring together. He probably would have written a poem about it in his head, just because, not even minding when it all vanished a moment later. Joan smiled when she opened the door, and kept smiling as he walked through the dark foyer. Sylvia looked at their reflection in the giant mirror hanging behind his head, and then followed him into the bright dining room. If Joan had a girlfriend, which he obviously did, she would know how to put on eyeliner. She would know how to give a perfect blowjob. She would know how to do everything.

"Tienes novia?" Sylvia asked, only half meaning to voice the question. "I mean, my mom was asking me. I told her I would ask you. She's really nosy. What's the word for nosy? You know, always in everyone else's business?"

Joan sat down and crossed his legs. In New York, only the gay boys crossed their legs. The straight ones made a point (especially on the subway) to sit with their knees as far apart as possible, as if whatever was between their legs was so enormous that they couldn't help it. Sylvia respected how little Joan seemed to care about seeming heterosexual. "Not really. When I'm in Barcelona." Joan shrugged. It was easy for him to find girls, of course. *Claro.*

There was a shuffling sound, and laughter, and then Charles and Lawrence stumbled into the kitchen, one of them clearly chasing the other. Charles reached the kitchen first and stopped short when he saw Joan.

"Hola," he said.

"Hola," Joan said back.

"Hola, Sylvia," Charles said again, his entire face a wink. He smoothed his forehead as if he were brushing bangs out of his eyes.

"Oh, Jesus, just leave us alone," Sylvia said, which set them off again, giggling like prom dates. Charles and Lawrence zipped through the kitchen and out the back door, setting themselves up nicely in the sun. Charles held their books, and Lawrence held the towels. Somewhere in the pile there was some sunscreen, and a hat to protect Charles's scalp from burning. Sylvia watched them settle in, feeling simultaneously envious and like love, in its best form, was something for comfortable adults, and something she might expect to find only decades down the road. *"Let's talk about the future,"* she said to Joan, who was staring off into space, perhaps contemplating his own beautiful existence.

Even though Franny was the cook in the family, Bobby and Jim both had very particular feelings about grilling meat. If Franny had minded surrendering the tongs, or found it at all sexist that the men in her family enjoyed sticking things into the fire, as all men had since the cave, she would not have relinquished her position. As it was, she had never much liked getting a face full of smoke, and was quite happy to let someone else do the lion's share for a change. Jim liked to make sure the grill was hot enough, to add newspaper or coals and occasionally douse the whole lot with a good squirt of lighter fluid. Bobby liked the cooking of the meat itself — the smell of the initial sear, the way the meat firmed up around his poking finger as it neared ready. Charles and Lawrence had no interest whatsoever and sat with the girls on the opposite end of the pool, Sylvia in the water doing somersaults.

They'd bought thin steaks (Franny had put a hand on her rib cage, along the diaphragm, at the butcher counter, a pantomime that seemed to have worked), and Jim had marinated them in some oily concoction all afternoon. The grill was fairly new, which made Jim grumble. It was the years of use that lent great flavor, like a cast-iron pan. He scraped the grill with a stiff metal brush he'd found, trying to generate some kind of friction that would elevate the meal. The day had started to cool — like clockwork, a western wind worked its way through the mountains every evening, forcing all but the most stubborn children out

111

of their swimming pools and into their clothes.

The house was exactly what Franny liked: beautiful and in the middle of nowhere. It was the sort of quirk that used to be charming — they'd go to some exotic foreign land, or to a boundless state like Wyoming, but without fail, the rental Franny had chosen would always be just far enough away from everything else that it was exactly like being at home, only with a different backdrop strung behind them. Jim gave the grill another good scrape. It was nearly hot enough — the heat made the air above the slats go wavy.

"It's ready," Jim said. "Should be three or four minutes on each side. We don't want to overcook them."

Bobby appeared at Jim's side. He peeled the first steak off the plate and lowered it onto the grill, where it let out a great hiss.

"That's good," Jim said. "We want that sear." It was like talking to an invisible camera on the other side of the grill, someone doing a documentary on father-son small chat. Jim was no good at it, he knew. He wanted to ask Bobby about Carmen, about what the hell he was doing in Florida, that rancid pit of a place. He wanted to tell Bobby what he'd done, how fuzzy the future

112

was, how he was sorry for letting them all down. Instead, Jim found he could talk only about their dinner.

Bobby lined up the other steaks, all in a neat row, and then stood back, beside his father. They were the same height, more or less, though Bobby still couldn't seem to stand up straight. Bobby had broader shoulders, and larger biceps, but he'd never lost his ragdoll posture.

"Any interesting properties on the market?" Jim asked. He crossed his arms over his chest, keeping his eyes on the steaks.

"Sure, oh, yeah," Bobby said. He'd been a real estate agent for years along Miami Beach, mostly renting but occasionally selling properties near where he and Carmen lived. They hadn't always lived together, but it had been a few years now of what seemed like a good domestic situation — the bedroom had blackout shades and a ceiling fan whirred away in the living room, and they were just a few blocks from the ocean. Franny so wanted Bobby to have a child — he was almost thirty, and had spent most of his twenties with a woman who had now aged out of her childbearing years. When they were alone at night, after half a bottle of wine, that was often what Franny wanted to talk about, wondering how Bobby had gone off course, and whether it was her fault. Jim wasn't sure the boy was ready. He might be, some years down the road, but not yet. Privately, Jim assumed that the blessed event would occur quite out of the blue, when some girl called him up some time after the fact and produced a very Post-like baby, his or her mounting bills tucked into the back of their adorable onesie. "I've got a really sweet two-bedroom on Collins and Forty-fourth, right across from the Fontainebleau. Travertine, glass, everything. Brand-new bathroom — it has one of those crazy Japanese toilets, you know, with the sprays and the heat? It's a nice one. And then there are a couple of houses over on the other side, in the city. Good stuff."

"And the prices? Coming back up?" Jim nudged one of the steaks with the end of his tongs.

Bobby shrugged. "Not much. You know, it's still pretty rough. Not everywhere is like Manhattan. I mean, like, your house is worth, what, six times what you paid for it? Five times what you paid? That's amazing. It's not like that in Florida."

"You could always move back, you know. You want to sell our house?" Jim laughed at the thought of it; he wasn't serious. Who sold a limestone on the Upper West Side?

Even if it was too big? Even if they got a divorce? Jim thought they would ride it all out, he was almost positive, and if they were going to ride it all out, they were going to do it in their house. Feet first, that's what they liked to say. Every time they repainted a ceiling or fixed the crumbling 1895 wires in the basement — feet first, that was the only way they were leaving the house. Now Jim didn't know. Franny had mentioned selling the house a dozen times, sometimes at full volume, and he had started to look at rentals in the neighborhood, but no, they wouldn't sell the house, they couldn't. It made Jim feel like his knees might buckle.

"Wow, I mean, that would be an incredible opportunity, Dad." Bobby looked at him through the fallen curls on his forehead. Jim hated it when Bobby had long hair — it made him look too soft, too young, like a goddamn baby deer. Just like Franny when she was in her twenties, only without the spitfire spirit that had made him fall in love with her.

"Oh, I wasn't . . . Moving back, yes. That would be lovely. I don't think we're quite ready to hand over the keys to the house, though, chum." Jim hoped his voice sounded light.

"Right, no, of course." Bobby pushed his

115

hair out of his eyes and reached for the tongs. "Mind if I flip?"

"Of course," Jim said, taking a step back, and then another, until he felt something prickly on his neck. He turned around and was surprised to find that he'd made it all the way to the trees at the edge of the manicured section of the yard, before the land dropped down steeply and led, eventually, to an ancient-looking town, where Spanish fathers and sons had tended olive trees and raised sheep together for centuries, working in tandem, like two parts of the same organism.

Bobby had retired quickly after dinner, claiming a headache, and Jim, Sylvia, and Charles had settled into the living room sofa for their umpteenth viewing of *Charade,* which Gemma happened to have on DVD. It was one of Sylvia's favorites. Cary Grant was sort of like her dad, plus or minus the chin cleft — high-waisted pants and a way of talking that was both flirtatious and belittling at the same time. It was what stupid girls in her grade liked to classify as "like, sexist," and she would have argued with them, but now she wasn't sure, maybe they were right. Sylvia sat in the middle, with her head on Charles's lap and her feet tucked up into her chest so that they didn't quite hit her father's thighs. It was a rare moment when Sylvia thought she might miss living at home, but they did exist, even when she was already so many thousands of miles away. Walter Matthau was chasing Audrey Hepburn, his droopy dog face the saddest thing for miles. Sylvia closed her eyes and listened to the rest of the movie, kept awake by the chuckles and exclamations of her two companions.

Part of the fun of going on vacation with so many people was supposed to be that you didn't all have to be together all the time — that was what Franny had imagined. She was clearing up the kitchen and the pool area — Carmen seemed to have been raised by actual humans, and put things away and helped wash dishes, but Franny couldn't say the same for her children. The pool was a mess — discarded plates with nubs of fatty steak left behind, all the better to coerce coyotes or dingoes or whatever the local wild dogs were out of their hiding places. "Let me help," Lawrence said, pulling the door to the kitchen closed behind him. They were in sweaters now. In New York, they would still be shvitzing, the concrete of the sidewalk and the buildings acting as heat conductors, keeping everyone glistening from June through September. It was a lovely night in Pigpen, clear and dark. Once the sun went down, the only lights were the ones in the house across the way and down the mountain's slopes. It reminded Lawrence of Los Angeles, only with a quarter as many houses and actual oxygen.

"Oh, thanks," Franny said. "My children are animals."

"Mine, too," Lawrence said, projecting into the future, his arms already wrapped around a small body swaddled in cotton. A tiny thrill shot up his spine. "I mean, you should see Charles's studio."

"Oh, I know," Franny said. "All ancient pad thai affixed to paper plates. It's his response to post-1980s expressionism excess, I think."

Franny sat down on one of the lounge chairs and picked up a pile of napkins and magazines and orange peels, Sylvia's detritus. "She's going to college. Ivy League. You'd think that she could throw something away."

Lawrence reached out for the garbage, and then held it against his chest. He stood between Franny and the house. If Sylvia and the boys were to get up, in search of more to eat, they would see only his silhouette against the rest of the dark.

"Listen," he said. "I'm really sorry about earlier. About saying something about the magazine, to Jim. I honestly don't know what happened, but I do know that I put my foot in my mouth."

Franny leaned back, drawing her legs up beneath her. She stretched her arms over her head, and then lowered them until they were blocking her eyes. She groaned. Franny had never felt older than she had in the last six months. It was true, of course, that was always true, that you'd never been older than you were at precisely this moment, but Franny had gone from feeling youngish to wizened and crumpled in record time. She could feel the knots in her back tighten, and her sciatic nerve begin to send out little waves of distress to the sides of her hips.

"I'm sorry," Lawrence said, not sure if he was apologizing for worsening Franny's mood or for whatever had happened with Jim at the magazine, or both.

"It's okay," Franny said, her eyes still hidden behind her arms. "I'm surprised Charles didn't tell you."

Lawrence sat down on the lounge chair next to Franny's and waited.

"He fucked an intern." She moved her hands and waved them around, as if to say

"Abracadabra!" "I know, that's it. Jim fucked an intern. A girl at the magazine, barely older than Sylvia. Twenty-three years old. Her father is on the board, and I guess she told him, and so here we are."

"Oh, Franny," Lawrence said, but she was already sitting up and shaking her head. He had imagined many scenarios for Jim's sudden leave from *Gallant,* and for the tension in the Post family — prostate cancer, early-onset dementia, an ill-timed conversion to the Jehovah's Witnesses — but not this one. Jim and Franny had always seemed happily solid, still capable of goosing each other in the kitchen, as off-putting as it sometimes was.

"No, it's fine. I mean, it's not fine, we've been married for thirty-five years, it is not fine for him to have sex with a twenty-year-old. A twenty-three-year-old. As if there's a difference. I don't know. Thank you. Sylvia knows some, but Bobby doesn't know anything about it, I'm pretty sure, and I'm trying to keep it that way for as long as possible. Maybe forever."

It was strange that Charles hadn't told him. Lawrence felt his cheeks flush with embarrassment, his own, not on Franny's behalf. How could Charles not have told him? Lawrence quickly imagined all the ways he could have mortified Jim and Franny over the next two weeks, without ever knowing what he was doing, all the ways he could have said the wrong thing.

Lawrence reached out and put his hand on Franny's shoulder. "I'm really sorry, Fran. I won't say a word to the kids, of course. And I'm sure Charles would be delighted to murder him for you, if you just say the word."

That made her smile. "Yes, I think so." She stood up. "At least one of us has a good husband. Come on, let's finish cleaning up before it's morning and the cretins destroy everything all over again. It's not the worst thing in the world not to have children, you know. Makes your life a terrible mess." And with that, Franny kissed Lawrence on the cheek, almost tenderly, and walked back inside. Lawrence turned and watched her through the window as she turned on the faucet and squirted soap onto the offending pile of dishes. Lawrence was still holding a stack of garbage on his lap, including a magazine left over from the airplane full of "Sex Tips He Won't Believe" and "What You REALLY Need to Know About Going Downtown." He couldn't believe Jim and Franny let Sylvia buy trash like that — it seemed as bad as openly reading an issue of

Hustler. He thumbed through to the article about oral sex, which was really more like a list, complete with reader suggestions. Straight girls really just needed to watch one or two gay porn movies in order to learn everything they needed to know, Lawrence thought. Maybe he'd tell Sylvia that one of these days. Something moved in the corner of his eye, and Lawrence looked upstairs. Carmen was staring back at him from her open bedroom window. They made eye contact, and Carmen put a finger to her ear, as if to say, *I didn't hear anything,* and then the light was out and the curtain was drawn and she was gone.

DAY FIVE

Franny and Sylvia drove with Joan, and Charles, Jim, and Lawrence followed behind them. It was Franny's idea to make a pilgrimage to the Robert Graves House in Deià, even though Franny claimed not to know anything about Robert Graves aside from the 1976 TV movie version of *I, Claudius,* which Jim said made her a heathen. That was right before they got into their separate cars and drove the forty minutes north. Sylvia was excited to get out of the house, but would have preferred a trip to the beach, despite the obvious drawback of having to deal with sand. This was like going on a school field trip with her mother, a pleasure she hadn't had since elementary school, when Franny routinely volunteered to accompany the class to the zoo or the Museum of Natural History, when she would then shirk her duties and run amok, waddling in front of the penguins like the rest of the children. At least Joan was along for the ride. Franny made him drive, of course, because he knew where he was going and wouldn't destroy the stick shift of the tiny tin box of a rental car, and also because she liked to sit in the front seat and be driven around islands by handsome twenty-year-olds. If Jim could objectify someone barely out of the teens, so could she.

"Sorry that we're all crashing your date with Joan today, Syl," Franny said, winking at her in the backseat. Joan checked her reaction briefly in the rearview mirror, his eyes faster than a snake.

"Let's try to stay adult here, shall we?" Sylvia said. "I'm sorry that my mother is sexually harassing you, Joan. *No le prestes atención.*" She crossed her arms over her chest, secure in the fact that her mother would be adequately annoyed and therefore stay quiet for the rest of the ride. Franny turned to look out the window and hummed something to herself, a song that had nothing whatsoever in common with the song playing on the car's cheap radio, a Céline Dion song that came and went as the mountain roads unfurled ahead of them. She rolled the window down halfway, enough for the air to send her short dark hair across her face.

Sylvia leaned back, curling her body into the corner of the seat. The car was the size of a pedicab, and about as secure. The chassis rocked side to side as they climbed a hill, and Sylvia closed her eyes, happy that if she was going to die on the mountainous roads of Mallorca, she at least would have had the last word with her mother. It wasn't fair to be annoyed with her, but Sylvia was anyway. Obviously her father was worse, and the one to blame, but Sylvia had been inside their marriage for long enough to know that it wasn't that simple, nothing was, certainly not a relationship twice as old as her. In the back of the car, with her eyes shut tight, New York felt farther away than an ocean, not that she missed it. Surely there were parties going on, *woo-hoo,* at someone's empty house, with bottles of booze and lemonade all poured into some giant vat of vaguely citrus-tasting awfulness, but she would never go to a party like that again. One would think that a lifetime of being a good girl followed by one stupid mistake would pretty much even out, but one would be wrong.

There were four people from her class also going to Brown, but two of them she would immediately never speak to again, an obvious and unspoken agreement based on the fact that they hadn't exchanged more than three words in all of high school. The other two were the problem: Katie Saperstein and Gabe Thrush. If Sylvia could have chosen two people to excommunicate for the rest of her life, to actually push a button and have them vanish off the planet, it would be Katie Saperstein and Gabe Thrush. Both together and separately.

Sylvia and Katie had been good friends — mud masks, sleepovers, shared Googling of half-naked movie stars. Katie was plainer than Sylvia; it wasn't cruel to say so — she had brackish-colored hair and a nose that always looked like she'd just walked into a plate-glass door. Once, when Katie was frustrated by how long it was taking to grow out her bangs, she cut them off at her forehead, creating, in essence, a small, growing horn. They both wore terrible clothes (that was the point) from the Salvation Army, ill-fitting jeans and ironic T-shirts advertising places they'd never been. Since tenth grade, they'd been close, eating lunch together most days on one of the stoops around the corner from school, with Sylvia ignoring Katie's blatant overuse of mayonnaise and Katie teasing Sylvia about her resistance to bacon. It was a good friendship, one that might have survived the leap across the chasm into college life. They'd talked about rooming together, even, but that was before Gabe ruined everything.

That was how it went, Sylvia had to remind herself. Even though she vastly preferred blaming Katie, the pug-faced slut, it was really Gabe who had done her wrong. They hadn't been exclusive, of course. No one was, except for the idiots who pretended that they were engaged and went home and had sex during their free periods because their parents weren't home and the maid wouldn't tell. Most people just floated around, too afraid to say what they wanted and too afraid to get it. Gabe had made a habit of coming to the Post house on a weekly basis. He and a few friends would ring the bell sometime in the afternoon, that magical zone during which Franny was bound to be working in her office and Jim was still at the magazine and no one would ask many questions. Sylvia thought it was hysterical how little her mother knew about her life, when her job was supposed to be about paying attention to details. Franny knew everything about how to make mole according to some Mexican grandmother's recipe that she learned in Oaxaca in 1987, but she had no idea that Gabe Thrush was coming over to lick her daughter's rib cage on a regular basis.

They hadn't had sex, obviously. Sylvia could scarcely imagine Gabe paying *less* attention to her, but having sex seemed like it was probably the one way to make that happen. He had tried once, she thought, but didn't know for sure. Mostly it was just rolling around in her bed with her shirt open or off, praying that no one walked in. Sylvia considered the romance the greatest achievement of her life to date, in that Gabe was good-looking (unlike some of the mutants she'd kissed out of boredom at summer camp) and popular, and when he called her on the telephone, they actually had amusing conversations. The problem was that Gabe Thrush was having similar relationships with half their class, including, it turned out, Katie Saperstein.

Unlike Sylvia, Katie had no mixed feelings about putting out. She walked into school on a Monday with a giant hickey on her neck and Gabe Thrush on her arm. Sylvia watched the two of them walk through the double doors, practically oozing postcoital smugness, and felt as snubbed as Katie's nose. That was in April, just before they all found out about who got in where. Since Sylvia was no longer speaking to Katie or

Gabe, she had to hear the good news from Mrs. Rosenblum-Higgins, their largely ineffectual college counselor — wasn't it just *great,* going to Brown with her friends? They were friends, weren't they? It was that weekend that Sylvia went to the party and got too drunk, that weekend when all the photos were taken, that weekend when Facebook exploded and she considered ratting out someone in the Mafia just to be put into witness protection.

The car did another shimmy, as if threatening to go on strike, and Joan turned abruptly up another steep hill — the road had no guardrails, no fences, nothing separating them from plunging to their depths if Joan had to suddenly veer.

"How far are we, Joan?" Sylvia asked. The scenery outside the car's windows looked much the same — sunny and bright, with houses the color of rustic pottery. They passed a field of gnarled and twisted trees, their branches heavy with enormous lemons.

"Deià is a few kilometers more. We are nearly there." Joan was dressed down, in a simple cotton T-shirt, but he was still wearing his cologne. Sylvia could smell it from the backseat. She thought about Gabe Thrush trying to wear cologne, standing in the middle of a crowded floor at Macy's, getting spritzed by hundreds of overeager young saleswomen, and laughed. If either of them tried to get anywhere near her in those lonely first days of college, she would set them on fire in their sleep. They didn't deserve her. No high school boy did. She was better than that, Sylvia knew, bigger and better and ready to shed her skin like a snake.

"Good," she said, arranging herself as sexily as possible in the backseat. "I'm sure my mom has to pee."

The house was just past Deià proper, on the road that led out of town. It had been a museum for just half a dozen years, but like many writers' homes that are open to the public, great pains had been taken to make the house look little changed since Graves's prime. If anything, newfangled items had been removed and replaced by their earlier counterparts, so that the house felt like something of a time warp, still punctuated by the clacking of typewriter keys instead of laptop computers. Jim admired the simplicity of the house, which was like most others in the area, a pale stone building with curved brick doorways and cool floors. They'd somehow beaten the native Mallorcan and the girls, and were already wandering around the small museum's grounds. A friendly woman led them around the two halves of the wide plot, pointing out the highlights of Graves's impressive garden. The heavy floral smell of jasmine floated over the bright faces of the zinnias and the massive tangles of bougainvillea. Charles fancied himself a naturalist and bent over to fondle the colorful leaves of the violets and the cosmos.

"I would kill to have a garden like this." Even at their summer house in Province-town, they had only window boxes. In the city, their apartment overlooked the Hudson River, but the patio was dark most hours of the day, pointing as it did into the cold backs of several taller buildings.

Lawrence laid a hand on his shoulder. "We could always move out of the city for real. Buy a bigger place on the Cape. Less dunes, more dirt." He could so easily picture Alphonse staggering among the planters, picking a tomato with his chubby baby hands. That was the kind of parent Lawrence wanted to be: encouraging and adventurous. Let the baby play in the dirt, let the baby explore.

"Please," Jim said. "Good luck getting him out of there." For a moment, Lawrence thought he meant the baby, but no, of course not. He looked toward Charles, relieved that their limbo status was still a secret. It was probably the way straight couples felt in those first tender weeks of pregnancy, when the egg and sperm had mingled but were so vulnerable that they might not take.

There was a hooting noise at the front entrance, and then a loud laugh as Franny scrambled up the shallow incline toward them. "Are we all moving here?" she asked. "Because I don't think I can do that drive again." She kissed Charles on the cheek, as if it had been weeks since she'd seen him last. "Poor Joan had to deal with us screeching and praying the entire time." She turned around and winked at Joan and Sylvia, now a few feet behind her.

"Would you like the tour of the house?" the docent said kindly, perhaps wanting to hurry them out of the way. Franny puffed out her lip and nodded enthusiastically, as if Robert Graves had been her favorite writer for her entire life and she could hardly believe her luck, being on this sacred ground. It was one of the things that drove Sylvia the craziest about her mother, the mad look on her face when she wanted someone to think she was paying special attention. The woman led the adults through to the house, and Joan and Sylvia followed behind.

When they were enough feet away from her parents that they wouldn't be able to hear her, Sylvia said, "I'm sorry about my mother."

"She's not bad," Joan said. "My mother is a little, eh, too." He wiggled a hand by his ear, the universal sign for crazy.

Sylvia couldn't imagine Joan having a crazy mother, let alone a mother at all. Or a father. Or ever needing to use the bathroom. Or blowing his nose. He stepped aside to let her follow the group into the house, and she got a mouthful of his cologne, which, mixed with the garden jasmine, made her breath catch in her throat. Joan was too much, a water fountain in the middle of the Sahara, a long-shot horse winning the Triple Crown. She couldn't take it. Sylvia hurried toward Charles and took his hand, elbowing Lawrence slightly out of the way.

They looked at the sparse living room, the kitchen with its gorgeous AGA stove, the pantry full of British cookie tins, their bodies crowding together in the roped-off sections of the floor. They trooped upstairs and looked at offices that could have been abandoned long enough to fetch a cup of tea. They marveled over the tiny bed, where

Graves had successively slept with two wives and a mistress.

"Can't be the same bed," Charles said. "No woman would accept that."

"This is not Manhattan, dear," Franny said. "I don't think there's a mattress store on the corner." She swiveled around, looking for the docent, but the woman had left them to their own devices. "I guess we'll never know."

"What do you think, Joan?" Franny said, making eye contact with the tutor. "Have you been here before?"

"On a school trip, yes," he said, nodding. "We learned one of his poems, 'Dew-drop and Diamond.' "

"Do you still know it?" Franny pumped her hands together, beckoning Joan toward her. He squeezed through the doorway, past Jim and Charles and Lawrence, until he was standing in the very center of the room, his body pulling the caution rope taut. "Go on," Franny said, "go on. I just love poetry." Sylvia shrank backward and stared at a spot on the floor.

" *'She like a diamond shone, but you / Shine like an early drop of dew . . .'* That's in the first part, I think. What is the word, stanza?"

Joan closed his eyes for a moment, running the words over again in his mind. "Yes, that's how it goes."

Franny reached out and grabbed his biceps. "Good Lord, boy." She let go and fanned herself. "Is anyone else getting warm?" She looked up at Jim and had a sudden flash of the girl, that stupid girl, and felt her cheeks get even warmer. She let go of Joan's arm.

Lawrence chuckled, and Charles gave him a look. "What?" Lawrence said. "That was hot."

Sylvia was glad to be near the door, and made a swift exit down the stairs, followed closely by her father.

They'd somehow missed the video presentation, a twenty-minute loop projected in a room as clean and bare as a Quaker meetinghouse, and so Jim and Sylvia went there, scooting in just after it began, joining another group of tourists. Franny wouldn't follow them in for fear of being bored to tears, and Charles would rather rub his hands against the rosemary bushes and imagine his life on a craggy mountaintop than sit in a dark room, so they were safe for the moment. Sylvia sat next to her father, but far enough apart that their hips didn't touch on the stark wooden benches.

The voiceover to the video ("I, Robert

Graves") seemed to be narrated posthumously, and Jim and Sylvia both laughed several times. Robert Graves came off like a hilarious eccentric egomaniac, with children riding donkeys down to the beach and an unstable mistress who had jumped out the window and survived. "This is better than reality TV, Syl," Jim whispered, and she nodded, in full agreement. It truly was an advertisement for leaving the city life behind, for finding a parcel of perfection and staying there, no matter how remote. Jim and Franny had never thought about leaving New York, not seriously. She would travel for periods of time while on assignment, but Jim's work couldn't exist elsewhere. He wondered if that was something Franny resented him for, shackling her to Manhattan. It didn't seem likely, but neither did the thought of Madison Vance.

She'd started the previous summer, just after her senior year at Columbia. The magazine had a solid internship program, with scores of bright young people doing menial tasks for no pay. They were at the copy machine, running back and forth to the supply closet, sorting the book room, taking detailed notes (for what reason, Jim was never sure) in meetings. The most promising interns were occasionally given things to do: fact-checking, research, reading the slush. In the fall, she'd been promoted to editorial assistant, a real job with benefits and a 401(k). Madison wore her long hair loose, and after she'd been in his office — this was well before anything happened — Jim would find strands of blond, like filaments of gold, stuck to his furniture.

It was embarrassing, how easily it had happened, how little effort he'd had to exert.

"Cool, huh?" Sylvia said.

"Yep," Jim said, his eyes refocusing on the screen. Instead of watching still images of Robert Graves at work, Robert Graves with his family, Jim saw Madison Vance's naked body. He'd been surprised the first time he'd reached his hand inside her skirt and felt her pussy, waxed and cool, as smooth as a hotel pillowcase. It was the kind of thing Franny would never have done on principle — she was full bush, always, and proud of it, like she was some kind of 1970s *Playboy* Playmate. Madison was the opposite, the slick result of youth raised on Internet porn. She'd groaned the second Jim slid his palm against her clit. When he was her age, he'd barely known what a clitoris was. He regretted so much of what happened, but there were moments that refused to leave his brain. Jim loved his wife, he loved his wife, he loved his wife. But it had been something, after so many years, to move his hand against someone new, not knowing how her body would respond, or how she would shift herself into his touch. He was sweating now, despite the air-conditioning. The film was long, and he was glad. The last thing he wanted was to look his daughter in the face.

Carmen didn't like missing workouts. For her clients, hitting the gym twice a week was the absolute minimum. That was maintenance. You lost muscle tone with any more time away. Taking two weeks' vacation was practically begging to return to sloppy squats and lots of panting. She'd tried to set her clients up with a substitute trainer while she was gone, but Carmen didn't trust the other professionals at Total Body Power not to try to steal them permanently. Jodi was the second-best at the gym, a real killer, and she'd been circling for weeks, after seeing Carmen's name crossed off the schedule. July in Miami was not a joke. Even though it was the off-season for Florida residents, the gym was busy with tourists who got passes from their hotels, and their bodies needed help more than most.

She was doing some circuit training by the pool. Push-ups, burpees, standing squat jumps, invisible jump rope. Bobby swam languid laps and occasionally called out words of advice.

"Atta girl. Explode!" Bobby was still learning the lingo.

They'd met at Total Body Power almost six years ago, when Bobby was two months out of college and still living off the Post credit card. He'd signed up for the premium package — twelve sessions with a trainer, twice a week, for six weeks. He told Carmen he was serious about getting into shape. He'd never been remotely sporty, and had no hand-eye coordination. Bobby's long body had been like a wilting zucchini, the same thickness from top to bottom. Carmen knew just what to do. She'd put him on daily protein powder and had him lifting more weight every week. Bench presses, dead lifts, kettle-bell swings. Bobby did pull-ups and push-ups and jumping jacks. She knew all the machines, and slid the key into heavier and heavier slots. By the end of the six weeks, Bobby's arms had nearly doubled in size, and his stomach, which had always been nearly concave, showed signs of an emerging six-pack. Carmen was an artist of the body, and she had made him from scratch.

They hadn't slept together until the very

end, that last week. Bobby was sorry that the sessions were coming to an end, and he knew that his father would object if he charged another thousand dollars at the gym. He asked Carmen out for a drink, not knowing if she poisoned her body in that way or any other. She said yes, and they met at the bar at the Del Mar hotel. Bobby had picked one of the less glitzy bars on the strip on purpose, not knowing how Carmen looked when she was out of her gym clothes, and not wanting her to feel uncomfortable, but he needn't have worried. She arrived five minutes late wearing Lucite heels and a white dress that ended only a breath below her firm, round bottom.

"Zip it," Carmen said, and started her squats. She pivoted her body so that she was facing away from the pool. She would be forty-one in a few months. Everyone at the gym said that forty was the new twenty-five, and they were right. She was thinking about running a marathon, or maybe doing a triathlon, or maybe both. The difference was in the muscle groups, and in the toning. To run, you needed solid hamstrings and quads, which were good for riding the bike, too, but once you got in the water, it was all about your back and your core. Carmen visualized herself in the water, a swim cap tight around her head. She imagined breaking the surface of water with each breath, drawing in exactly as much energy as she needed to take the next stroke. She would finish in the top of her age bracket, if not higher, that much she knew for sure. Lots of her clients at the gym were in their forties, bodies pouchy from childbirth or laziness. Carmen would never let herself be like that, soft and passive. She was strong.

Bobby hoisted himself out of the pool and lay down, dripping wet, on the recliner closest to Carmen. The sun was directly overhead, but he didn't mind. His whole family pretended they were vampires or cancer victims, deathly afraid of a little vitamin D, but Bobby liked getting some color.

"So," Carmen said, stretching out one calf and bending herself in half over it, her toes lifted toward the sky, "what's up with your parents?"

"What do you mean?"

"You know what I mean." She pulled her left leg back and straightened out the right one. "Tension much?"

Bobby rolled over onto his stomach. "They're always like this."

"My ass."

"Oh, I'm sorry, were we talking about your ass? Because I am way more interested

141

in that conversation." Bobby lifted his head and raised his eyebrows.

Carmen walked over and sat down next to Bobby, both of their bodies too big for the narrow lounge chair. "I'm serious. Are your parents okay? They seem so, I don't know, touchy."

"They're fine. They're always like that. I don't know. It's a transition, you know? My dad just retired. Can you imagine retiring? That's like saying, 'Okay, world, I am officially too old to be of any use. Put me on the ice floe, or whatever.' "

"What are you talking about?"

"You know, like Eskimos? Anyway. I'm sure that's all it is." Bobby shifted onto his side, to make more room, and Carmen lay down in the space, curling her dry, warm body next to his wet one.

"Why did he retire, then, if you don't think he wants to feel like an Eskimo, or whatever?" Bobby put his wet hands around Carmen's waist and pulled her close. She smelled the tiniest bit like sweat, which he'd always found sexy.

"I have no idea," Bobby said, "but I'd really rather talk about something else. Like getting you out of these pants." He slid one wet hand into the waistband of her Lycra shorts.

Carmen squirmed away from him, pretending to be disgusted. She stood up and shook herself off, ridding herself of imaginary cooties before slowly peeling off all of her clothes. "We should go on vacation more often," she said, and jumped into the pool. Bobby was hard before he could follow her, and tripped over his bathing suit as he followed her in with a great big splash.

After Joan was dropped off at home and the rest of the group was fetched, everyone set out for dinner in Palma proper. Joan had recommended a tapas restaurant, and Franny had taken copious notes about what to order. This was her area of expertise, her chief joy in life, figuring out what to put in her mouth next, and when. It was out of the question to go before nine, but Bobby was starving to death and Sylvia was moping, so Franny rounded up the troops and loaded the cars and barked directions to the city.

The plan was to walk around town before dinner, which seemed to be everyone else's plan as well. They parked the cars on a narrow street by the cathedral, a massive gray pile just off the beach. After a few days in Pigpen, Palma felt like being at home — the city was lively, the streets filled with couples and families and dogs, everyone strolling slowly and drinking at small tables outside. Bobby and Carmen walked ahead, holding hands.

"Look," Franny said to Jim, who shrugged. "Maybe it's love after all?"

"She's fine," Jim said. "She doesn't bother me."

Franny glared at him. "You're a bad liar." She had liked this about him for most of their marriage, but now, as she said it aloud, it occurred to Franny that this was a flaw.

The cobblestone streets were pitched, heading up- and downhill. There was a little shop selling Mallorcan pearls, and Franny ducked in, Charles and Lawrence trailing behind her. She bought two strands, both blue and satisfyingly lumpy, and strung one around her own neck and one around Sylvia's.

"Mom," Sylvia said, fingering her new necklace, "I think my stomach is actually going to eat itself. Like, my stomach is going to think that the rest of my body is trying to kill it and it will attack the rest of my organs like parasites. And then I'll be dead in an hour."

"You're welcome," Franny said, and hooked her elbow in Sylvia's. "Let's follow the lovebirds."

"Oh, please," Sylvia said. She looked over her shoulder to make sure no one else was close enough to hear. The pedestrian-only streets were filled with well-dressed people of all ages — dapper white-haired gents in thin sweaters and loafers, rambunctious teenagers licking each other's necks. They made it a block before they hit Bobby standing by himself in front of a clothing store.

"Ditched her?" Sylvia said.

"She's in there," he said. The store was blasting dubstep so loudly that they had to raise their voices to be heard. "I couldn't take it."

The mannequins in the window were wearing asymmetrical dresses printed with three different patterns, clothing that Frankenstein might have sewn.

"Barf," Sylvia said. "This is clothing for blind strippers."

"Well, she likes it, Sylvia, okay?" Bobby crossed his arms.

"You know, I'm going to go in and check on her," Franny said. "It's no fun to shop alone."

Charles and Lawrence were trailing behind, and Sylvia watched as they walked in and out of a sunglasses store, a shoe store, a candy store. They did everything together. She wondered if her parents had ever been like that, even before Bobby was born. It seemed unlikely.

"Where's Dad?"

"I don't know," Bobby said. "Didn't say anything to me."

"Are you okay?"

"What do you mean? Of course I'm okay." Bobby's hair was getting long, and the dark curls hung to his eyebrows.

"Jeez, nevermind." Sylvia peered into the dark hole of the clothing store that had just eaten her mother.

The store was dense with racks of skimpy, sweatshop-manufactured clothing. Franny walked through, touching things as she went, recoiling from all the shiny, stretchy fabrics. She finally found Carmen in the back, near the dressing rooms, with a pile of stuff over her arm.

"Can I help?" Franny said, putting out her hands. "Here, let me hold all that while you look."

Carmen shrugged and offloaded the stack into Franny's waiting arms.

"You and Bobby have fun today? We missed you at the Graves House, it really was something. I think secretly every writer imagines their house becoming a museum. Or having a plaque, at the very least. So many plaques."

Carmen gave a half-smile and continued to paw through a rack of sequined tops. "Oh, you know, museums aren't really my thing."

"Well, it's not really a museum, it's just a house. Where a writer lived. So it's more about snooping around than looking at art."

"I don't read that much."

Franny smiled with her lips closed, a tight line. This was a grown woman, she reminded herself, a person who supported herself and made her own decisions. This was not her family. This was not her problem. "Mm-hmm."

"Oh, you know, I did just read a really good book, though, on the plane," Carmen said, pausing with her hand on the hanger of a spectacularly ugly dress. Franny's heart leapt, even as she was trying to convince it to temper its expectations. "It's called *Your Food, Your Body.* I think you'd really like it, actually."

"Oh, yeah?" Franny said. It could be sociology, she thought, or anthropology, a study of cultural norms through their natural dishes, an investigation of stereotypes through the meals our ancestors have given us. Franny loved books about food — maybe this was it, the moment she'd been waiting for, the moment that Carmen opened her mouth and proved that she'd been paying attention all along.

"It's about what kind of diets work best for your body type — like, for example, I'm small and muscular, which means no complex carbs. My Cuban grandmother would murder me if she was still alive, no rice and beans!" Carmen opened her eyes wide. "It's really interesting."

"That does sound very informative," Franny said. "You ready to try some things on?"

Carmen shrugged. "Sure." She plucked a single dress out of Franny's arms, made out of transparent plastic, like a garment made out of Saran wrap. "Isn't this one cute?"

"Mm-hmm," Franny said, unable to say more.

The tapas bar Joan had recommended was in the tangle of small streets near the Plaça Major, which also had a Burger King and a pizza place, both of which were crowded with Spanish teenagers. There was a crowd spilling out of the restaurant, which made Sylvia fold in half like a toy with dead batteries. Determined, Franny wiggled her way through the packed bar to the hostess, and they were seated before long — Joan had made a phone call on their behalf. As he'd mentioned to Franny, his parents knew the owners. It was a small island, after all. "What a sweet boy!" Franny said over and over again, to no one in particular. "What a sweet, sweet boy."

"Yeah," Bobby said. "Too bad his name is Joan," pronouncing it like an American, rhyming with *groan,* a woman's name. His mother socked him in the arm.

"Joe-*ahhhhhn.* And you're getting awfully muscly," she said. It wasn't a compliment.

Bobby and Charles began to order by pointing — an overflowing plate of blistered green peppers covered with wide flakes of salt, toasted pieces of bread with dollops of whipped cod, grilled octopus on a stick. Plates appeared and were passed around the table with great moans of pleasure. Franny looked at the menu and ordered more — *albóndigas,* little meatballs swimming in tomato sauce; *patatas bravas,* fried potatoes with a ribbon of cream run back and forth over the top; *pa amb oli,* the Mallorcan answer to Italy's bruschetta.

"This does not suck," Sylvia said, her mouth half full.

"Pass the meatballs," Bobby said, reaching across her.

"Más rioja!" Charles said, raising his glass toward the center of the table, clinking

glasses with no one, because everyone else was too busy eating. Franny and Jim sat next to each other on the far side of the table, the backs of their chairs wedged against the wall. Charles and Lawrence got up to go look at the tapas in the glass cases along the bar, and the children were occupied with the food still in front of them. A sizzling plate of steak landed on the table, and Bobby speared an enormous piece with his fork and then dangled it over his mouth like a caveman.

"So?" Franny said. Jim rested his arm on her chair, and she let it stay, just to see how it felt.

"I think it's a success." Jim's face was only a few inches away, the closest it had been in what felt like months. He hadn't shaved in a couple of days, and he looked the way he'd looked as a young man, blond and scruffy and handsome. Franny was caught off guard, and jerked her chair forward, knocking his arm away. Jim recovered quickly and knit his hands together on the table. "At least, I think so."

"The kids are good," Franny said. "Though I really don't know about that girl." Carmen had eaten only the peppers, which she complained were too oily.

"Have you seen her powders?"

"What does that mean?"

Jim smiled a very small smile and lowered his voice. "She has baggies full of powder, and she puts it in everything she eats. In water, in her yogurt. I think it might be Soylent Green."

Franny surprised herself by laughing, and fell a few inches closer to Jim's chest. "Stop," she said. "I'm not ready to laugh with you." She thought of the girl, younger than Bobby, her baby boy. Her jaw stiffened so quickly that she thought it might crack.

Jim raised his hands in surrender, and they both turned back to the far end of the table. Charles and Lawrence were on their way back, each carrying two plates of tiny, gorgeous bites.

"Get that over here," Franny said, patting the empty table space in front of her. "I'm starving."

Day Six

Jim drank his coffee by the pool. It was already warm outside, and the tall, narrow pine trees stood static against the backdrop of the mountains on the other side of the village. It had been almost a full week, and he was still tiptoeing around Franny, still breathing quietly, still doing whatever she said. If she had wanted him to sleep on the floor, he would have. If she wanted him to turn off the light when she was tired, he did. They had been married for thirty-five years and three months.

The first divorces happened quickly — a year or two into an ill-planned marriage, and they were done. The second wave happened a decade later, when the children were small and problematic. That was the one that the child psychologists and playground moms fretted about, the kind of divorce that caused the most damage. It was the third wave that Jim hadn't seen coming

— the empty-nester crises of faith. Couples like him and Franny were splitting up all over the Upper West Side, couples with grown children and several decades of life together behind them. It had to do with life expectancy, and with delayed midlife meltdowns. No one wanted to believe they were midlife when they hit forty anymore, and so now it was the sixty-year-olds buying the sports cars and seducing the younger women. At least that's what Franny would have called it. Clear as day, a simple case. But of course nothing was ever simple when the lech in question was your own husband.

The back door clanged shut. Jim looked over his shoulder and was surprised to see Carmen heading over to join him. She was wearing her workout clothes, which she seemed to have in place of pajamas or blue jeans, whatever else one would wear casually around the house. Carmen always looked ready to drop to the ground and do fifty sit-ups, which Jim supposed was the point.

"Morning," she said, setting her tall glass of green liquid down next to his mug on the concrete. "Mind if I join you?"

"Of course not," Jim said. He tried to remember a moment when they had been alone together, but couldn't. It was possible that they'd been left alone in a room while Bobby went to the bathroom, maybe, but even that seemed unlikely. He gestured to the chaise longue beside his, and she sat, knitting her fingers together and stretching her palms away. Her knuckles cracked loudly.

"Sorry," she said. "Bad habit."

They both took sips of their drinks and stared out at the mountains, which had taken on a bluish tint from the cloudless sky above.

"So," Carmen said. "I'm sorry about what's been going on with you and Franny." She placed one hand flat over her glass. Jim wondered if it tasted like sawdust, or if it had the flavor of chemicals, a thousand vitamins ground to dirt. "It must be hard on both of you."

Jim ran a quick hand over his hair, and then did it again. He pursed his lips, unsure of how to proceed. "Huh," he finally said. "I'm sorry, did Fran talk to you?"

"She didn't have to," Carmen said, lowering her eyes. "The same thing happened with my parents. Bobby doesn't know, but I can see it. Don't worry, I won't say anything to him."

"Huh," Jim said, still at a loss. "Thanks."

"No problem," she said, the words coming out faster now. "I mean, I was in high school, just a little bit younger than Sylvia, and it was really hard. My parents were going through this really tough time, but didn't want us to know, but of course we knew, and my brothers and I were all in the middle of it, even though they thought we had no idea."

"I'm sorry to hear that." His coffee was getting cold. Jim looked back toward the house, hopeful that someone else was stirring, but there was no sign of life.

"If you ever need to talk to anyone about it, you can talk to me," Carmen said. She put her hand on Jim's shoulder. "Just between us."

"Thank you," Jim said. He wasn't sure what he was thanking her for, or what she knew. All Jim was sure of was that he wanted to be rescued by a small plane. They didn't even have to stop, they could just swing by and lower a rope. He would climb up all on his own.

There was no food left in the house. Franny had forgotten how much food her children could consume, and everyone else, too, always nicking little pieces of the bread she was saving for the next day's panzanella.

"Who wants to come grocery shopping

with me? I'll throw in lunch. Who's with me?" she asked the room at large — Charles and Lawrence were off exploring a nearby beach, and Carmen and Bobby were off running up and down the mountain. Jim was reading in the living room. Only Sylvia was standing near enough to hear, directly in front of the open refrigerator door.

"God, yes. Please."

Franny hadn't driven a stick in several decades, but those muscle memories never really went away. Jim offered a three-minute refresher course, slightly alarmed at the thought of Franny driving on foreign roads, but she insisted that she knew what she was doing. Sylvia crossed herself as she lowered her body into the car. "Just get me back alive in time for Joan."

"As if I'd kill you without giving you the chance to see him again," Franny said, and turned the key in the ignition. She put her left foot down on the clutch, and her right on the gas, but the movement was not as fluid as it had once been, so many years out of practice, and the car lurched forward. Franny's face purpled, and Sylvia screamed. Jim was still standing outside the car, his hands gripping tightly at his elbows. *Gallant* men always drove stick, and taught their children. It was an important life skill, like having good knives and speaking a foreign language. Franny waved Jim off and backed out slowly, her spleen somewhere in her throat. "It's fine," she said, more to herself than to Sylvia. "I know what I'm doing. Everyone relax."

According to Gemma's notes, there was a super-sized grocery store about thirty minutes away, closer to the center of the island, larger and better stocked than the one Franny and Charles had gone to in Palma. Franny felt better once they were on the highway — there had been a few gentle stalls at stop signs on the road through Pigpen, but so what, no one was grading her. Once they were moving at a good clip, she felt her legs relax into a good rhythm, this one down, this one up. Sylvia hit buttons on the radio, which seemed to play only dance music and seventies American pop — Franny cried out for Sylvia to stop when she got to a station playing Elton John.

"It's like the land that time forgot," Sylvia said.

"I think you mean it's like the land that forgot time. This is the way it should be — Elton John on the radio and the best ham in the world. And family."

"Nice afterthought, Mom." Sylvia rolled her eyes and stared out the window.

The highway downgraded when they hit the outskirts of Palma, slowing to a one-lane road with stoplights, which meant that Franny had more opportunities to make the car stutter, die a little death, and then be revived. They were sitting at a red light, just a few miles before they were to hit the grocery store, when Franny noticed a large compound to their right — the Nando Filani International Tennis Centre. Without thinking, she made the turn.

"Pretty sure this isn't the grocery store," Sylvia said.

"Oh, zip it. We're having an adventure." Franny slowly pulled through the tennis center's open gate and into the parking lot.

Nando Filani was Mallorca's best and only hope at a grand slam or a gold medal. Twenty-five and surly, he stalked the edges of the court like Agassi or Sampras, hitting enormous serves that aced his opponents more often than not. He'd gotten in trouble a bit on the tour — someone's teeth had been knocked out, which he swore was an accident with an errant ball — and this tennis school was his way of paying reparations. Tennis players, after all, were supposed to be ambassadors of goodness, all white shorts and silver platters. It was a sport for the civilized, not merely the athletic. Franny

158

had played a bit in high school, though she'd never been much good, but it was the only sport that all four Posts could stand to watch, which in turn meant that it was the one sport they could talk about with one another. Sylvia cared about it the least, of course, but every few years there was a player handsome enough to keep her minimally engaged.

The air was full of thwacks and grunts — the sounds of balls hitting racquets, of tennis stars in the making. Franny hurried around from the driver's side of the car to a fence just beside the main buildings. Through the fence, she could see a dozen rows of tennis courts, many of them filled by children. Franny murmured appreciation for a diminutive brunette's excellent serve, and then hurried back across the parking lot. Sylvia leaned against the side of the car.

"Mom."

Franny grasped the fence on the other side, which hid another row of courts, these less populated by children.

"Mom!"

Franny turned, her face open and confused, as if Sylvia had woken her from a dream. "What is it?"

"What are we doing here?" Sylvia slowly peeled herself off the car and trudged over to her mother's side. It was warmer at the bottom of the mountain, and the sun was shining directly overhead. "It's too hot."

"We're looking for Nando, of course!" It was smack between Wimbledon (which Nando had won the previous year, though this year he was runner-up to the Serb) and the US Open (which he hadn't ever won, being better on both clay and grass), and so it seemed possible that he actually might be at home, training. "Come on, I want to go inside."

Sylvia slumped onto Franny's shoulder. She'd been taller than her mother since she was eleven. "Only if you promise that if, for some ungodly reason, Nando Filani is standing directly inside that door, you will not speak to him, and we can turn around and go directly to the grocery store."

Franny lifted a hand to her heart. "I swear." They both knew that she was lying.

The office was clean and modern, with a large dry-erase schedule on one wall and a pretty young woman sitting behind a counter. Franny grabbed Sylvia by the elbow and marched straight up. *"Hola,"* she said.

"Hola. Qué tal?" said the woman.

"Habla inglés? My daughter and I are enormous fans of Filani's, and we were

wondering about lessons. Is it possible to sign up? We're in Mallorca for about ten days, and we'd just love the chance to play where he played. You must be so proud of him." Franny nodded at the idea of all that national pride, wrinkling her nose for all the mothers in Mallorca.

"Lessons for two?" The woman held up two fingers. *"Dos?"*

"Oh, no," Franny said. "I haven't played since I was a teenager."

"One?" The woman held up a single finger. "Lessons for one?"

Sylvia twisted her body into a pretzel. "Mom," she said. "I respect that you're trying to do something here, but I'm not exactly sure what it is, and I'm pretty sure that I have no interest. Or sneakers." She pointed to her flip-flops and waggled her slightly dusty-looking toes.

"Do you have a list of instructors?" Franny put her elbows on the counter. "Or any reading material? About the center?"

The woman slid a brochure across the counter. Franny picked it up, pretending to read the Spanish until she realized the reverse was printed in English. Her eyes skimmed the short paragraphs and the glossy photographs of Nando Filani until the very bottom of the page. In a large photo, Nando had his arm thrown around the shoulder of an older man. They were both wearing baseball hats and squinting into the sun, but Franny could make out the other man's features clearly enough.

"I'm sorry, *perdón,* is this Antoni Vert?"

The woman nodded. *"Sí."*

"Does he still live in Mallorca?"

"Sí." The woman pointed north. "Three kilometers."

"Mom, who is that?"

Franny fanned herself with the brochure. "Does he offer lessons? Here? By any chance?"

The woman shrugged. *"Sí.* More expensive, but yes." She turned her chair toward her computer screen and hit a few buttons. "He had a cancellation tomorrow afternoon, four p.m.?"

Sylvia watched her mother quickly dig through her purse, swearing a few times before finally landing on her wallet. "Yes," Franny said, not looking at Sylvia or the receptionist, only the photo in the brochure. "Yes, that will do." After she signed her name, she turned around and walked calmly out the door, leaving Sylvia standing at the counter with an open mouth. "Weren't you in a hurry?" she called from outside. Sylvia made a face at the woman behind the counter and hurried back to the car, unsure of what she'd just witnessed, but positive it was something she could tease her mother about for decades to come.

Franny refused to say anything about Antoni Vert other than that he'd been a tennis player in her day, Spain's last best hope before Nando's aggressive rise, but Joan was more forthcoming. He and Sylvia were theoretically working by the pool, but really they were just eating a giant bowl of grapes and an equally giant bowl of Franny's homemade guacamole, despite the fact that Sylvia had teased her for making Mexican food in Spain, as if all Spanish-speaking cultures were the same. Joan sat with his legs crossed, his sunglasses perched on the top of his head. Sylvia sat with her feet in the pool.

"He was very famous," Joan said. "All the women loved him. My mother, she loved him. Everyone. He was not as good as Filani, but he was more handsome. In the early eighties. Very long hair."

"Huh." Sylvia kicked her legs back and forth. "I mean, how interesting. My mother basically had a heart attack, but not as much of a heart attack as she's going to have when she tries to actually play tennis." The pool water splashed onto her legs, which she hoped looked carefree, like a *Sports Illustrated* swimsuit shot, and not like she had just peed down her thigh.

Joan laughed, and then tossed a grape into his mouth. "What about you, Sylvia? No boyfriend at home in New York?"

Sylvia dunked a chip into the guacamole and then lowered it gently onto her tongue. It was hard to try to be seductive when they were talking about her actual life. She shook her head and chewed. "Everyone in New York sucks. Or at least everyone at my school. Do you say that, sucks? What's the word for that?" She swallowed.

"*Me tienen hasta los huevos.* It means I've had it up to my balls. Same idea."

"Yeah," she said. *"Me tienen hasta los huevos."*

A small airplane flew across the sky, a trail of white smoke behind it, a blank skywritten message. Sylvia watched as the thin white line bisected the otherwise perfectly clear blue sky. It looked like a math equation — x plus y equals z. Avocado plus onion plus cilantro equaled guacamole. Skin plus sun equaled burn. Her father plus her mother equaled her.

It had been a weird spring at home. Franny was Franny, like always, the central figure in her own solar system, the maypole around which the rest of the world had to dance and twirl. It was Jim who had been acting strange. It didn't make any sense when he'd suddenly retired. *Gallant* was his oxygen, his entertainment, his everything. Sylvia would wander through the house and find him sitting in a new room, or in the garden, staring off into space. Instead of interrupting him, as she normally would, she would avoid him. He looked so deep in thought that disturbing him seemed as dangerous as waking a sleepwalker. That was before she knew. The longer he was home, the more conversations she could hear through the hundred-year-old walls and floors. It came in pieces at first, a few words louder than the rest, and then all at once, when her mother decided that it was too hard to pretend that things were hunky-dory. Franny had put it like this: Her father had slept with someone, and it was a Problem that they were trying to figure out, as if the whole thing could be solved with a giant calculator. Sylvia didn't know who the woman was, but she knew that she was young. Of course, they were always young. Jim had not been present for the conversation — it was better that way for everyone.

Parents got stranger when you got older,

that was obvious. You could no longer take for granted that everyone else's family worked exactly as yours did, with the bathroom doors open or shut, with the pinch of sugar in the tomato sauce, with the off-key but effective bedtime lullaby. Sylvia had spent the last few months watching her mother ignore her father unless she was scolding him, and Jim was not someone who took well to scolding. Sylvia sat in her chair at the kitchen table and watched them silently spar. She wondered if it had always been this way, or whether it was only her more mature eyes that recognized the cold breeze between her mother and father. Sometimes in books she would come across a mention of his-and-hers bedrooms — old movies, too; TCM was full of women waking up alone in their dressing gowns — and think that maybe it wasn't such a bad idea. What were parents anyway, except two people who had once thought they were the smartest people in the world? They were a delusional species, as tiny-brained as dinosaurs. Sylvia didn't think she ever wanted to get married or have children. Forget about the ozone layer, and tsunamis — what about dinner? It was all too much.

"Let's go inside," she said. "I'm finding all this sunshine very depressing." She pulled one leg out of the pool and then the other, watching them drip dark spots onto the concrete.

Joan picked up the bowls of food and followed her into the dining room.

It was siesta time. They'd all been delighted to acclimate to the custom, and now everyone dragged themselves to their separate corners right after lunch, eyelids already heavy. Carmen slept on her back, while Bobby curled up like a seashell next to her, his mouth open. Jim fell asleep on the sofa in the living room, a book on his chest. Sylvia slept on her stomach, her face turned to one side like a swimmer. Lawrence slept like a child, with the covers up to his neck. Only Charles and Franny were still awake, and they were in the master bathroom, Franny in the tub and Charles on the closed lid of the toilet.

Gemma had all the best bath products, of course: shampoos and conditioners, exfoliating scrubs, bars of soap with sprigs of French lavender embedded in them, bath gels, bubbles, loofahs, pumice stones, the works. Franny planned to soak for an hour, even if it meant using all the hot water in Pigpen. The tub wasn't very long, but neither was Franny, and her straight legs just barely touched the far end.

"So?" Charles said. He was flipping through a magazine, one of Sylvia's trashy ones from the airplane. "How's it been?"

Franny had a washcloth over her eyes. "You've seen it."

"I mean when it's just the two of you." He turned the page to a spread of women in sequined evening gowns.

"It's like this," Franny said, and then kept her mouth shut for a beat. "It's like nothing. It's like I want to punch him in the eyeball almost as much as I want him to actually apologize. I can't tell you how many times I've truly considered murdering him in his sleep."

"So you're not mad?" The next page was the entire contents of an actress's purse, spilled out and identified piece by piece. Chewing gum, a nail file, some makeup, a mirror, another pair of shoes, headphones, a BlackBerry. "What does she read when she gets bored?" he said to himself.

Franny explored the drain with her big toe. "I'm beyond mad. I truly didn't know this space existed, where he could do something so terrible that the word *mad* wouldn't begin to cover it. Do we really do it? Do we sell the house? Does Sylvia become totally unstable and crazy because the minute she goes to college, her parents get a divorce?" She shook the washcloth off into the water, and it made a little splash. "What would you do if Lawrence cheated on you? Would you get a divorce?" She turned around to look at him.

Friendships were tricky things, especially friendships as old as theirs was. Nudity was nothing more than a collection of hard-earned scars and marks. Love was a given, uncomplicated by sex or vows, but honesty was always waiting there, ready to capsize the steady boat. Charles closed the magazine.

"I cheated on him once. With one person, I mean. More than one time."

Franny sat up and swiveled ungracefully in the tub so that she was facing Charles directly. Her breasts were half above the water, half below, her heavy flesh settled into tidy rolls underneath. Charles wanted to ask her if he could take a photo to paint from later — she would say yes, she always said yes — but realized it was not the time.

"Excuse me?"

Charles leaned back against the toilet tank. There was a small square window on the short wall of the bathroom, and Charles looked through it onto the mountains, which seemed to wave through the ancient glass. "It was in the beginning. Almost ten years ago. We were already living together, but it wasn't that serious. It wasn't that serious to me, I should say. Lawrence, bless his little heart, he always thought we were in it for the long haul. He's the settling-down type, you know, with his real job and his supportive parents. He always wanted to get married, even before it was legal. Whatever documents we could get, he wanted them.

"This was when I was with Johnson Strunk Gallery, remember, on Twenty-fourth? And Selena Strunk always had the cutest boys working for her, the art handlers, kids who looked straight out of some gym-bunny porno, all beefed up and adorable, with little beards they'd just learned how to grow. I don't know why they liked me — I was already, what, forty-five? But some of them wanted to be painters, I suppose. Anyway, one of them, Jason, he started hanging around the gallery when he knew I'd be there, and he was a nice kid, so I took him out for coffee. When we sat down, he grabbed my dick under the table. Lawrence is such a WASP, he would rather die than admit he even *had* a dick in public. So I was, you know, surprised. It only happened a few times, over the next few months, at my studio."

Franny made a noise. "Involuntary," she said, then covered her mouth with the washcloth and waved him on.

"Lawrence was so young, I didn't think it could really be *it.* I didn't even know if I believed in *it.* So I fucked around. I felt terrible about it, of course, and the whole thing was over quickly, but I never told him. So."

"So? So? So you never plan on telling your husband that you had sex with someone else? What the fuck, Charlie?" Franny crossed her arms over her chest, which had a lesser effect than it might have, due to her nakedness, and that she slipped a bit into the tub, and had to pull herself back upright.

"No," Charles said. "And I'm not telling you because I think that what Jim did wasn't awful, because it was. I'm just telling you because you asked. I wouldn't want to know. And if he did, and I found out, I would probably forgive him."

Franny rolled her eyes. "Well, obviously you would, now." The water in the tub had cooled, and she turned the hot water back on, refilling the room with a warm steam.

"Even if I hadn't, Fran, that's the truth. Marriage is hard. Relationships are hard. You know that I'm on your side, whatever your side is, but that's the truth. We've all done things."

171

"That is bullshit. Yes, we've all done things. I've done things like put on thirty pounds. He's done things like put his penis inside a twenty-three-year-old. Don't you think one of those is significantly worse?" Franny stood up, her body dripping, and grabbed a towel. She stayed put, the now dingy water sloshing against her calves.

"I am on your side, sweetie," Charles repeated. He walked over to the side of the tub and put his hand out, which Franny accepted, stepping over the lip like Elizabeth Taylor playing Cleopatra, her chin lifted from her shoulders, her dark hair wet against her neck.

"Well," she said, once she was safely on dry land. "Secrets are no fun for anyone. Keep that in mind." She kissed him on the cheek and padded into the bedroom, listening for the sounds of snoring coming from all the other rooms.

DAY SEVEN

Waiting for a baby was like waiting for a heart attack — at a certain point, you had to just surrender and make other plans, not knowing if you'd have to cancel. Charles and Lawrence had taken a trip to Japan the previous year but had put off Paris when it seemed — for no real reason, Lawrence had just had a feeling — that they might be chosen. They had spent holidays at home alone, their anxiety too toxic to make small talk. The hoops prospective adoptive parents had to jump through were legion: writing letters, making websites, culling flattering family photographs without any wineglasses in them. The goal was to make your family sound stable and appealing, to have the birth mother imagine her child having a better life in your arms. Gay men were attractive options, Charles was surprised to learn, in part because there would never be any competition as to who the child's real mother was. They'd never actually been chosen before, though, and this time the waiting had taken on a surreal quality, like being told that you were going to win the lottery, maybe, just hang on for a week and see if the numbers actually match.

It had been Lawrence's plan from the beginning, and after they were married, there was no stopping him. Charles, on the other hand, had never truly visualized himself with a baby. He had Bobby and Sylvia, after all, and other friends had pipsqueaks for whom he could buy expensive, dry-clean-only clothes and other impractical gifts. Wasn't that one of the perks of being homosexual, being able to adore children and then hand them back to their parents? Lawrence didn't see it that way. Some of their friends had gone through lawyers, which were more expensive but also more private. Lawrence said they'd try that, too, if the agency didn't work. They went to informational meetings at Hockney, at Price-Warner, everywhere gay couples were welcome. They sat in brightly colored waiting rooms as quiet as an oncology ward, trying not to make eye contact with the other hopeful couples in the room. Charles was surprised that the carpet wasn't polka-dotted with holes burned by a thousand downcast stares. There were no balloons or cheery smiles in the waiting rooms, only in the glossy brochures.

Now the best they could do was keep themselves busy. Lawrence wished for a Rubik's Cube, or knitting needles, not that he knew how to use either. Mallorca would have to suffice. It was a hot day, and Bobby and Carmen and Franny seemed happy enough to stay in the pool. Jim read a novel in the shade. Lawrence couldn't take another whole day of nothing, and the Miró museum was nearby, a fifteen-minute drive down the mountain. They took Sylvia and went.

The museum itself wasn't remarkable — a few large, cool rooms, and Miró's playful paintings and drawings on the walls. One room had an exhibition of other Spanish artists, and they walked through quickly, pausing here and there. Lawrence liked one painting of Miró's — oil and charcoal on canvas, large and beige, with one red spot in the middle — that looked like a giant swollen breast. Charles took his time in the last room, and Lawrence and Sylvia waited for him outside.

Outside the museum, below the city, the ocean was enormous and blue. The day smelled like jasmine and summertime. Sylvia put her hands on Charles's and Lawrence's shoulders, and said, "This'll do." Up a hill and around a corner were Miró's studios. They crunched along the gravel and peeked inside his rooms, set up as though he would be home any moment. Easels held canvases, and half-used, rolled-up tubes of paint sat uncapped on his tables. Charles loved visiting other painters' studios. In New York, the younger artists moved farther and farther out in Brooklyn, to Bushwick and corners of Greenpoint that nearly kissed Queens. His own studio was neat and white except for the floors, which were spotted with so many years of accidental drips. In Provincetown, he worked on the sunporch, or in a small, bright room that had once been an attic. Had Miró had any children? Charles leafed through the small pamphlet they'd been given at the door, but it didn't say. Lots of artists had children, but they also had wives, or partners, someone to stay home. Why hadn't they talked about that? Lawrence could take some time off, of course, a few months, but then wouldn't he go back to work? Who was going to watch the baby? Charles wished that the social worker had sent a photograph, but they didn't do that — as they'd explained in the meetings, it's just like when people have a baby biologically. You see the child when it's put into your arms.

Lawrence tilted his head and walked around to the room on the other side of the studio, so respectful of this man's sacred space. Charles loved that about his husband, his willingness to see what other people couldn't, that art was both mining and magic, a trade and a séance at once. It hadn't been easy to convince Lawrence to come — two whole weeks with the Posts was not everyone's idea of a vacation. Charles reached over and petted Lawrence's head. They never had time like this in New York, when Lawrence was always running to the office. When they were in Province-town, Charles would walk over to the bakery to get them breakfast, or would be in his studio while Lawrence slept in. It felt luxurious, the two of them just wandering through a museum on a weekday. Sylvia walked back out onto the gravel lookout, leaving them alone. Maybe it would have been easier to imagine if the child — Alphonse, his name was Alphonse — was a girl.

"Hello, there," Lawrence said, circling back toward Charles. He crossed his arms over his chest and leaned his head down so that it rested on Charles's shoulder. It wasn't comfortable — Lawrence was three inches taller — but it was good for a moment.

"I was just thinking about how nice it will be to go home," Charles said.

"What have you done with my husband?" Lawrence said, laughing.

"What?" Charles pinched him in the side, sending him scooting a few inches away. "You act like I've been ignoring you."

Lawrence groaned. "Of course you've been ignoring me."

Charles poked his head outside, checking on Sylvia, who was lying prone on a bench, ignoring the other tourists, who were all taking photographs of the view. "Honey, no."

"*Honey,* yes." Lawrence stayed put. He recrossed his arms.

"Lawr, come on. How have I been ignoring you? We're with half a dozen other people. What am I supposed to do, pretend I don't hear or see them?"

"No," Lawrence said, walking slowly back to Charles's side. A German couple tromped in, and they lowered their voices. "I'm not asking you to be rude. I'm just asking you to be slightly less of a bloodhound, always three inches behind Franny's ass."

178

"Your ass is the only one I want to be three inches behind."

"Don't try being nice to me now, I'm mad at you."

Charles had often thought that if they'd had the wherewithal or the money to actually produce a biological child, a boy or a girl made with Lawrence's sperm, he wouldn't feel remotely conflicted. How could he not love anything that had a face like that?

"I'm sorry," Charles said. "I'm sorry. I know I get distracted when I'm around her. You are more important to me, I promise you." This was not the first time they'd had this conversation, but it always surprised Charles. Luckily, he knew what Lawrence needed to hear. Whether he believed him or not was another story. Sometimes he did, and sometimes he didn't. So much depended on Lawrence's mood, on the hour of the day, on whether their most recent sex had been good or merely passable.

Lawrence closed his eyes, having heard what he'd needed to hear. "Fine. I think we're both just anxious, you know? This is it, don't you think? Can't you just feel it?" He shivered, and then Charles did, too, as if an icy breeze had somehow made its way through the studio.

"Of course," Charles said.

Franny hadn't packed proper exercise clothes, but luckily her feet were the same size as Carmen's, so she could borrow a pair of sneakers, and Carmen was so happy to lend them that it seemed like she might levitate. Fran wore leggings and a T-shirt she liked to sleep in, even though it had small, soft holes around the neckline. Her hair was too short to put into a ponytail, but she didn't want it flying in her face (Franny imagined herself moving as quickly as a Williams sister, zooming from one corner of the court to another), so she'd also brought along the stretchy black headband she used when she washed her face.

Antoni Vert was standing behind the desk, just behind the receptionist. As in the photograph, he was wearing a baseball cap pulled low on his forehead, and a pair of reflective sunglasses hung on a neoprene cord around his neck. His face, though wider when she had seen it so often on a television screen, still looked to Franny like a Spanish movie star's — the dimple in the chin, the black hair. She smiled and rushed toward the counter.

"Hello, Mr. Vert, Antoni, it is such a pleasure to meet you," Franny said, holding out her right hand, the borrowed sneakers in her left.

Antoni swiveled at his hips and pointed at the wall clock. "You're late."

"Oh, am I?" Franny shook her head. "I'm *so* sorry. We're still getting to know the island roads, I'm afraid." Franny said this knowing full well that Mallorca had the most clearly marked highways she'd ever been on, gigantic signs with arrows and plenty of space. The royal *we* seemed to help her cause, as if she were blaming her lateness on some invisible chauffeur.

"We start now," he said. "You need a racquet, yes?"

"Oh, shoot," Franny said. Gemma had had a closet full of sporting equipment, of course. She was nothing if not healthy and industrious. There were probably cross-country skis hidden somewhere in the house, just in case the earth stopped spinning on its proper axis and the mountains were suddenly covered with powdery white snow. "It's in the car!" She waved the sneakers at Antoni and then bolted out to the parking lot. "I'll be right back!"

Franny laced up while Antoni waited, clearly irritated at the delay. What was three hundred euros a lesson? Franny chose not to do the math. It was a priceless experience she was giving herself, a gift that could not be bought at any other time or place. She double-knotted, trying to remember the last time she wore sneakers. Her best guess was sometime in 1995, when she was trying to get back into shape after Sylvia was born, doing *Buns of Steel* in the living room. "Ready."

"Come," Antoni said. He opened the door and waited for Franny to walk through it. She had to get so close to his body in order to pass, and she walked sideways, as slowly as possible, a happy little crab.

The courts seemed more crowded once she was on the other side of the fence. On television, they always looked so enormous, with these lithe young bodies scurrying around, but in reality a tennis court wasn't very big. In fact, the courts were so close together that Franny worried she might hit balls into someone else's game or, worse yet, into someone else's face. Luckily, Antoni kept walking until they'd reached the final court in the row, which had a few courts' cushion from their closest neighbors, a boy of about twelve and his coach.

"So, you know how to play?" Antoni spoke with a thick accent, his voice low and his tongue heavy.

"I watch everything," she said, lying.

"Even the small tournaments." Franny tried to think of one to name, but couldn't. "I have an excellent grasp of the rules."

"And the last time you played?" Antoni reached into his pocket and pulled out a tennis ball. Franny wished that Charles had come along and was close enough to make a joke. It was strange, having this experience alone, when it would clearly (so clearly) become something that she would write about, a story she would codify into a moment on the page. There would be a witty and slightly naughty joke from her best friend, *right there.* Only he wasn't. Franny could tell him all about it after, he would make the joke then, and after that, it was a matter of editing.

"Oh," Franny said. "Ages ago. A decade?" One of the women in her detestable book club played tennis every week in Central Park, as spry and mean as a goose, and she and Franny had had a game one morning. The woman pelted her with ball after ball, always giggling afterward in faux apology. The bruises had lasted for weeks. "I'm not an athlete. I'm a writer. You know, there haven't been very many good books about tennis. Do you ever think about writing a memoir? I have a lot of friends who have ghostwritten sports books. We should talk, if you're interested."

"Okay, we start easy," Antoni said, ignoring her. He walked over to the far side of the net. "Ready?"

Before Franny knew it, Antoni had served a ball. She watched it land three feet ahead of her and laughed. "I'm sorry," she said. "Did you want me to return that? It just seems so funny, actually playing with you."

"This is not playing. This is practice. Warm-up." He hit another ball, and Franny was surprised to find her feet moving and her racquet outstretched. She connected — the racquet smacked the ball back over the net, and Franny was so thrilled by her own sporty prowess that she jumped up and down, ignoring the fact that Antoni was, of course, going to hit the ball right back. He did, and the ball skidded by her, its bouncing path to the fence undisturbed. "Sorry, sorry," Franny said. "I'm ready now. Sorry! I just didn't know that that was going to happen. Ready." She dropped into a half-squat like the players on television did, waving her hips back and forth.

Antoni nodded, his eyes hidden behind the reflective panes of his sunglasses. He arched backward, throwing a ball high into the air. Franny had watched him play for so many years, she knew the motion of his body. It wasn't an OCD tic, like some of the younger players had (Nando Filani was notorious for turning his head to the side and coughing, which McEnroe always likened to a prostate exam). Antoni's body moved purposefully, his shoulders as wide as a swimmer's. He threw another ball up and hit it slowly, as gently as a mother to a child. Franny bounced from side to side, waiting to see where the ball would land, and then hurried toward it, getting the edge of her racquet underneath it just in time to send it back over the net. They volleyed lightly for a few more strokes before Franny missed a shot, and she panted happily, exhilarated.

"Not bad," Antoni said. Franny wiped her forehead with her fingertips. "Let me see a serve." He walked over to her side of the net, coming deliberately behind Franny. He slid his sunglasses down his nose and then crossed his arms. "Toss, then serve."

Franny bounced the ball a couple of times and was relieved to find that it felt good in her hand, familiar. There had been a time when this was a normal function for her, and she willed all the atoms in her body to remember those days, standing outside in Brooklyn, the girls from her high school team all cackling and yelling. She threw the ball into the air and swung her racquet overhead. Franny heard a loud crack, and then she wobbled forward a few feet, and the next thing she knew, she was staring into Antoni Vert's shadowy face, lying on her back in the middle of the tennis court. At last, he looked as delighted to see her as she was to see him.

Bobby and Carmen were out by the pool doing their exercises, and normally that would have made Lawrence do an about-face and sit in the bedroom reading for a couple of hours, but the day was too beautiful to stay indoors. He put on his hat and sunglasses and headed outside, a novel tucked under his arm.

"Hey," Bobby said from the deep end of the pool. He was treading water in the most athletic way possible, bouncing up and down like a spring, the damp ends of his curls weighty and dark.

"Hey!" Carmen said, mid push-up. She dipped down halfway, stopped, and then went even closer to the ground before straightening her arms and rocketing back up to a plank position. Lawrence was impressed.

"You are really good at that," he said, and then kicked off his flip-flops and settled into one of the lounge chairs.

"Thanks!" Carmen said without stopping. "I can show you, if you want."

Lawrence squeezed out a dollop of sunscreen into his palm and began to cover himself — arms, legs, cheeks, nose — with a thin coating. It was the expensive stuff, chalky white and impermeable.

Bobby stared. "What is that? Zinc?"

"What, this?" Lawrence said, turning the tube over. "I don't know. It's made of things I can't pronounce."

"Don't you ever want a tan?" Bobby swam over to the side of the pool. "Sometimes I go to the beach with just tanning oil and fall asleep. It's the best. You wake up and you're totally bronzed. Like, a statue."

"That sounds like an excellent way to get skin cancer."

"Well, yeah, I guess." Bobby did some flutter kicks, his feet sending little plumes of water into the air. Lawrence tried to imagine having a baby and then watching the baby grow into someone who used tanning oil. It wasn't as bad as smoking crack, but it did seem to signify major differences in ideology. Bobby dunked his head underwater and then hoisted himself out of the pool. "I'm gonna hit the showers, guys. See you in a bit."

Carmen grunted, and Lawrence nodded. For a few minutes, they stayed in silence, Carmen doing her push-ups and Lawrence doing nothing at all, just staring off into space and watching craggy faces emerge from the mountains, which happened as often as they appeared in clouds. There was a man with an enormous beard, a cat curled up into the shape of a doughnut, a Samoan mask, a sleeping baby.

"How long have you guys been together now?" Lawrence heard himself ask. He didn't want to read the novel he'd brought outside. It was the next movie he was working on, a period-piece adaptation. Nineteenth-century Brits, lots of party scenes with scores of extras, lots of horses. Those were always the worst. Every page turned into nothing but dollar signs — Lawrence read the cost of crinolines, of vintage lace, of imported parasols. Werewolves weren't great, either, but packages of fake hair were less expensive than real dogs for a hunting scene. His favorite movies of all were the tiny ones where the actors all wore their own clothes, brushed their own hair or didn't, and everyone rented a country house for a week and slept all piled on top of one another like a litter of newborn kittens. He could do the accounting for those in his sleep.

"Me and Bobby?" Carmen sat with her legs wide open in straddle position and leaned forward. "Seven years, almost."

"Wow, really?" Lawrence said. "Was he still in college?"

Carmen laughed. "I know, he was a baby. He only had one set of silverware. One fork, one knife, one spoon. And then a drawer full of plastic ones that he got from take-out places. It was like going out with a kid in high school, I swear." She swung her torso over one leg and then crab-walked her fingers to the toe of her sneaker. "Fucking hamstrings."

"Not to be rude, but how old were you when you met? We have a big age gap, too, and people ask me all the time. I don't mean to be offensive." Lawrence didn't actually know if he meant to be offensive or not, but he was curious. He hated when people asked him the same question — young men phrased it in such a way that meant they thought Charlie was old, and old men phrased it in such a way that meant that they thought that Lawrence was nothing more than a blow-up toy, available for sex at all hours, in any orifice. It was nothing like either of those things. Lawrence never thought about the ten years between them except when they were playing Trivial Pursuit and Charles suddenly knew which actors were on which television shows, and who had been whose vice president. In their practical, daily life, the age difference mattered as much as who finished the toilet paper and needed to remember to replace it with a fresh roll, which is to say, if it ever mattered, it was only for a split second, and then it was forgotten. They had worried about Charles's age, for the birth mothers, and now that they'd made it past the first round, Lawrence hoped that it wouldn't be the thing standing in their way. They could change apartments, or neighborhoods, lots of things, but they couldn't change that.

"Well, I'm forty now, so I guess I was thirty-four? Maybe thirty-three? I can't remember what month he joined the gym."

"And were you pretty serious right away?"

"I guess." Carmen closed her legs. She reached up and pulled the elastic out of her ponytail, shaking her hair loose. It hung in awkward damp curls around her shoulders, kinking out at funny angles where the rubber band had held it in place. "We try to keep it casual, but with respect, you know?"

Lawrence didn't, and shook his head.

"I mean, we're exclusive, but for the first few years, it was more like, we'll see. Now we're really solid, though."

"I gotcha." It sounded like bullshit, like the sort of thing men with several second-string girlfriends might say. Lawrence had a dozen friends of just that description, men who refused to commit, because what was the point? But his friends were older, and only a handful of them were interested in having children. Life would be so much more interesting if one could ask all the questions one wanted to and expect honest answers. Lawrence just smiled with his lips closed.

Carmen pushed herself up to stand. It was still light, but the needles on the pine trees had started to shift from glittery to dark, which meant that the sun was saying fare-well for the day. "What about you? When did you guys decide to get married? I mean, when did you know you were ready?"

"When we could." Lawrence would have had a thousand weddings to Charles. They'd had a party each time a law passed, and one with their parents at City Hall, followed by a giant party at a restaurant in SoHo where Charles had drawn murals on the walls, so they were all surrounding themselves, smiling in two places at once, Lawrence and Charles and even Franny. That was one thing Lawrence hadn't known when he was young, when he had fantasies about his Dream Wedding, back a hundred years ago when he'd stolen all of his sister's Ken dolls and laid them on top of each other on his bunk bed, way up there where no one would see. Lawrence didn't know then, and wouldn't know for decades, that marriage meant sealing your fate with so many other people — the in-laws and the grandfathered-in friends of the bosom, the squealing children who would grow into adults who required wedding gifts of their own.

"That sounds nice," Carmen said. She wasn't really listening anymore, but instead halfway into her own Dream Wedding. It would be a small affair, maybe on the beach, with a reception inside afterward. All of her Cubano relatives would want a band, and so they would have one, the men in their guayaberas, the women with flowers behind their ears. Even though Carmen herself didn't eat sugar, her mother would insist on a cake — *tres leches* — and everyone would have a piece. Bobby would pretend to shove it into her face, but instead feed her the tiniest bite, knowing full well that each swallow meant fifty more jumping jacks the next day. But on their wedding day, she would eat a whole piece and not care, she'd be that happy. Together, she and Bobby could be a training team, maybe someday leave Total Body Power and start their own gym. Carmen had already started thinking about names.

Clive. Clifton. Clarence. Lawrence had always imagined the baby being a boy, maybe because they were both men, maybe because he wanted a girl so badly that it felt like bad luck to even daydream about the possibility. Alphonse wasn't right, but they could change it. *C* names felt natural, and slightly old-fashioned in a way that he liked. For a girl, he liked something more whimsical: *Luella, Birdie,* or maybe even something cinematic: *Scarlett.* A couple they knew had recently been chosen by a birth mother and were now delirious from lack of sleep, happy as clams. That was all Lawrence wanted — the chance to stare through bleary, four a.m. eyes at a slumbering Charles, wishing that he'd wake up and feed the baby. He could smell the sour spit-up, the foulness of the soiled diapers. He wanted it all.

Sometimes it was pleasant to sit in silence with a near stranger, both of you lost in your own thoughts. Once the pressure to speak was gone, the quiet could hover for hours, covering you in a sort of gossamer cloak, like two people staring out a moving train's window. Both Lawrence and Carmen found that they liked each other far more than they imagined they might, and they quite happily sat together without speaking until the sunset was complete.

Franny was in bed with an ice pack on her head, where a large goose egg had already formed. Antoni had driven her home himself, a ride that she dearly wished she remembered for more than just her own throbbing skull. Antoni tried to explain to Charles, who answered the door, what had happened, but there wasn't much to say. She had hit herself in the head with the butt of her tennis racquet and briefly knocked herself unconscious. She would be fine, Antoni was sure, though he admitted that he hadn't seen it before, not such a direct hit on one's own scalp. Antoni had been very sweet about the whole thing — when Antoni had his sunglasses and baseball hat off, Charles could see what had made Franny's heart go aflutter. He was still gorgeous, and spoke so quickly with his beautiful mouth, Charles almost didn't even care what he was saying, just so long as he kept talking. She had a strong swing, Antoni said, and smiled. They would reschedule, if she wished, and he would call to check on her. Antoni wrote down the name of his personal doctor for Charles and then left, getting into a waiting car driven by one of his employees, who had followed them up the mountain.

They'd cooked and eaten dinner without her — Charles delivered a plate to her bedside and returned when Franny had taken a few bites. Carmen was eager to help with the dishes, even more so in Franny's absence, but Jim shooed her away from the sink. He pushed his sleeves up to his elbows and turned on the faucet. "You go on," he said. "I'll do it." Jim spoke with authority, and Carmen backed away, hands raised.

"You wash, I'll dry," Charles said, setting out a dish towel on the countertop. Bobby had vanished into his bedroom, and Sylvia was sitting at the dining room table, hypnotized by her laptop. The house was as quiet as ever, though outside the wind was picking up, and occasionally branches tapped against the windows.

Jim dampened the sponge and dove in. They worked silently for a few minutes, an assembly line of two. At the table, Sylvia gave a loud snort and then a louder laugh. Both Jim and Charles turned to her for an explanation, but her eyes stayed glued to the screen.

"I do not understand the Internet,"

Charles said. "It's a giant void."

Jim agreed. "A limitless void. Hey, Syl," he said. "How's it going over there?"

Sylvia looked up. She had the crazed expression of a child who'd stared directly into the sun, blinking and temporarily blind. "What are you guys talking about?"

"Nothing, dear," Jim said, laughing. Sylvia went back to the computer screen and started typing quickly.

Charles shrugged. "At least she could always get a job as a typist."

"I don't think those exist anymore. Administrative assistants, maybe, but not typists."

"Franny seems okay." They made eye contact for a moment while Jim handed off a dripping plate.

"Does she?" Jim wiped the back of his wet hand across his forehead. "I really can't tell anymore. You'd know better than I."

Charles clutched the plate in both hands, turning it over and over until it was dry. "I think she does. That bump isn't pretty, but it'll heal."

"Do we need to sue that tennis player, whatshisface? I never liked him. That awful ponytail, now this." Another lawsuit would balance out his own, force them to band together. Jim imagined himself and Franny striding into a Mallorcan courtroom, the bump on Franny's head now the size of a tennis ball, hard proof of Antoni's negligence.

"And how are you?" Charles asked. He purposefully looked toward the dishes, now dry and ready to be put away, and toward his wet hands, which he toweled off.

Sylvia had started playing a video, the sound of which blasted out of her tinny computer speakers. She was off in teenager land, content and miserable in equal measure, oblivious to the trials of any human heart that wasn't her own. Jim turned the sink back on, though there were no more dishes to wash.

"I have no idea," he said.

Charles placed his hand on Jim's shoulder and gave it a squeeze. He wanted to tell Jim that everything would be fine, and that his marriage was as solid as it had ever been, but lying seemed worse than offering a small show of sympathy.

Day Eight

The previous evening's threatening wind had blossomed into full-on rain. Gemma hadn't warned them about the possibility of inclement weather, and Franny was furious. She hobbled from the bed to the window and watched skinny raindrops ping against the taut surface of the swimming pool. It was Saturday, one of their few weekend days in Mallorca, not that there was much of a delineation between the week and the weekend. Still, Franny felt cheated, and planned to go downstairs and complain. First, she hobbled back around the bed the long way and into the bathroom, where she was so shocked by her own reflection that she actually yelped. After waiting a moment to make sure that no one was coming to her rescue — another thing to complain about — Franny moved closer to the mirror.

She had somehow managed to hit herself with her racquet, that much Franny understood, hard enough to knock herself to the ground. The bump rose out of her center part, a lone volcanic mountain in an otherwise peaceful valley. "Ugh," Franny said. She tied her black robe more tightly around her waist, as if that would distract anyone, and swanned her way down the stairs as slowly as Norma Desmond, wishing for the very first time that she'd thought to pack a turban.

The chest in the living room had been well stocked with board games: Monopoly and Risk, Snakes and Ladders. Charles had made a brief but impassioned speech in favor of a game of charades but was quickly shot down. They decided on Scrabble, and Lawrence was winning, being the best at math, which everyone knew was all it took to truly succeed. He knew all the two-letter words, the *QI* and the *ZA,* and played them without apology, even when it made the board so dense that it was difficult for anyone else to take a turn. Bobby, Sylvia, and Charles all stared hard at their letters, as if simple attention alone would improve their odds.

"I'm pretty sure you're cheating," Bobby said. "I wish we had a Scrabble dictionary. Sylvia, go look one up on your computer."

"Screw you. You're just mad you're losing," she said, rearranging the tiles on her rack. She had two *O*'s. *Moo. Boo. Loo. Fool. Pool. Polio.* Sylvia always played the first word she saw, and didn't care if she set up the next player for a double word score. She laid down *MOO.* "Give me seven points, please."

Lawrence rubbed his hands quickly over his face, up and down. "Sylvia, sweetheart, you're driving me crazy. You can do better than that, I know you can."

"Let her play how she wants to play, Lawr," Charles said, swatting him affectionately on the wrist. "Now, let's see . . ." He played *BROMIDE,* crisscrossing Sylvia's *MOO,* a bingo. Charles and Sylvia both cheered.

"You so don't get it," Bobby said.

Carmen was not a fan of word games, or of board games at all, and she'd been sitting in the chair on the other side of the room, flipping through Sylvia's airplane magazines. She'd read them already, and knew the pictures by heart — this television star was looking skinny, this one was looking fat, and they were wearing the same bikini! Every few minutes she would get up and slowly walk behind Bobby to look at his letters, and the board, and then circle back to her chair like a discontented house cat. The last time they'd gone on vacation, two winters previous, Bobby and Carmen had gone to an all-inclusive resort called Xanadu. The resort was on a Caribbean island, and because all the food and alcohol had already been paid for, they felt like high-rolling celebrities, exactly as the resort's brochure had said they would. They had six margaritas at once at one of the swim-up bars, and when Bobby later threw up all over their hotel room, they didn't particularly mind, because it had all been free, and they weren't responsible for cleaning it up. They rented Jet Skis and went parasailing. They had sex in a cabana at the far end of the beach — twice in one day. The other people at Xanadu had been great — all other couples like them, ready to dance until dawn and maybe slip a tongue down someone else's throat when their girlfriend or boyfriend went to the bathroom. It was just *fun.* Nothing serious, nothing boring. Even though mostly they'd just sat around on the beach, it still felt like doing something. They were tanning, they were drinking, they were dancing. That was a real vacation. Being locked up in this house on Mallorca felt like the day in the fourth grade when Carmen's mother had forgotten to pick her up at the library after school.

"Bobby, can I talk to you for a minute?" she said, standing up again and letting the magazine flutter from her hand to the floor.

Bobby looked at the board, and at Lawrence, and at his sister. "Play slowly," he said, and followed Carmen out of the room and into the kitchen.

"Did you talk to your parents yet?" she asked, once they were out of earshot.

"What?" Bobby looked over her shoulder, making sure no one else was close enough to eavesdrop. It had always been one of his sister's talents.

"About the money. It's really not that much. And if you could just pay it all off now, the interest . . ." Bobby stopped Carmen by clamping his palm over her mouth. "Hey," she said, and peeled it off.

"Listen, they're my parents, okay? I know how to talk to them." Bobby crossed his arms over his chest and blew an errant curl off his forehead.

"Okay, if you say so," she said. "It's just that we've already been here awhile and you're sort of running out of time. And why didn't you tell me about your father's job? I didn't realize he was really leaving the magazine, like, for good."

"Yeah," Bobby said, "me neither. I mean,

I guess my mom told me, but I wasn't really listening. It's fucked up. I don't know, maybe now's a bad time." A great chorus of shouts carried over from the living room. "We'll talk about this later, okay?" He didn't wait for her to respond, and pushed past her back into the living room. Carmen sat by the window and watched the rain, all the while trying to figure out a way to make a bolt of lightning go through the window, through the walls, and directly into Bobby's chest. She was only trying to help. They never spent more than an afternoon with her family, and they were twenty minutes away. Carmen thought she might make a list of everything she did for him, just to have it written down on paper so that she could actually see it in black and white. The Posts weren't that great, if they'd never taught Bobby how to treat a girl. The rain didn't stop until after the sun went down.

Bobby needed to get out of the house. After the Scrabble tournament (Lawrence in first place, Charles in second, a reluctant Jim in third after a single high-scoring game, Bobby in fourth, and Sylvia in a distant fifth) and a low-key dinner, Franny was in high gear about a movie marathon starring someone Bobby had never heard of and was sure he couldn't give two shits about. He needed to get out of the house. Carmen was ignoring his little touches, still irritated, and so he asked his mother for the keys.

"Sylvia," he said. The thought of a night out alone in Palma was intoxicating, but he didn't know where to go. "Send your tutor an e-mail and ask him where the best bars in town are. Somewhere fun." Across the room, he saw Carmen's eyebrows flicker upward, but he chose not to acknowledge it. She wasn't invited.

Joan was quick — he sent over a list of three spots in a place called Magaluf, a town just outside Palma known for its clubs. They were for tourists, he said, but when there were really good DJs, all the Mallorcans went, too. The best one, Joan said, was called Blu Nite, and tonight there would be a DJ called Psychic Bomb. Sylvia begrudgingly admitted to having heard of him, and Bobby had seen him spin lots of times at home.

Bobby didn't like going out by himself — in Miami, if he wasn't with Carmen, he'd be with a whole posse of his boys from the gym, other trainers and some select clients, or sometimes even his college friends, though he didn't see them as much as he used to. Some of them had gotten married, and one had even had a baby. *No, thank you* — that was Bobby's philosophy. The idea of Carmen coming along and harping on him without his mother around to muzzle her up was so awful that Bobby really had only one choice in wingperson. It was hilarious how the Posts all probably thought that Carmen was mute, when all she did was tell him what he was doing wrong. At the gym, at the laundromat, in bed.

"Syl, you want to come with me?"

Sylvia was locked again into her computer screen, marveling at the thought of Joan somewhere nearby doing the same thing. Bobby had never asked her to do anything with him before, except maybe order burritos from the place around the corner, and she wasn't quite sure she'd heard him correctly.

"You want to come with me?" he repeated himself.

"Um, yeah, sure," Sylvia said, slowly closing the lid of her laptop. "Give me a minute to get dressed." She hurried upstairs and threw open her suitcase, rooting around like a pig in hopes she would find a treasure trove of things she hadn't actually packed. The thought occurred to her that she could find something truly perfect to wear to a cheesy nightclub if she snuck into Carmen and Bobby's room, but Carmen had been acting like a freak all day, and if she wasn't going with them, something must be weird. So Sylvia picked out her tightest jeans and a T-shirt she'd had since the fifth grade with a picture of the Jonas Brothers on it and hoped for the best. She hadn't even meant to pack it, but it was small and tight, and she hoped the Spanish were as into nostalgic irony as she was.

Blu Nite was on a corner, down the block from a sushi restaurant and a bar that promised karaoke. Sylvia was wearing her nicest shoes, a pair of black ballet flats, and she couldn't help but notice that every other woman she saw was stalking around on a pair of stiletto heels like they were trying to irrigate the sidewalk. It had stopped raining, but the streets were still slick with water, with lots of little reflective pools just waiting to soak your feet. Bobby didn't seem to notice that Sylvia kept leaping over puddles, and was hurrying to keep up with him.

"Do you have a fake ID?" he asked, barely turning around to look at her.

"I only have to be eighteen. Which I am. So, no." Sylvia jogged for a few strides until she was next to him.

Bobby was wearing what he would wear out in Miami — a nice pair of dark jeans, an untucked button-down shirt with the top two buttons undone, and a silver necklace that Carmen had given him for Christmas. He glanced at Sylvia, clearly regretting his decision to invite her along, and then nodded toward the door of the club. "Whatever. Let's go in. I need a drink."

Blue neon tubes lined the walls, which struck Sylvia as a little bit too obvious of an interior decorating choice. It was still early, and so the crowd was fairly thin, but there were several clumps of girls dancing together in the center of the large room.

"Is this all a club is?" Sylvia asked, but the music was loud enough that her brother either couldn't hear her or could ignore her without seeming rude. She'd been expecting a light-up dance floor like in *Saturday Night Fever,* or, at the very least, a velvet rope. Blu Nite was one giant room with black leather sofas along the walls and a cluster of high glass tables near the bar, where the single men seemed to congregate. They were all dressed like Bobby, with shirts covered in printing at odd angles, as if all the clothing in Spain had gotten mangled in the printing machine, and now the logos were creeping over everyone's shoulders instead of being square in the middle of their chests. It was the classic Euro look — shiny and well groomed to the point of New Jersey. She was still looking around when she realized that Bobby was across the room, belly up to the bar.

"Get me something," she said, hurrying behind him.

Bobby nodded and raised two fingers at the bartender. *"Dos!"*

The DJ booth was at the far end of the bar, on a raised platform. Sylvia could see only Psychic Bomb's head bobbing in time to the music — he'd just faded from something into a Katy Perry song she recognized, and the girls on the dance floor all squealed.

"Here," Bobby said, pushing an enormous glass into her hands.

"What is it?" Sylvia sniffed at the rim — it smelled like cough syrup.

"Red Bull and vodka."

Bobby had one, too — they stood there for a minute, Sylvia sucking the sweet drink through a long straw, and Bobby gulping his back with large swallows. Bobby's glass was empty almost immediately, and he returned to the bar to get another.

"Thirsty?" Sylvia said, when he came back.

"I was just really needing to get out of the

house, you know?" Bobby spoke without looking at her. He scanned the room, his head moving in time with the music. "Carmen was driving me fucking crazy."

"And Mom?"

"And Mom." Bobby looked at her, finally. "I can't believe you still live with them."

"Only for another month." Sylvia tried to sound chipper.

"Honestly?" Bobby said. "I have no idea who they are. When I was a kid, they fought all the time, and when you were a kid, it was like sunshine and rainbows. I have no idea. At least now they're looking more like people I recognize."

"I'm pretty sure they're fighting all the time," Sylvia said. Had they really not told him anything? Bobby had always seemed so grown-up, so adult, that she'd assumed he would have known everything long before she did. "It's pretty bad."

"Yeah?" Bobby said, but he wasn't really listening to her. Sylvia felt sorry for him, sorry enough to keep her parents' secret. He lived so far away, what was the difference? When he visited for Christmas, they would all go out to dinner and be civil and her parents would still be her parents and her house would still be her house, if only in Bobby's imagination. "I'm going to

209

dance," he said, and left her sitting there. Psychic Bomb faded into a song with a faster beat, which sounded like something that would have poured out the open window of a packed car with Jersey plates.

Sylvia stayed put, stunned, and watched as Bobby quickly finished his drink, set the empty glass down on the bar, and then made his way onto the dance floor, swiveling his hips like a gyroscope. Sylvia opened her mouth and let it hang there, voluntarily slack-jawed. Bobby moved quickly into the orbit of two distinct groups of dancing girls, and both circles opened up to let him in. The girls on the left were taller and blonder, and seemed to be speaking German. The girls on the right were smaller, mousier — Brits, maybe. (Sylvia was not surprised that the native Spaniards did not yet seem to be in attendance — it was still their dinnertime, after all.) Bobby shimmied into the center of the circle on the right, eliciting even more squeals. One squat girl, with a dark brown bob that swung from side to side as she danced, seemed particularly excited about Bobby's arrival, and reacted as if she'd been expecting him. She positioned her body in front of Bobby's, her knees straddling his left leg, so that it looked like they were in a two-person limbo contest. Sylvia turned toward the bar, unable to watch any more.

There were some stools at the high glass tables, and Sylvia sat down. It wasn't that Sylvia didn't like to dance, it was more that she'd never really learned how, and even if she had, she didn't see the point in grinding against total strangers. It reminded her of the photos, and how they would never go away; even though she'd untagged herself and flagged them for inappropriate content, there would always be someone new who'd seen them, or who had been at the party, waving another camera in her face. Dancing was something for luckier, less stupid people. Sylvia wished, for the millionth time, that she'd been born in a more civilized century, when dancing was about learning steps and executing them en masse, like a drill team, everyone waltzing together. The twentieth century had been bad (the flappers, the hippies), but the twenty-first was even worse. Sylvia thought of Tolstoy, and Austen's grand balls, with protracted wistfulness. What was unfolding in front of her was a pathetic travesty. A cocktail waitress swanned by, and Sylvia flagged her down, pointing to her now empty glass and nodding. Another.

■ ■ ■ ■

An hour later, Blu Nite had started to fill up. There was as much Spanish being spoken as German or English, which made Sylvia feel less like a colonizing imperialist. She'd lost Bobby in the crowd — he'd surfaced once at her table, sweating and panting and smiling, and once at the bar, when she was going for a glass of water, but other than that, he was just another body making the place into a massive, thumping *Romper Room* for adults. Two hours later, Sylvia was getting tired. She'd had two glasses of sangría after the disgusting vodka and Red Bull, which wasn't a lot, but given the lack of moisture in the room and the uncharacteristic lack of snacks (the Spanish were *excellent* at snacks), Sylvia was feeling a little bit drunk and more than a little ready to go home. She slid off her stool and made her way across the room to the bathroom. She'd pee first, then find Bobby and convince him that the place sucked and that they should leave.

There was a line for the women's restroom, which was not surprising. Sylvia shuffled against the wall and took her place. All the other girls were glued to their phones, texting and e-mailing and on their Facebook pages. Sylvia had a small pang of grief at not being able to do the same thing. She missed her phone, despite the fact that she hated most of the people she knew and didn't care what they were doing all summer. She would have checked her e-mail to see if Joan had written back. She would have looked at the clock to see what time it was in New York, what time in was in Rhode Island (which was the same as in New York, of course, but it felt good to think of it as so separate and far that it be acknowledged as such). Sylvia shifted from foot to foot. She was getting sweaty, not from actually moving around but just from being next to so many bodies, and she stuck her nose toward her armpit to check on her smelliness. The girl behind her gave her a look, and Sylvia rolled her eyes. Across the very narrow hall, a short line had started to form for the men's room, too, which Sylvia found satisfying in a vaguely feminist way. She was all for equality. The men weren't sure what to do, though, not having trained for moments like this throughout their entire lives, and the guy in front banged on the door.

A minute later, the lock turned, and Sylvia watched as her brother and one of the mousy Brits tumbled out, their faces still attached like two warring vacuum cleaners. Her lipstick was smeared on his cheeks and neck. They squeezed past the guy who had banged on the door, who sneered at them less aggressively than Sylvia would have done, had she been in his position.

"Um, hello?" she said, tapping her brother on the shoulder.

"Oh, hey, Syl," he said, sounding remarkably casual. He pulled back, leaving the Brit gaping like a caught fish. His shirt was open at the neck, unbuttoned almost to his navel, and the Brit dug her fingers into his sparse chest hair. Bobby's eyes were having trouble focusing on Sylvia, and she had to force herself not to look away.

"What the fuck are you doing?" All the other women waiting for the bathroom had let their phones fall to their sides, happy to have a live show instead.

"This is my new friend. She's on vacation, too. Right?" The girl looked up from Bobby's chest and nodded.

"This is fucking gross, is what it is. Do you know that he has a girlfriend? Who is here with us? Who no one likes, but he brought her anyway? Do you even know her name?"

"I'm Isabel Parkey!" Little Isabel cocked her head to the side, confused about who to be annoyed with. "We were just having some fun," she said in a British accent, as posh as someone in a BBC miniseries.

Bobby kissed her on the cheek and then physically turned her around and pushed her back toward the dance floor. "I'll meet you out there — let me talk to my sister for a minute." Isabel shrugged. A new song came on — a golden oldie, maybe Kylie Minogue — and she jumped up and down, her troubles forgotten. "Let's go," Bobby said to Sylvia, his voice now so low that she could barely hear him over the thumping and the singing along. She could tell that the other women waiting for the bathroom were straining to hear him, too.

"Not yet, I still have to pee," she said. "But that does not mean that we're not going to talk about this. You are gross, you know that? Who does that?"

Bobby wiped off his cheeks and mouth with his shirttail. His belt was unbuckled, and he refastened it. "Whatever, Sylvia. I'm not married to her. It's not that big of a deal."

"But you *live* together. She is your girlfriend. You force us to hang out with her. And then you treat her like this? That is so fucked up. Like, the worst kind of fucked up."

If he were a nice brother, the kind who asked her questions about her life, he might know about Gabe Thrush and her stupid friends and how she was never, ever going to have sex with anyone in her entire life because of boys like him, but he didn't know anything at all. If he were a nice brother, and less pathetic, she would have told him all about their parents and how the whole world was ending and no one seemed to care. A lightbulb went on over Sylvia's head. "You do this all the time, don't you?"

Bobby couldn't resist smirking with pride.

Sylvia could no longer contain her rage, and began to pummel her brother in the stomach. The other girls on line for the bathroom shrank back against the wall, getting themselves as far out of arm-swinging range as possible. Those who were merely keeping their friends company but didn't really have to go fled back onto the dance floor. No one stepped in to rescue Bobby, possibly because Sylvia's punches were cartoonishly amateur and didn't seem to be wounding him in the slightest. After a little while, she stopped. "My knuckles hurt, you asshole."

"Let's go," Bobby said, and this time Sylvia slumped after him, furious and still having to pee so badly, but ready to not have so many people staring at her. They wound their way through the club — even more packed now — careful to avoid Isabel and her friends, who had yet to relinquish their corner of the dance floor. They'd made it all the way to the front door before someone stepped in front of them, purposefully halting their progress. Sylvia closed her eyes, sure that it was going to be the Spanish police, arresting her for assaulting her brother in a public place.

"*Ciao,* you found it!" Joan kissed her on both cheeks and clapped Bobby on the shoulder. "It's a good place, yes?"

Sylvia smoothed out her shirt, which she had only recently realized was in fact so small and tight that you could see the indent of her belly button, which was almost as bad as being able to see her nipples. Could he see her nipples? Sylvia's cheeks burned. He had kissed her. His face, his mouth, had been right next to hers. Her stomach lurched as it had when driving down from Pigpen, the small car flying around wet corners, dangerous and fast.

"Yeah, it's pretty cool," Sylvia managed.

"Hey, we were just on our way out, man, but we'll see you," Bobby said. "Ready, Syl?"

Joan stood there expectantly. She couldn't

217

figure out a way to ask him for a ride home, or tell him how badly she had to pee, or to say that her brother was an asshole, and she'd only just realized it, so Sylvia leaned in close and whispered to him in Spanish, *I wish I could stay.* She tried to look wistful, the kind of face that a French actress would make before stepping onto a train, never to be seen again, and then walked out of the club as quickly, scissoring her legs together so hard that she was sure the denim would wear out.

Sylvia held it until they got to the car, a few blocks away, and then unzipped her pants and dropped into a squat in between cars. Her pee was warm and splashed against the cobblestones, running in a ragged stream down the sloped street. Sylvia would have cared, but it felt too good. She thought about Joan coming after her, like someone in a romantic comedy, and finding her with her jeans pulled taut against her thighs and her bare butt wedged between two bumpers. Bobby was already in the driver's seat, waiting. He could wait.

Men were terrible, that was the truth. Men would do anything, say anything, just to get a girl to take her clothes off. They were liars and cheaters and awful people, all of them. She'd always thought of her brother as an older version of herself, a test batch of genetic material, but lately she wasn't sure. Maybe there was something else that came with having a penis, a partial moral blindness located in a secret chamber of the heart. It made her feel like there were bugs crawling all over her, like someone was standing too close behind her and breathing heavily. Bobby's behavior was disgusting, even as identified by someone currently urinating on a public street. Her sordid behavior was out of necessity, like when you'd see mothers letting their little boys pee against trees in Central Park. They didn't think they were watering the plants, they were avoiding carrying around a piss-soaked child for the rest of the day! Sylvia had made a decision. Bobby had done no such thing. He had let himself slip and slip and slip. He didn't even feel guilty! At least their father seemed to realize that he'd done something wrong. She shook off, relieved and empty, and stood up, careful to step out of the puddle.

A group of women rounded the corner, headed to Blu Nite or another place like it, and Sylvia watched as they teetered along together, speaking Spanish quickly and tossing their long, dark hair over their shoulders.

European women had it so much easier. All they had to do was open their mouths, and they sounded smart and sophisticated, and they always had small hips and big boobs, like sex robots made in a laboratory. Sylvia looked down at the ground as they passed. Joan's sort-of girlfriend probably looked like that, like someone who could unselfconsciously meet strangers while wearing only a bikini. Sylvia hoped they couldn't smell her pee.

After they'd passed, Sylvia hurried the long way around the car and folded herself into the passenger seat. Bobby was holding his head in his hands, pitched forward so that his moppish hair was dangling over the steering wheel.

"You're not going to tell her, are you?" He spoke without moving.

Sylvia fastened her seat belt. "I don't know yet." She could hardly keep track of what secrets she was keeping for whom.

This made Bobby shoot up straight. "No, Syl, you can't!" His breath was boozy, and his eyes were red. Sylvia had never seen her brother like this. He was always so composed, like their father, even-keeled and amiable. She didn't know what to make of him in this new state, cracking like a discarded Easter egg. "Please," he said.

"I'll think about it, okay?"

"Okay," he said, and turned the key in the ignition. He wasn't good at driving the stick shift, either, and they stalled four times on the way to the highway, each time making Bobby slouch lower and lower in his seat, as though the accumulated humiliations were physically hurting him. It took an hour to get home, and when they pulled into the driveway, Bobby put out his arm, preventing Sylvia from getting out. "Wait."

"What?" Sylvia was glad to have gotten home alive, and was dreaming of her bed, maybe checking Facebook to see if she needed to hate anyone more than she already did. The Internet was excellent for confirming one's worst fears about the human race.

"I'm really sorry you had to see that." Bobby paused. "I mean, I'm really sorry you had to see that side of me. When I see you guys, I like to pretend that part of me doesn't exist, you know, like it stays in Florida. Shit, I don't know."

There was a light in Sylvia's bedroom window, which she'd left on by mistake. Otherwise the house seemed quiet; everyone had likely retreated to their own corners for the night. Sylvia felt sorry for Bobby, that he'd have to crawl into bed with Carmen,

221

his guilt coming off him in stinky waves like a cartoon skunk. But not so sorry that she would sit in the car with him and wait it out. It wasn't her job to make him feel better.

"Sucks for you," Sylvia said, opening the door. "But it sucks even more for her. Or, actually, you know what? It sucks more for you. Because she could get a new boyfriend. But you can't change the fact that you're an asshole. I love you, Bobby, because you're my brother, but I honestly don't like you very much right now." And with that, she slammed the door and huffed inside, not waiting for him to move or even respond. He wasn't her problem.

DAY NINE

The curtains were open and the sunlight streamed in through the window, onto Bobby's pillow. He tried to turn away, but the whole room felt lit up like a film set. He frowned, peeling his eyes open as slowly as possible, as if the light would hurt any less.

"I guess you don't want to come for a run with me, huh?" Carmen said. She was standing at the foot of the bed, already in her exercise clothes and sneakers. "Have fun last night? It was great when you came in. I'm sure you don't remember. It was really something else. What were you drinking? The whole room still smells. That's why I opened the window."

Bobby did remember: he remembered his sister's disappointment, and the British girl's tongue on his dick, and the way the Red Bull tasted when it came back up. "Ugggh," he said, not wanting it to happen all over again. He turned onto his stomach, burying his face in the pillow.

"Oh, I'm sure you feel like crap," Carmen said. "So I'll just see you later, I guess, yeah? I wanted to go on a cruise to the Bahamas, okay? So this is not about me, Bobby. This is on you." He heard her pivot on her rubber soles and squeak out of the room, pulling the door closed behind her. The reverberations sounded like a truck running over his skull. All he wanted was more sleep — sleep could do anything. It could make him feel human again, it could make him forget. Before he drifted off again, Bobby felt a lurch in his stomach and scrambled out of bed and into the bathroom as quickly as he could, almost making it to the toilet before throwing up again, and littering the bathroom floor with tiny pieces of everything left in his stomach, which wasn't much. He thought, for only the first time that day, that if he had to choose between living and dying, dying might be easier.

Sylvia was awake but pretending not to be. The only thing she was looking forward to was that it was Sunday, and therefore Joan would not be coming over, which of course was a bad thing, because it was the only thing making the trip even remotely enjoyable, but if he had come over, it would mean that he would have to see her hungover, which wasn't pretty. Not that Sylvia ever felt actually, clinically pretty, but there were those odd days when her skin behaved and her clothes behaved and the mirror behaved. This was worse than normal, though. The inside of Sylvia's mouth felt like it had been dried with paper towels all night long, her saliva blotted into nonexistence. She reached for her telephone, the poor dead soldier, and held it over her face. If it worked, she would have swiftly pressed a few buttons and started scrolling away, but all she could do was look at the icons for the apps. The Wi-Fi didn't work upstairs, and it wouldn't have mattered anyway. She could imagine what she had missed: new pictures of Gabe and Katie kissing like brain-damaged guppies or pressing their cheeks together like they *couldn'tstandtobeapartforasecondlonger.* Everyone else would be posting pictures of the parties they were at, or vacations with their families, everyone at the beach and tan and flaunting it. There might even be new and embarrassing pictures of someone else, someone to take the spotlight away from her. She swung one leg out of the bed at a time, crab-walking out as far as she could without raising the rest of her body.

Standing up straight made her head feel wobbly, but it wasn't so bad. She'd had worse hangovers — twice. The first time was when she was fifteen and the whole family went to a wedding of one of Franny's friends in Northern California wine country, and every table (including the teenage table, where Sylvia was sitting, miles away from her parents and everyone else she knew) had bottles of wine that were replaced with a rapid frequency. The second time was when she and Katie Saperstein accidentally drank too many wine coolers before a school dance "as a joke" and spent the whole night in the school bathroom, the same place where they had to pee a hundred times a day, reminding them of their mistake forever and ever, or at least until graduation. This wasn't as bad as either of those times, but it was bad enough that Sylvia knew she'd have to dig through her mother's bag for some aspirin.

Sylvia shuffled to the door of her room, opened it, and stuck her head out as an exploratory venture. There were sounds coming from downstairs — Charles and Lawrence, she thought — but no movement on her floor. She shuffled farther into the hall and put her ear against the door to her parents' room. They would both be awake by now — her father never slept past seven, and her mother was incapable of feeling left out, and so even she rose early when there were other people around. Sylvia knocked once and waited. There wasn't any sound, so she opened the door. The bed was empty, as she'd suspected. "Mom? Dad?"

When there was no answer from her invisible parents, Sylvia shuffled the rest of the way into the room, and into their bathroom. Her mother traveled with a small pharmacy — sleeping pills, ibuprofen, acetaminophen, antacids, antidiarrheal tablets, Benadryl, calamine lotion, Band-Aids, Neosporin, floss, nail clippers, nail files, the works. Sylvia rooted around until she found the pills she wanted and swallowed them down with a gulp of water from the sink, which felt so good that she did it a few more times, lapping straight from the tap like a dog. She looked at herself in the mirror and began a semi-thorough investigation of her pores. Her face was blotchy, and there were little pimples on her nostrils. She smiled widely, and then bared her teeth. As long as Bobby didn't try to speak to her, she'd be fine. The thought of seeing Carmen wasn't appealing, but then again, it never was. Sylvia turned around and wobbled back in the direction of her bedroom.

Her parents' bed had been hastily made, with the thin cover pulled up to the pillows, but nothing tucked in. On Franny's side (it was the left side, with the messy stack of books and magazines and two half-full glasses of water), the pillows were dented and askew. On Jim's side, they were perfectly straight, as if her father's head hadn't moved all night. Sylvia walked around to his side of the bed and sat down. She pulled back the cover and put her hand on the bottom sheet, feeling for warmth. There was no trace of her father in the room except for his empty suitcase and a pair of his shoes tucked neatly beside the dresser.

Sylvia had always known that her parents had issues — that was the word people liked to use. They fought, they belittled each other, they rolled their eyes. Everyone's parents were like that when no one was watching. Sylvia had never actually confirmed that with any of her friends, but it had to be true. It was like discovering that Santa didn't exist, or the Easter Bunny, or that no one actually liked their extended family. This was doubly true for parents who had been married as long as Franny and Jim. It was a normal part of life, being annoyed at the person you were always with. Healthy, even. Who wanted parents like on fifties television, with pot roasts and implacable smiles? Even so, Sylvia had never even entertained the possibility that one of her parents had cheated on the other one until she started hearing the whispered fights through the walls. Now instead of seeming normal, it all just seemed sad. Her head still throbbed, and her mouth was dry again. Sylvia pushed herself back up to standing, even more mad at Bobby for helping the whole world go to shit, instead of just their parents.

The werewolf movie had gone back for reshoots, which meant more work for Lawrence. He wasn't surprised — it was the bad movies that needed the most coddling, from the actors to the producers to the location scouts. He stood with his back to the fridge, laptop in his arms. The director had had a last-minute change of heart about the ending (Christmas for all, werewolf love) and had instead shot a version in which Santa Claws had leapt to his death from the sleigh. Reshoots were necessary, and the remainder of the fake hair had already been returned. It was the sort of thing that would have taken him days even if they were at home, but from Mallorca, with the spotty Internet, Lawrence saw the rest of the vacation sliding from mediocre but tolerable to actually hellish. They should have just gone home when they got the e-mail, whatever the end result. Charles seemed to be slipping, too, purposefully avoiding conversations they'd spent the last year having incessantly, and Lawrence worried that he'd changed his mind.

Franny and Charles were sitting at the kitchen table, munching on pieces of fruit and reading magazines — Franny had finally come into possession of Sylvia's airplane reading material, and was glued to an article. Charles had his sketchbook out and was drawing, but Lawrence doubted he was paying much attention, choosing instead to read over Franny's shoulder. Franny was one of the earliest hurdles in their relationship — Charles's parents were ancient and infirm, unlikely to put up a fight about his suitors, but Franny was vocal. Her opinion mattered. They'd gone to a dinner party at the Posts', the table filled out by another couple (the Fluffers, Franny called them later — "Just pretty window dressing, so that you wouldn't notice me taking notes"), whom they hadn't seen since. The food was divine — Franny had cooked for days, and it showed, with dishes more elaborate than anything Lawrence had ever eaten except on holidays at his grand-mother's house. There was a salad with pieces of grapefruit in it, and asparagus wrapped in pancetta, and a rack of lamb with the kind of mustardy crust that Lawrence thought you could get only at a restaurant. She'd been friendly and warm, as Charles had said she would be, but there was no mistaking the glint in her eye. Franny was judging every word that came out of his mouth, the way he cut his meat, the way his hand searched out Charles's thigh under the table. Not for anything funny, of course, just to squeeze, for re-assurance.

Franny pointed to something on the left-hand side of the page, and Charles erupted into laughter. She leaned into his shoulder, an easy, comfortable motion she'd done thousands of times over almost forty years, since two years before she and Jim were married. Lawrence and Charles had been together for almost eleven. Even now that they were married, sometimes it felt like he could never catch up. Lawrence was just about to interrupt their cozy moment and ask what had been so funny when Bobby, looking significantly worse for wear, shambled into the kitchen.

"Good morning," Franny said, sitting up

straighter. "Do you want some breakfast?" She scooted out from behind the table and around to the fridge, where there were now three people crowding into a very small space.

"Sorry," Lawrence said, "let me get out of the way." He swung his laptop over his head, like a suitcase he didn't want to soil after jumping overboard, and waded back to Charles.

Bobby opened the fridge and stood there, red-eyed and blurry. "There's nothing to eat."

Franny made a noise. "Don't be ridiculous. What are you in the mood for? Want some pancakes? French toast?"

"That makes you fat," Bobby said. "I need protein."

Without bristling at his surly tone, she continued. "Eggs? Maybe some bacon and eggs?" Franny looked up to him for approval. Bobby's eyelids hung at half-mast.

"Fine," he said, but he didn't move or close the door. Franny reached around him to grab what she needed from the refrigerator shelves. He stood still, a statue that smelled of dank armpits and a night of fitful sleep.

"I think Carmen's already up and at 'em," Charles said, nodding his chin toward the window. They all turned to look. She was alternating between jumping jacks and burpees, up down, up down, out in, up down, up down, out in. Bobby turned the slowest of all, and let out a thin wheeze of air when he saw her.

"She's pissed," he said. "She only does doubles when she's pissed."

"What'd you do, tiger?" Charles said, amused.

Bobby shrugged and dragged himself over to the table. Lawrence scooted over to make room, and Bobby collapsed into the nearest seat. "Nothing. *God.* Nothing."

"Women," Charles said, rolling his eyes, then quickly shrugging toward Franny. *I don't know,* he mouthed.

"You know what they say about women . . ." Lawrence started, but the look on Bobby's face made it clear that whatever joke he was about to tell wouldn't be worth it. They all sat in silence, waiting for Bobby's breakfast to be ready.

Carmen took a break and squatted down until her butt hit the ground, extending her legs out in a straddle position. If Bobby had asked her to go with him, she would have. If he came outside right then and told her that he loved her and kissed her on the cheek and apologized for interrupting her night's sleep, she would have forgiven him. If he had waved out the kitchen window even, and smiled at her! Carmen folded over the space between her legs, resting her hands on the rough concrete. He didn't understand anything at all.

A certain learning curve was to be expected — she was an adult when they met, and he was something else, half boy, half man. Maybe more than half boy, if she was being honest with herself. The first few years hadn't even counted, not really. He was learning how to balance his checkbook, how to order wine at a restaurant, how to separate his lights from his darks. Bobby had been so sweet, gobbling up every piece of practical information. She was an oracle of the real world! Franny and Jim Post paid someone to clean their house, so no wonder Bobby was confused when his toilet bowl began to show signs of use. They paid someone else to do their taxes, so no wonder he didn't know what he could deduct, which receipts to save.

And still, the Posts looked down at Carmen. She could feel it, she wasn't stupid. Certainly not as stupid as they thought she was. She heard their muttered remarks, saw their rolling eyes. She had given up trying to impress them years ago, thinking that it was her newness, her eagerness, that got under their skin. Now she wasn't sure that she'd ever had a chance. It was a strange feeling, to be someone else's lightning rod, the glinting piece of metal in the storm. The scapegoat's scapegoat. She saw how hard it was for Bobby to relax around his parents, and she wanted to help. But she couldn't help if he didn't let her.

Carmen rolled back up to a seated position and slid her head from side to side, stretching out her neck. He had five minutes to come outside and talk to her. She could see them all through the window, smiling and laughing. He had five minutes.

Jim wanted to spend the afternoon alone, so he drove one of the cars down the hill to Palma. The countryside was satisfying for only so long. Palma was big enough to get slightly lost in, with narrow streets and dead ends, just the way he liked. There were still some Moorish buildings, and some leftover evidence of the conquering hordes, and some interesting architecture tucked beside the chain restaurants. Let Franny plan the itineraries — Jim was happy to stroll with no destination in mind. He had a notebook in his pocket in case anything occurred to

235

him, but the notebook had stayed in his pocket thus far.

The last time Jim had applied for a job, he was twenty-two years old. Loyalty was more common in the old days, when fact-checkers became writers became editors, none of this bouncing from career to career like younger people seemed to do, as if art school and business school made sense on the same résumé. *Gallant* had been his professional home for decades, for his entire adult life. It had been another marriage, just as complicated and nearly as satisfying. But now here he was, a cool sixty, with no Monday mornings ahead. He turned left and walked up a cobblestone street that led into a small plaza with some cafés and outdoor seating. Jim chose a table in the shade and ordered a coffee.

His thoughts moved in spirals: If this, then that. If they divorced, then they'd sell the house. If they sold the house, then he'd have to move. If he moved, where would he go? If he stayed on the Upper West Side, was that pathetic? Was it aggressive? Was he supposed to surrender the zip code? Was Riverside Drive too far, too remote? Could he live in the nineties? He remembered the nineties when they moved in, how anything above 86th Street felt like it was overrun with drug dealers on stoops. If they didn't divorce, would they ever have sex again? And then Madison Vance appeared again, as she often did, her hair still wet from the shower but already wearing her makeup, her naked body pressing against his leg like a blind saluki. She licked his neck and then his earlobe. She began to whisper. Jim took a sip of his coffee and tried to make Madison disappear.

Telling Franny was worse than the conversation with the board. It wasn't easy to surprise someone after thirty-five years of marriage, but he'd done it. She'd laughed at first, thinking he was joking, the way they had often joked about murdering each other's parents, or accidentally amputating a digit while making dinner. They were sitting in bed, Franny with her nose tucked behind a book, her back slumped down like always. Half a dozen chiropractors had scolded her, but what was she going to do? Stop reading in bed? When he started talking, she held her finger between the pages, keeping her spot, but as he went on, she turned the book facedown onto her thighs. When Jim thought about the worst moment in his marriage, he thought about watching Franny turn her book over, the straight line of her mouth. It was what he'd avoided

237

thinking about when Madison was in front of him, when he thought he might be twenty-five again, if he wanted it badly enough. But there was no getting out of one's only life. Franny was a fact, and Madison was a mirage. She should have been a mirage. She should have been a jerk-off fantasy, a pretty picture, but instead Jim had let her walk through the looking glass and into his arms, and he couldn't take it back.

Jim tried to take another sip but discovered the coffee had gone cold and thick. He dropped a few euros on the table and wandered on, turning right and left and right again, eventually finding himself standing across a busy road from a crowded beach. He was sweating through his shirt by now, his long sleeves curled up and cuffed. He jogged across the street, dodging cars, and took off his shoes and socks. The sand was hot, and Jim stepped lightly over people's towels, side by side like floor tiles, until he stood at the water's edge. The water lapped in lightly, covering his toes. He absently wished that Franny had come with him, almost looking for her in the crowds of people in their bathing suits. But he would have to get used to doing things on his own.

Carmen insisted on helping Franny make

dinner. Together they tore the ends off green beans, mixed a vinaigrette, roasted a chicken, and made a pie. Franny was surprised at how easy it was — Carmen had fair knife skills and wasn't afraid of using salt or fat, as long as it wasn't for herself. They passed bowls back and forth, and ducked around each other to reach into cabinets or to open the oven door. Sylvia helped out in the kitchen when pressed into service, but would happily have eaten takeout every night instead. It was pleasant to have another body beside her, helping without complaint.

"I think we're all done!" Franny said. She broke off a tiny, crunchy piece of fatty chicken skin and let it dissolve in her mouth. "Mmm."

"Table's set." Carmen was nothing if not efficient.

"Thank you," Franny said. She was moved by the tiniest gesture — it had been a longer week than she'd anticipated, being the chief of an unruly tribe. It would not have been much of an exaggeration to say that she might have cried, if only Carmen had been a little bit younger and a more suitable match for her son. "Soup's on!" she called into the living room and up the stairs. One by one, they trickled in, Sylvia and Bobby from their respective bedrooms, Jim and the boys from the living room, where they'd been drinking some cocktails. Maybe it was easy, after all, having everyone together. Maybe everyone just needed a few days to settle into their new space, to relax. Maybe they were all going to start having the best vacation of their lives, right now. Franny brought the chicken to the table with a smile on her face. When Sylvia came into the room, still wearing her pajamas, Franny gave her a kiss on the forehead.

Everyone filed in, sitting mostly in the seats they'd assigned themselves at the beginning of the trip, the way students in a classroom will always sit in the same place, whether or not they've been told to do so. People were all creatures of habit, the Posts no exception. Franny and Carmen brought all the food in, and Charles moaned with pleasure as he usually did, no matter what had been prepared. It was important to have at least one enthusiastic eater on hand at all times. After all the food had been set down, Carmen slid behind the row of chairs to take her spot beside Bobby, wedged in between his right elbow and the wall. He was barely speaking to her, still, even though she was quite sure that it was her right to be annoyed, not his. This was what Bobby did when he felt wounded — he turned all the hurt feelings inside out, so that his pain at having *caused* pain was tantamount. No matter what Bobby had ever done, it would be Carmen's job to soothe him. An apology was not forthcoming.

Jim carved the chicken and sent the platter around. Lawrence slid a few spears of asparagus onto his plate and then passed the platter in the opposite direction. The meal worked like clockwork for a little while, everyone taking what they were hungry for, if not a little bit more, not saying much except polite *thank you*s when a serving dish appeared in front of them. This was what Franny liked the most about being on vacation, the moments when no one was worried about what they should or should not be doing and just did exactly what was right.

Sylvia ate one asparagus spear at a time, letting the long green stalk hang out of her mouth as she made it disappear bite by bite. Jim tried not to be amused. There was little noise except chewing and the clinking of forks and knives. Franny made an excellent roast chicken. Even Carmen was eating, which Franny considered enough of a coup to comment on it from the far end of the table.

"So glad you like it, Carmen! It's nice to see you dig into something other than your green juice." Franny mimed the mixing of the powders, a mad-scientist-gone-bodybuilder. "Not that there's anything wrong with green juice, of course. I did a juice cleanse once, for a week, for a magazine. Remember that, Jim? I lost four pounds and my sense of humor." Franny laughed at her own bad joke, another sign that things were improving.

Carmen glared at Bobby. He didn't look up from his plate. None of this was her fault — she had done nothing wrong. Carmen wanted to be the kind of woman who was above pettiness, who didn't believe in taking an eye for an eye, but she wasn't. They had talked about how he was supposed to behave with his family, how he was supposed to present her, how he should treat her, and here he was, acting like a teenager. Carmen had done so much work to make him into the right kind of man. If he didn't respect her enough to not behave like an asshole, well, then she wouldn't respect him enough to carry on his little charade.

"Bobby sells them, you know."

This made him look up. His eyes widened, and he shook his head back and forth, imploring her not to. No matter what he'd done, Bobby never thought that Carmen would sell him out, not like this. Not at the dinner table, without warning. She plowed ahead.

"Bobby sells the powders, I mean." Carmen straightened up and tossed her hair over her shoulders, enjoying the sensation of having everyone listen to her for once. She thought she might never stop talking.

Franny puffed out her lower lip. "What do you mean?"

Sylvia froze with half an asparagus spear sticking out of her mouth, a green cigar.

"He sells them at the gym, at Total Body Power. But also at other places, like fitness conventions. You know Amway? It's kind of like that." Carmen had an aunt and uncle who sold Amway, and it wasn't really the same thing, but she knew the look it would put on Franny's face, the way the word would sound in her ear, cultish and cheap.

Sylvia spat out the uneaten half of her asparagus. "Wait, what?"

"What is she talking about, Bobby?" Franny said, knitting her fingers together under her chin. "This is crazy!"

Jim leaned back in his chair. The feeling he experienced wasn't surprise or disappointment, but a very slight letting out of air, like a balloon slowly emptying. It was the sensation of Franny's focus shifting away from him and onto their son, the kind of feeling no father ever wanted to admit that he enjoyed. His poor son was doing him a righteous favor, whether he wanted to or not. Jim half wanted to try to kiss Franny right then, to see how distracted she'd become, but no, that might ruin it. Instead, he remained quiet and tried to focus on what was being said.

Bobby's stare remained fixed on his plate. He held his fork in his left hand, and his napkin in his right. He didn't turn back to Carmen, or direct his chin upward to face his family. She was doing this to him on purpose. He told the truth to the moist chicken now cooling in front of him.

"It's not that big of a deal. It's just to make some extra money. The market's been slow for the last couple of years, and Carmen thought . . ." Here he paused, closing his eyes. "It's not her fault. I needed to make some money, and she got me a job at the gym." Bobby looked up and made eye contact with his mother, who was still holding her hands as if in prayer. "I'm an assistant trainer, and I sell the Total Body Power Powder. It's not bad. I'm much healthier than I was before."

"Tell them the rest." Carmen made a tiny

smacking sound, satisfied. She wasn't going to let herself smile, but she sure as hell was going to make sure everything came out that she thought should come out. He'd made her wait long enough.

"There's *more*?" Franny made a noise like a fish on dry land.

"Take it down a notch, Fran," Jim said, jeopardizing his newly secure position.

"Wait, so you're a personal trainer now, too?" Sylvia said. "Like, people pay you to force them to do sit-ups? Like a gym teacher? Do you have a whistle?"

"What's in the powders?" Lawrence wanted to know. "Is it that Xendadrine stuff that's supposed to give you a heart attack?"

"Jesus!" Bobby said, pushing his chair back from the table. Carmen looked smug. Everyone else waited for him to continue. It wasn't that working at a gym was so sordid, it just wasn't what people like the Posts *did,* that's what they were all thinking. Charles and Lawrence experienced pangs of guilt at this internal admission, having been dis-criminated against for their entire lives, and still occasionally hollered at on the sidewalk by morons in passing cars. Franny felt like a failure. Sylvia was trying to imagine her older brother wearing a sweatband and a Britney Spears–style microphone, doing dance steps at the front of an aerobics class. Jim, who had paid for Bobby's college education, was the most disappointed, though he knew enough to mask such feelings. He had long suspected that Bobby's career might not be going quite as gangbusters as he wanted everyone to think, and wasn't entirely surprised by this new information. "Fine," Bobby said, shaking his head. His soft curls bounced, as pretty as they'd always been, and Franny began to tear up.

"I started selling the powders because it seemed like a good way to make money more quickly, but in order to do that, I had to buy them in bulk, like, really in bulk, and they haven't been as easy to unload as the manager at Total Body Power made it seem. They're really good, all whey protein, but the shakes come out kind of grainy if you don't mix them with enough liquid, and there's an aftertaste."

"You get used to it," Carmen said. "Bobby doesn't even drink them anymore, but I do. They're really good for your muscle recovery after a workout." Bobby gave her a sharp look, and she stopped talking.

"Eww," Sylvia said, and Franny pinched her, hard.

"Anyway, I used my credit card to buy the

powders from the distributer, and I haven't been able to pay off my card in a while, and so it's just getting a little, you know, expensive." Bobby's cheeks were the color of the wine, a red so deep they were nearly purple.

"How much are we talking, honey?" Franny leaned forward and reached for Bobby's hands. The room was completely silent while everyone waited to hear the number.

"A hundred and fifty. Or so." Bobby let his mother stroke his hands but wouldn't look at her.

"A hundred and fifty?" Franny wasn't thinking. She'd begun to brighten, and looked over her shoulder at Jim, confused. He frowned.

"A hundred and fifty *thousand*?" Jim asked.

Carmen was the only one who didn't make an audible reaction, because she already knew the figure in question. It was $155,699, actually, but Bobby was rounding down. He hadn't told her until it was nearly half as much, and that was a year ago, shortly after he began to work at the gym. It had been sweet watching him, Carmen wanted to tell his family that — seeing him holding a heavy bag steady for a middle-aged woman who wanted to get rid of her upper-arm wattle was nice, and Carmen liked that she could teach him things. Give him pointers. Some of the trainers had been to kinesiology school, but most of them were just gym rats who'd stuck around long enough to make a good impression. Bobby was neither, a pale New York City half-Jew who'd never done more than jog on a treadmill. The ladies found him unintimidating, and he reminded them of their sons up north. He was popular. If he'd only stuck to that, it would have been fine. They probably would have been married by now, maybe even living closer to the beach. But Bobby had liked the idea of easy money, and what was easier than making a milkshake?

Bobby nodded. The purple in his cheeks had shifted into a slightly greenish tint.

"Hmm," Jim said. "We'll talk about this later, son, okay? I'm sure it'll all be fine." He spoke with his most solid voice, then Franny withdrew her hands, and stood up, searching for a tissue. Sylvia laughed — she'd never heard so large a number said out loud so casually. Her bank account had approximately three hundred dollars in it. She used her parents' credit card whenever she needed to, which wasn't often. Charles and Lawrence held hands under the table.

Charles wanted to remember to tell Lawrence that this was one of the possible perils of having children — having to bail them out. The chicken smelled heavenly, like butter and garlic and some tiny green things that Franny had snipped out of the planters by the pool, and he was starving.

"Well," Charles said. "Would someone pass the wine?" Bobby lunged for the bottle on the table, delighted to have something else to do. "Lawrence, how are your werewolves coming along?"

Lawrence began to talk at length about the reshoots in Canada, about the waylaid bags of fur, and though everyone peeked at Bobby in their own time, even Franny made a show of listening to Lawrence talk about the movie, listening as if their lives depended on that rickety sleigh.

Franny and Jim lay next to each other, side by side on their backs, staring at the ceiling. Even before Jim had left *Gallant,* a hundred and fifty thousand dollars would have been a large sum, but now that there was only Franny's inconsistent income and even more inconsistent royalties coming in, it was enormous.

"We could cash out some stocks," Franny said.

"We could."

"But is it our responsibility?" Franny flipped onto her side, making the bed buck like a small ship on a choppy sea. She rested her face on her hands, and looked as young as she ever had, despite the worried lines between her eyebrows.

"No, it's not," Jim said, and rolled over to face her. "Not directly. Not legally. He's almost thirty. Most young people have debt. Anyone who goes to law school has three times as much debt as that."

"But they're lawyers! And can make it back! I just don't know if this is one of those times when we're supposed to let him figure it out for himself. Clearly he meant to — he didn't bring it up, she did. *God,* that woman. And to think, all night, I was really starting to like her. But she did that to him on purpose!" Franny was getting agitated. "I know, I know," she said, lowering her voice. "They're right next door."

Seeing his wife in such a state should not have thrilled Jim, but it did. It was rarer and rarer for Fran to get so riled up about something that she could discuss only with him — now that the children were so old, they no longer needed to have the endless conversations of their late youth and early middle age, wherein they would talk about their offspring's friends and teachers and punishments and all the ensuing guilt and pride for days on end.

"We'll figure it out," he said, and reached out to stroke her face, but she was already rolling back toward the windows, settling in for sleep, and so he reached only her back, but when she didn't shrug him off, it felt like a small gain.

All the lights were out — even Bobby and Carmen's, Sylvia could tell from the dark crack of air underneath the door. Something was off, in addition to Bobby's bank statements. She didn't know what it really meant to be in debt, but Sylvia imagined men with fedoras and briefcases knocking on the door and threatening to cut off meaningful body parts.

At home, she knew all the noisy stairs, which wooden planks creaked and which ones didn't. Here, she had to guess and so just stayed close to the banister, placing each foot carefully and slowly before moving down to the next step. She wanted to check the living room sofa. There was no evidence that her father hadn't been sleeping in bed with her mother, but their room had just felt *strange,* that's how Sylvia would have described it, had anyone asked, which they wouldn't. It felt strange in the same way some places felt haunted, when she just knew that there were ghosts present who were friendly or not but definitely dead.

The downstairs was all dark, too, except for a single light in the dining room that someone had left on by mistake. The house was cool, and Sylvia shivered. She nudged her way over to the wall between the foyer and the living room and squinted into the darkness. She could make out the couch, but not well enough to see if there was anyone sleeping on it. She took a step closer but felt like she'd stepped into the middle of an ocean, completely unmoored and lost, and so she retreated to the wall, touching it with both her hands. "Dad?" she said, quietly. There was no response. Even if he'd been asleep, her father would have answered her. Sylvia waited for what felt like forever and then repeated herself.

Of course he wasn't there. Everything was fine, except the things that weren't. Her parents were screwed up, but maybe not as screwed up as she thought. Sylvia was relieved, and embarrassed that she'd even wanted to check. When she was a little girl, and had a nightmare, her father had always been the first one on the scene, opening closet doors and poking his head under the bed. That's all she was doing — making sure that the monsters were pretend. Sylvia felt immediately tired, though she'd been wide awake until just that moment. She could hardly make it back up the stairs and into her own bed before falling asleep, so secure was she in her fact-finding mission.

DAY TEN

Franny busied herself in the kitchen, making Tupperware containers of snacks that wouldn't melt in the sun. Gemma had the glass ones, of course, nothing plastic. Franny would have to be careful loading up the beach bags. No one wanted shards of broken glass with their grapes. The plan — her plan, which she hadn't yet shared with anyone but Jim — was to take a field trip en masse, the whole group. They would drive to the nearest beach, which wouldn't be so crowded on a Monday morning. They'd sit and bake there all day, splashing around and eating *jamón* and *queso* sandwiches from the local vendors. Gemma had two large beach umbrellas, and mesh folding chairs with low seats built for sunbathing. Franny would wear her large straw hat, and Bobby would be as happy as he'd ever been. She wouldn't take no for an answer.

One by one, her guests trickled out of

their bedrooms. Charles and Lawrence liked the beach and were easy to convince. Sylvia was nervous about seeing Joan and was more than happy to put him off for the day. Bobby said yes, and Carmen said yes, though they appeared in the kitchen separately and seemed not to be speaking to each other. It wasn't even nine o'clock before Franny had the two cars packed up for the day, and they were off.

Gemma recommended three beaches: Cala Deià, opposite the Robert Graves House, which was remote and rocky and "rather magic" (no bathrooms, no snack shops); Badia del Esperanza, a wide "golden sandy paradise" (high possibility of children/tourists); and Cala Miramar, "a functional beach within a half-hour's drive. Lots of Spanish families. Less-than-glorious bathrooms on-site." (No more exciting than a trip to Brighton Beach.) How could they argue with paradise? Surely children wouldn't be at the beach at this hour, when they should be napping or parked in front of cartoons. Franny plotted out directions to the Badia del Esperanza, and gave a copy to Charles, who was driving the other rental. Sylvia sat in the backseat of her parents' car. At the last minute, Bobby had joined her, as if choosing to do so at the last moment would mean that no one would notice. Sylvia raised her eyebrows but didn't say anything, and neither did Bobby, who immediately wedged a towel behind his head and fell asleep, or at least pretended. Jim and Charles drove in tandem, going slow around the hairpin turns, willing the tiny cars to climb and descend the winding hills with ease.

The beach was a twenty-five-minute drive over the mountains — up, up, up, then down, down, down. Jim drove under Franny's close supervision — *Watch out, watch out, watch out* or *Oooh, look, guys, sheep!* depending on how harrowing the roads were. Sylvia read her book until she felt like she was about to barf, and by then (she had a strong stomach when she wasn't hungover, and she'd slept as well as she ever had the night before) they were nearly there.

"Hey," Sylvia said to her brother, and jostled his leg.

"What?" Bobby said, and looked at her warily.

"What did you say to Carmen? Clearly you told her about the girl. Otherwise, why would she have done that to you, right?" Sylvia was genuinely curious — she tried to imagine Gabe Thrush coming to her and telling her about his stupid indiscretion, instead of just showing up at school holding hands with Katie Saperstein. She might even have forgiven him.

"I didn't." Bobby raised a finger to his mouth and shushed her. Then he pointed to their parents.

"Oh." Sylvia scrunched up her face. "So why was she so mad?"

"Shit, Syl, I don't know, because I went out without her, and got drunk, and came home and puked. Do we really need to talk about this right now?"

"We're not listening," Franny said from the front seat.

Bobby rolled his eyes. "Great."

They were close — the air was saltier. Sylvia decided to let it drop. It was strange to see Bobby this much — when he came back to New York, he never stayed more than a few days at a time, and even then he was always running around with his friends from high school. They never saw each other for more than a meal. She wondered if he'd always been this surly and defensive, or whether something had changed — those looming dollar signs — more recently. There was no way to know. She'd always thought that siblings were pretty much the same people in differently shaped bodies, just shaken up slightly, so that the molecules rearranged themselves, but now she wasn't sure. She would have told Carmen the truth. As it was, Sylvia felt the information starting to rot inside her, like a dead rat on the subway tracks.

Jim parked in a slanted spot on the side of the road, and Charles pulled in two spaces behind them. They all loaded up their arms with Franny's supplies and humped the lot of it down a steep set of stairs to the sand, walking past a barrier of narrow pine trees.

Gemma was right — the beach was glorious. Once they were through the trees, the beach opened up like an unfolded map, with more and more clean, bright sand in both directions. There were several clusters of people — umbrellaed colonies here and there — but on the whole the beach was quiet, and the water was nearly empty. The water! Franny wanted to run toward it with her hands clasping open and closed like a lobster's claws, to hold on to it, a shimmery dream. The Mediterranean was richly blue, with tiny waves lapping in and out. One woman stood some ten feet out, her legs submerged up to her knees and her hands on her hips, elbows winging out to the sides. There was no music playing, no beach volleyball. These were serious sunbathers, the early risers, and dedicated swimmers.

Franny led the troops halfway down to the water, and carefully set down her bounty. She flapped out her towel and unfolded an umbrella. She lathered herself with a low-SPF sunscreen — what was the point of coming to a beach and not leaving with a bit of a tan, after all? — and looked around, satisfied. There was sweat on her upper lip, and she wiped it away with a finger.

"I'm going in!" she announced, and peeled off her gauzy cover-up. She dropped it onto her towel and turned away, hoping no one was looking at her thighs. There was a pitter-patter of running feet behind her, and before Franny knew it, Carmen was in the water, sloshing through with high knees until it was deep enough for her to dive, and then she was gone.

Sylvia curled up like a sleeping dog in the narrow and shifting shade offered by the umbrella.

"You know that the sun will not actually set you on fire, right?" Bobby said. He was lying on his back, with his T-shirt thrown over his face.

"I'm a delicate flower," Sylvia said. She stuck out her tongue for emphasis, but Bobby was no longer looking. On her other side, Charles and Lawrence had set up shop on an impressive scale — magazines, chairs, their shoulder bags weighing down the corners of the beach towels. They were both reading novels, and Charles had his camera in his lap, in case he saw anyone he'd like to paint. Lawrence had also brought his laptop on the off chance that the beach had Wi-Fi, which it didn't. There was a large hotel just up the road, and he planned to duck away at some point to send some e-mails, or really just to hit the refresh button in hopes that the agency had written again with some news, asking them to call. The beach was too lovely to ignore, though, and Lawrence was more than happy to loll around for a few hours. The water was warm enough to swim in but brisk enough to be refreshing, and so they took turns splashing around and then baking on the sand.

Franny stood in the water and tried to look as European as possible. She wasn't going to take her top off, but she could do the rest — sunglasses, a simple suit, an air of nonchalance. Carmen was swimming laps again, the current bringing her farther from the shore, but she seemed determined, and Franny doubted that she would need to be rescued. She had a good, strong stroke, dragging the water underneath her with every motion.

"Maybe she'll drown," Jim said, appearing next to Franny. "Would that make things better or worse?" He was wearing a thin cotton polo, which the wind pushed against his lanky torso. Jim's resolute refusal to gain weight like a normal middle-aged person was always high on the list of things that drove her crazy. Bobby and Sylvia both seemed to have been born with this gene, which made Franny wish that it were possible to give such things in reverse, though she'd long held on to the idea that being chubby gave one character. Being thin led to nothing but cockiness. Maybe that's why Bobby was in this pickle. If he'd been an overweight child, perhaps it could have been avoided.

"Oh, stop," Franny said. She crossed her arms over her soft middle, pushing together her breasts. It felt absurd to still be conscious of her body in front of her husband, but after that girl, *that girl,* Franny had reverted to the behavior of a bulimic teenager, minus the purging — eating a second helping of dinner after Jim had gone upstairs for the evening, or when he wasn't looking. Sneaking in an ice cream cone when she ran errands. Putting on her Spanx in the bathroom, with the door closed.

"So it sounds like Bobby did more than get too drunk the other night," Jim said.

Franny quickly looked over her shoulder at her kids, some twenty feet away. Bobby was sitting up and staring at the water, his elbows resting on his knees. "I couldn't tell what happened, could you?"

"Didn't sound good."

Bobby stood up, dusted off his bottom, and walked slowly into the sand. He nodded at his parents when he passed them, but kept going. Franny and Jim watched him wade slowly into the sea before he inelegantly dropped to his knees. He flipped onto his back and began to float, his body just a few inches above the sand and bits of seashells. Franny watched her son bob for a few minutes before his whole body began to thrash around as if he were being attacked by an invisible shark.

"Fuck!" Bobby said. "Fuck, fuck, fuck!" He struggled to stand up, and began to hobble back to his towel. The other beach patrons turned to look. "I think something bit me." He was clutching his calf, just above his right ankle. Carmen had heard the commotion and swum closer, her head and shoulders above the surface.

Jim hustled to his son's side. "Here?" he asked, pointing to where Bobby was clutching his leg. The skin was raised and turning red, in a lacy pattern. Bobby lost about twenty-five years immediately, his face as open and expressionless as a baby's right after its very first shot — that wide surprise. Growing up in the city meant little exposure to stings and bites of the natural variety, unless they were ornery pit bulls walking down Broadway. Franny pushed Jim out of the way, and knelt in the sand next to Bobby.

"Sweetie, are you okay?" She reached out for his leg but then withdrew her hand. "Can I touch it?"

Sylvia had rolled onto her side and was watching with some amusement. "Did karma bite you, Bobby?"

"Sylvia!" Franny shouted. They never yelled at the children — it just wasn't in their nature. They cajoled, they teased, they wheedled, but they never yelled. Sylvia recoiled as if she were the one who'd been stung, and hid underneath her umbrella.

Jim weighed his options. He'd seen it done before, and it would make the burning sensation stop, but being peed on by your father would sting, too. He led Bobby, limping, off to one side of the beach.

"Just do it," Bobby said. He turned his

263

head, defeated. "Like this could get any worse."

"Let's go in the water," Jim said, "out of the way. Just watch where you step."

They walked on the dark, damp part of the sand until the very end of the beach, where they stood against the rocks. Bobby closed his eyes and winced in anticipation. Jim pulled down the waistband of his bathing suit and slid his penis out, aiming for Bobby's leg. He *had* seen it done before, but never like this. He wanted to explain to Bobby that he was still his child, that even though Bobby had made mistakes, and he had made mistakes, there were years and years of love built up between them, that they could go without speaking for decades and Jim would still love him. Jim wanted to tell Bobby about how much shit he had cleaned off his bottom when he was a baby, about all the times that Bobby had shot golden arcs of urine directly into his face. This was purposeful, this was nothing! But it didn't feel like nothing. Jim sighed, and a warm stream was released.

The piss worked like a charm. Bobby's leg was still patterned with raised skin, but it didn't actually feel like it was on fire anymore. He and his father rinsed the small puddle off the beach as well as they could, and then headed up the sand toward the bathrooms and the snack shop to clean up.

The bathrooms put New York City to shame — a slightly sandy floor, but otherwise sanitary and orderly, with extra rolls of toilet paper and paper towels on view, the kind of things that would have been bolted down if they were in Manhattan. Bobby soaked a few paper towels with soap and water and cleaned himself off. Jim stood back and watched after washing his own hands.

"What's going on, Bobby?" Jim made eye contact with his son in the mirror, which Bobby quickly broke, angling his face back down toward his wounded calf.

"Nothing," Bobby said. "I mean, you guys heard all of it. I wasn't making enough money, so I got another job. It's not *that* much debt. I'll be fine. I was going to ask you guys to help me, but it's fine, I can do it myself."

"I meant with Carmen. What was Sylvia talking about in the car?"

Bobby let out an exasperated moan. He turned around and leaned against the lip of the sink. "God! It was nothing. Some girl at the club. It was nothing. I know that you and Mom have been together since you were younger than me, and you guys have a great marriage and all, but things are different now. I don't know. Carmen is fine, she's good, you know? She and I get along really well. But I don't know, forever? Probably not. So why pretend? It's not like she's gonna know."

Jim and Franny had agreed not to tell the children about Madison, about Madison's upturned nose and her blond hair and the way she had wrecked Jim's life. The way he had let her ruin his life. No, that still wasn't it. Jim had been the agent of his own destruction. It was the way he had wrecked his life by choosing to have an affair with a woman so young. By choosing to have an affair at all. Affairs seemed so old-fashioned, like something his own father would have done, and no doubt did do, over and over again. They didn't threaten the marriage, because the marriage was a scrim, a false curtain pulled tight over the turbulent inner lives of his parents. Jim had never wanted a marriage like that, and he didn't have one. He and Franny had struggled and fought throughout, especially when Bobby was young. It was never a foregone conclusion that they would stay together — that was something from the stone ages, not the seventies. They'd seen free love (at least on television) and still chosen to get married.

Their eyes were open. It was impossible to keep the information (the basics, only the basics) from Sylvia, because they were all under the same roof, but it had been easy to keep the truth from Bobby. It made it nicer to talk to him on the phone, now that Jim and Fran, separately or together, could pick up the telephone and travel back through time to a better marriage.

"Bobby, I cheated on your mother. It was a horrible thing to do, and I don't want to sound cavalier about it. The only aspect of the entire situation that I know I did right, however, was to tell her the truth." Parenting was a terrible curse — it was about subjugating your mistakes so well that your children didn't know they existed, and therefore repeated them ad nauseam. Was it better to be a hypocrite or a liar? Jim wasn't sure. Either way, he wished that Franny was standing next to him, in this beachside Mallorcan men's room. She'd be furious at him all over again, but she would know what to say to their son.

"This is a joke, right?" Bobby looked confused, like he was vacillating between pride and disappointment. His face eventually settled into a half-smile, the look that Jim had most hoped he'd avoid.

"It's nothing to be happy about, Bobby."

Jim flattened his own mouth into a thin, tight purse. He motioned toward the door.

"No, come on," Bobby said. He slapped the remaining water off his leg and shook it out. "It's just that I didn't know that. About you. It's kind of funny. I mean, you're my dad."

Jim looked at him quizzically. A Spaniard in a very small bathing suit walked into the bathroom and headed for the urinal in the corner.

"Maybe it's genetic," Bobby said.

"Don't be an idiot," said Jim.

Franny ducked under Sylvia's umbrella to apologize.

"Sweetie, I'm sorry I snapped at you," she said. Sylvia looked at her warily. Franny wasn't much for apologies, and her daughter clearly suspected there was more coming. Franny shrugged her shoulders and relented. "What's going on with your brother? Can you tell me?" Franny looked back at the water. Despite the presence of electric fish, Carmen was still swimming. She was going to go back to America weighing three pounds, all the exercise she was doing to avoid spending time with the family, and for the moment, Sylvia didn't blame her.

"I don't think you want to know."

"Of course I do," Franny said, but she wasn't sure. The debt was enough, and the job at the gym. She didn't want to feel like a snob; she was the daughter of a truck driver and a housewife — how could she be a snob? And yet she wanted more for him. She wanted him to want more for himself. She and Jim had had so many whispered conversations over Bobby's crib when he was a baby, even before that, over her stretching belly when she was massively pregnant. They had planned his future — as a politician, a writer, a philosopher. A personal trainer with a sideline of whey had not been on the list.

"He cheated on Carmen. The other night. I saw him. It was gross."

"What do you mean? Dancing with girls, like?"

"Mom." Sylvia sat up, her spine uncurling. Slumped over, her baggy T-shirt hung to her knees, her bathing-suited body hidden well beneath it. "Please. I saw a lot more than that. Like, tongues. Eww, can we not talk about this? It was gross enough to watch it happen once. I'm not dying to relive the moment." She squinted toward the sun. "I can feel the skin cancer beginning to form."

"You actually saw him with another girl?"

Franny's breath shortened. There was that sickening satisfaction at hearing gossip for the first time, swiftly followed by the realization that she'd done everything wrong, everything important. She leaned to the left so that she was able to see where Jim and Bobby had gone. They weren't at the far end of the beach anymore, and she couldn't see them elsewhere on the sand. Maybe they'd heard Sylvia open her mouth and had run, knowing what was to follow.

Jim didn't know it was possible to see actual wavy lines of anger around someone's head, like a cartoon come to life, but when he saw his wife pacing back and forth on the sand, there they were, clear as day. Charles and Lawrence were standing on her left, and Sylvia was still tucked under her umbrella on the right. Carmen had made her way out of the water, and stood awkwardly in the background, her wet hair clinging to her shoulders like a cape. When Franny saw Jim approaching, she huffed her way up the beach to meet him. She made it just past the edge of Sylvia's towel, kicking a little sand onto her daughter by mistake.

"Do you know what your son did?" Franny was hysterical, her eyes wild and searching.

"I do now." Jim was in no mood for this. What Bobby had done wasn't his fault — it had nothing to do with Jim or his own poor choices.

"He had sex with another girl, practically in front of his sister. In a public place! Should I be happy that you at least had a hotel room?"

Sylvia peered out from under the umbrella, her pale eyes tracking her mother's movements.

"Fran, let's talk about this at home," Jim said. He stretched out a hand toward her, but she slapped it away.

"At home? In New York? When the kids are gone and you are, too, and so who cares anyway, you mean? I think they all deserve to know. It was crazy to think that we could keep a secret like this." She pretended to look worried. "Oh, no, are there reporters here? Is anyone here from *The New York Times*?" The other patrons of the beach were staring, and Franny waved. "I think that woman's from the *Post*."

"Mom, we don't have to do this here, okay?" Sylvia's voice was quiet. She rolled onto her hands and knees and then pushed herself up to stand. She looked so thin to Jim, so delicate, just the way she had as a baby. He hated what she would hear next,

271

and the way she would turn toward him, wanting it so badly not to be true.

"Your father slept with an intern. Your brother slept with a stranger." Franny stopped, calculating how cruel she should be. "I don't know how this happened."

"People sleep with interns all the time," Bobby said. "And strangers! Especially strangers! What's the big deal?"

"She was not an intern, she was an editorial assistant," Jim said. Franny looked at him and bared her teeth.

"The big deal is that she's barely older than Sylvia, which makes me ill. The big deal is that your father and I are married to each other. The big deal, my love, is that you don't seem to understand why this is a big deal. That is the biggest deal of all. Because my husband may have disappointed me, but if I haven't even taught you that much, then I have disappointed myself." Franny spun around and began to cry at a very high pitch, the sound of an insistent smoke alarm. Charles hurried over and tucked her into his arms. Lawrence shook his head in sympathy.

"I think it's time to head back to the house," Lawrence said, quickly gathering as many things as he could carry. "You get the rest," he said to Jim.

"Franny, come on," Jim said. "You're acting like a crazy person right now. Just relax."

Charles spun Franny out of his arms like a dancer sending his partner twirling across a ballroom floor. He marched up to Jim, stopping when he was two feet away. Charles gritted his teeth.

"Don't you tell her she needs to relax, after what you did," Charles said.

"I think we *all* need to relax," Jim said, softening the air with his hands. He looked around at his children, seeking their support. "Am I right?"

"You have always been such a motherfucker," Charles said. He pulled back his right arm, strong from decades of hoisting canvases and gallons of paint, and let it fly, directly into Jim's right eye socket. Jim stumbled backward, surprised, and clutched his face.

"Let's go, Fran," Charles said.

Franny was shaking as if she were the one who'd been hit. She gave Jim a pleading look and then let herself be scooped back under Charles's arm. They started to walk to the car.

"Wait!" Sylvia said. "Don't leave me here with them." She wanted to say more to her father but couldn't. There was no air inside her lungs. Sylvia pictured the couch in the

273

dark — maybe he had been there after all, not last night, but the night before, and for who knows how long before that. Everything was worse than she thought. She tried to remember New York, and all the nights since her father had stopped working, all her mother's dates with her awful book club. There were too many things to think about all at once, and Sylvia felt like she might throw up. She dug her feet into her shoes, which were half filled with sand, and clomped after Charles and her mother.

Lawrence drove, and Sylvia sat in the front seat, giving Charles and Franny the entire backseat in which to cuddle and moan. Sylvia had never heard her mother wail like this — Franny sounded like a circus animal being trained to jump through a fiery hoop. Sylvia tried to face forward and ignore whatever was happening behind her. Out the window, palm trees waved hello, gigantic pineapples wearing grass skirts. The morning was bright, and Sylvia cupped her hands around her eyes like a horse wearing blinders. Lawrence turned on the radio, and Elton John's voice once again filled the car.

After a minute, Franny's sniveling tapered off. "I love this song," she said, and started to sing along. Lawrence and Charles joined in — "Bennie and the Jets" in a fractured, off-key three-part harmony. Franny tried to sing the highest but couldn't, and so Lawrence launched into an impressive falsetto. Charles sang bass and played along on an invisible guitar. The song went on interminably, their voices getting louder and louder, until they were all screaming. After Elton, the DJ said something in German and then played some Led Zeppelin. Lawrence turned down the volume.

"You guys know that song is terrible, right?" Sylvia said, though she was very glad that her mother had stopped crying. She swiveled around in her seat and clutched the back of her headrest. "You okay, Mom?"

Franny reached up and squeezed Sylvia's fingers. "I'm okay, honey. I'm just, I don't know." She turned to Charles. "I can't believe you really hit him."

"You would if you knew how long I've wanted to do that." Charles looked at the back of his hand, already sporting a pale bruise.

"Yeah," Sylvia said. "I kind of wanted to do it, too. Men are fucking dirtbags. No offense, guys."

Charles and Lawrence shook their heads. "None taken," said Charles.

"Are you getting a divorce?"

Franny had asked herself the same question hundreds of times — when Bobby was small and they couldn't stop arguing, when he was eight or nine and they were deciding whether to stay together, when he came home and told her about Madison, and on all the days he said or did something that she thought was annoying, like fart in a small elevator. That was marriage.

"I don't know, honey, we're still sorting it all out. We both love you and your brother. It's just a little messy at the moment." Franny wiped at her cheeks. "I must look like a wreck."

Sylvia laughed. "You should have seen yourself at the beach. It was like you turned into Godzilla. Momzilla. You were Momzilla. Momzilla and Gayzilla Strike Back."

"I like that," Franny said. She leaned back into Charles's chest. "Find something else we can sing along to, Lawr."

Lawrence hit the dial a few times, hurrying past anything recent or in a foreign language (ignoring the fact, of course, that English was a foreign language in Spain), and eventually came to Stevie Wonder. Franny began to belt out the words, and hummed along with the harmonica solo, and so without waiting for further approval, he turned the volume up and kept driving.

■ ■ ■ ■

Jim hadn't been hit since he was a teenager. He'd had that kind of face then, a soft chin and puppy-dog eyes that turned down at the corners. He'd been thrown into lockers and teased for his willingness to do extra-credit homework. It wasn't until he had his final growth spurt in the eleventh grade that the girls ever noticed him, other than wanting him to come to their study sessions in the school library. His eye stung, and though there hadn't been any blood, he knew he would have a shiner. Did people still use the word *shiner*? He felt like an old man — the transition was swift. Just that morning, he'd woken up feeling young again, like he and Fran could make it work, that everything would be all right and he would have his life back.

Two burly men in leather jackets walked toward him on the beach, their heavy black boots trudging awkwardly through the fine sand.

"Saw ya get punched there," one said.

"Didn't take it too bad," said the other.

Jim looked at them with his left eye, keeping the right one shut tight under his cupped palm. Bobby and Carmen took a step closer, wondering if they were going to have to intervene, to keep Jim from being a human heavy bag. Bobby felt his pulse quicken — he'd taken some kickboxing classes at Total Body Power and thought he could defend himself, if given the opportunity.

"You were on our plane," Jim said, recognizing the patches sewn onto their leather jackets — young Elvis, fat Elvis, a vintage motorcycle. " 'The Sticky Spokes,' " he said, reading off the larger man's biceps.

"Were we? That's a riot," the man on the right said. He was shorter, with closely cropped red hair. "Just a blokes' vacation, we do it every few years. Get on some bikes and ride around. Don't get to do it as much as I'd like at home anymore. I'm Terry. Want me to have a look at the eye? I'm a pediatrician."

Bobby unclenched his fist.

Jim nodded, and Terry stepped in closer. It hurt to open his eye, and Jim blinked away some involuntary tears. Terry pressed two fingers very gently around the socket, and felt along Jim's cheekbone.

"You'll be fine, nothing's broken," Terry said. He reached into his back pocket and pulled a handsome calling card out of an elegant leather wallet, attached to his belt with a thick chain. "Call me if you need something, though. We're here until August."

"Will do, thanks," Jim said. "What kind of bike do you ride?"

Terry's whole face perked up, widening into a near-perfect circle. "You know bikes? At home I've got a Triumph Scrambler. Nineteen sixties body with a twenty-first-century heart. This week I'm on a Bonneville, gold and gleaming and quick as lightning." He patted Jim on the shoulder. "You'll be fine. Keep it cold."

Bobby, Carmen, and Jim all thanked Terry and his silent friend and watched them stalk back through the sand. They were set up at the very edge of the beach, nearest the parking lot. Jim could just make out the outline of a motorcycle through the pine trees.

The umbrellas were difficult to close properly, and there were so many towels and tote bags that they had to make two trips to the car to pack everything up. Jim sat in front with Bobby behind the wheel, a still slightly cool water bottle pressed to his eye. Carmen reluctantly shared the backseat with the rest of Franny's myriad snacks, some of which had spilled out of their containers and onto the beach towels. The car smelled like cut strawberries and suntan lotion. Jim and Bobby made no indication that they would speak, which was good. A half-hour of silence seemed like the very least they could all give each other. Carmen rolled down the window, despite the air-conditioning, and let the fresh air in. Moving felt like a step in the right direction.

Day Eleven

The house was big enough for all of them, barely. Jim's black eye allowed him to take up more space, and after a bad night's sleep clinging to his edge of the bed, as far from Fran as he could get without sleeping on the floor, he planned to spend the morning in Gemma's handsomely cluttered office. She was an interior designer, or an amateur milliner, or a certified Reiki practitioner in addition to owning a gallery in London. Jim couldn't keep it straight. Her books were varied to the point of insanity — one shelf devoted to Eastern religions, one to fashion, one to World War Two. He'd known women like Gemma before, rich girls with brains but no focus, good-looking and well-meaning dilettantes. He took a book on Buddhism off the shelf and opened it at random.

Out the window, Franny and the boys were having their breakfast by the pool. The day was misty but getting warmer, and Fran, her back to Jim, was wearing one of her gauzy dresses that he loved. Fran had all the usual feelings about her body's changes, about menopause, but to Jim, she still looked just as beautiful as she ever had. Her bottom was still round and shaped like a generously large fruit. Her face was still full and soft. He felt himself getting older, but Franny would always be younger than he was. There was no good way to tell her that, not without the name Madison Vance coming out of her mouth soon afterward.

At first it was just friendly office banter, the kind Jim had always enjoyed. There had been numerous other women he'd flirted with at *Gallant,* and it had always been innocent. There was the one whose large glasses took up half her face, and the one who had a fiancé in Minneapolis, and the lesbian who flirted with Jim anyway, because she flirted with everyone, a wonderful quality in a person of any orientation. He hadn't for a second considered sleeping with any of them, even when he and Franny were having problems. Sure, had he pictured their bodies once or twice when he and Franny were having sex? He had. But he had never so much as picked an errant hair off their sweaters or stood too close to them in a crowded elevator. Jim was loyal to his wife.

She was telling a story — Franny picked up her fork and twirled it in the air like a baton. Charles and Lawrence, both facing Jim's window, threw back their heads and laughed. Jim wished he could join them outside, just open the door and walk out and sit next to her.

Madison Vance had appeared like a lump of kryptonite, as suddenly as if she'd fallen out of the sky. She was forward, and brave, and when she told Jim she wasn't wearing any underwear, he shouldn't have raised his eyebrows in amusement. He should have called human resources and then tucked himself in a ball under his desk like an air-raid drill. Instead, he had smiled and involuntarily run his tongue across his lower lip. True youth was something magnificent to behold — not the youth of thirty-five or forty-five or fifty, all still young and vital when viewed from the other side, but the unimpeachable youth of the early twenties, when one's skin hugged the bones and glowed from the inside out. Madison let her long blond hair hang loose over her shoulders, and it swung side to side, each tiny strand both delicate and wild. She had made it clear that she wanted him, *in that way,* in that ancient way, she wanted him. And Jim wanted her, too.

The moment he walked into the hotel bar to meet her, Jim knew he was making a mistake. Up until then, he had convinced himself that it was all in good fun — he was taking this young woman under his wing. She was a pip, a go-getter! And they would sit at the bar and have drinks and talk about journalism and novels, and then she would go on her merry way, taking the subway back to Brooklyn Heights, where she was sharing a sublet with a roommate. Once he walked into the bar, though, and saw what Madison was wearing, her pale thighs extending out from under her impossibly short dress, Jim knew that the situation wasn't even close to the one he'd let himself believe.

He had walked to the desk, he had asked for a room.

He had tipped his face down to meet hers.

He had unzipped her dress and watched the fabric slide over her narrow hips.

Jim turned away from the window and let his head drop toward his chest. His eye ached and he wished that the rest of his body was as marked, one giant bruise, because he deserved it.

■ ■ ■ ■

When she was in high school, Carmen had thought long and hard about her options. There was a boy in her class who loved her, and she loved him, too. They'd lost their virginity to each other in his twin bed, and their mothers were friends who liked to sit together on plastic chairs on the beach. When she was at Miami Dade, there was a guy she met at Starbucks and slept with on and off for the next six months, until it turned out that he had another girlfriend back home in Orlando. There were always lots of guys at every gym she'd ever worked at, eyeing her while she worked out. Miami was an easy place to meet someone if you cared about your body.

Bobby was different. The first time they went out, he told her about his family and New York. He was still in college, but seemed so much younger than when Carmen was his age. She'd been supporting herself since she was sixteen, and at twenty-one, Bobby's parents still paid his rent, though she didn't know that yet. What was clear was that he came from somewhere else, a different planet of wants and needs. She loved hearing about his mother — a writer! It sounded like a job from the movies, going around the world and writing about what she ate. Carmen started buying magazines that she thought his mother might be in, and sometimes when Bobby came over to her house, he'd confirm her suspicion, saying, *Oh, I think my mother was in that one,* and sometimes he'd say, *Oh, my mother hates that one — total assholes,* and Carmen would pretend that the magazine had been a gift from a client, disowning it quickly.

She tried so hard to get them to like her. She stayed quiet at their dinner parties and smiled blankly when they talked about something she didn't know anything about. She wore her most conservative clothes and tried not to complain about the cold. But nothing she did ever seemed to be right.

The kitchen was warm — all the blinds were open. If it had been her mother's apartment in Miami, all the shades would have been closed until just before dusk, but the Posts didn't seem to mind the house heating up like an oven. She wasn't going to say anything, it wasn't her decision.

"Morning," Bobby said. He'd been sleeping late. Carmen wound her hands around her orange juice. It was the first morning in a year that she hadn't had a protein shake, but he didn't seem to notice.

"Good morning," Carmen said. Everyone else seemed to be by the pool, and Sylvia was surely still asleep. The house was theirs alone. "Will you take a walk with me? Just a walk." He hadn't been saying much, and neither had she.

"Sure," Bobby said, staring out the window at his family. He didn't want to be around them any more than she did. They tugged on their sneakers and were out the door before anyone knew they were gone.

Pigpen was straight down a narrow road — a two-way street only when absolutely necessary, and they walked in single file, Bobby in front. There were all sorts of things like that — lessons Bobby hadn't learned. Was she supposed to teach him? She'd tried. Walking on the outside in case a car jumped the curb or went through a puddle, letting her pass through doorways first. He didn't do any of those things. If she'd asked, he would have said something about how they were equals, but really, he'd just never thought about it. Carmen stooped down to pluck a flower, and tucked it behind her ear.

The town was only a few streets long, the cobblestone blocks curling in and around one another in a tight knot. They walked past the small grocery store, and the Italian restaurant, and the bar that sold sandwiches. When they reached the end of the block and rounded the corner, Carmen was just about to open her mouth. Instead, they turned left and then stopped abruptly.

The street ahead of them was filled with people — one man with a guitar, some children throwing things into the air, and a few older women standing around beaming. The cars on the street were stopped, but the stymied drivers didn't honk their horns or even look impatient. Carmen pulled Bobby closer to the action, and they watched from across the street — at the center of the group, standing outside the doorway of a small building, were a bride and groom. Another man stood just behind them on the steps, making proclamations. Carmen could understand most of what he was saying — *This is a joyous day, God has given these two people each other* — but it wouldn't have mattered if the man was speaking Swahili. It was a wedding, in any language. The bride, a plump woman near Carmen's age if not a bit older, wore a short dress with a lacy bodice, and a wrist corsage. Her new husband wore a gray suit and a tie, his mostly bald head gleaming in the sunlight. They gripped each other's hands tightly, rocking back from side to side as their friend spoke. The woman let out a peal of laughter, and her husband kissed her on the mouth. The old ladies shook their handkerchiefs in the air, and the children screamed happily, consumed by their own role in the festivities. Carmen felt her stomach pump once, then again, and realized that she was crying.

She reluctantly turned away from the happy scene and toward Bobby. He stood with his arms crossed, an impatient expression on his face.

"Train wreck," he said. "Did you see the size of her arms? She could use an hour or two of some triceps pull-downs. Like four times a day for the rest of her life." He chuckled. "Ready?"

Carmen felt as if she'd been slapped. "She looks beautiful." The bride and her groom were dancing now, in between the stopped cars. She twirled out, then in, out, then in. Each time she came close, her husband kissed her, so clearly thrilled at his own fortune. "You know, I always thought that you'd grow out of this."

"Of what?" Bobby shook his curls off his forehead.

"Of being afraid."

Bobby looked confused. "Listen, if this is

289

about something my sister said —"

"I don't care, Bobby. It's not about anything your sister said, or didn't say. It's about you. I always thought that you would need some time, you know, to grow up, but I think I just realized that it's never going to happen, not while I'm sitting around waiting for it. I'm gonna go home."

"You want to walk back?" Bobby started to turn.

"No, you don't understand," Carmen said. "Back to Miami. Without you. This is over. I should have done this years ago. Don't you see how happy they are?" She pointed to the bride and groom, still hugging their families, their smiles stretching their cheeks. It didn't matter that the bride's dress was too tight or hadn't come from Vera Wang — she was *happy*. She wanted to be with this man for the rest of her life, and he felt just the same way. They had chosen to make the leap and, having leapt, were delighted to find that the world was even more beautiful than they'd hoped. Carmen knew right then that Bobby was never going to marry her. He was never going to leap, at least not with her at his side.

"You're breaking up with me?" Bobby asked. She couldn't tell if he looked confused, relieved, or both. There were lines on his forehead, but the corners of his mouth had begun to twitch into a nervous smile. "Right now?"

"Right now, Bobby. And I think you should take a little time off from Total Body Power, too. I'll make sure your clients are covered. Take a few weeks to figure out what you're going to do next, okay? You're not a personal trainer, not really. And the powders don't work unless you're a bodybuilder. There's just too much bullshit, you know?" With that, Carmen spun around and started walking back up the hill. She would call a taxi from the landline and figure out her flight when she got to the airport. She'd never been to mainland Spain — maybe she'd go there. She didn't turn around to see if Bobby was walking behind her, because it didn't matter. She would pack up her clothes and leave the powders in the kitchen. She was done.

Everyone was so excited about Carmen's premature departure that even Sylvia forgot about Joan. He rang the bell twice before anyone thought to let him in. Sylvia opened the door and said, "Oh! Hi!" and then quickly ushered him into the dining room.

"Sorry," she said. "It's been a little crazy. My brother's girlfriend just went home."

Joan slid onto his seat and ran a hand through his hair. "She was too old for him anyway, no?"

"Maybe," Sylvia said. "But I don't think that was the problem."

"So, you liked Blu Nite? It's a good club, right?" Joan did a little dance, shimmying his shoulders and biting his lower lip.

"It was okay," Sylvia said, feeling like she was going to be a virgin forever no matter what, and that Joan wouldn't touch her for a million dollars, because why would he, and that she should just give up. "How about we do irregular past participles?" She opened her workbook. They had only a few more days on the island, and she was starting to feel like it was the end of summer camp. Her pathetic seduction had failed. If it hadn't happened yet, it wasn't going to, and so she should just do some work and maybe place out of a few Spanish classes at Brown. She should have packed some makeup, and some high heels, and a whole other personality.

"Okay," Joan said. He was wearing a pink shirt, and it made his tan skin look like brown sugar covered with honey. "And maybe tomorrow, we have our lesson out? I want to show you the rest of the island, yeah?"

"Okay," Sylvia said. Her face was on fire instantly, actually burning and painful. She picked up her glass of water and pressed it to one cheek and then the other. "Whatever."

Jim was still hiding out in the office next door, on the other side of a very thin wall, but Charles didn't think he could wait any longer. He sat on the edge of the bed and waited for Lawrence to come out of the bathroom. Lawrence opened the door, his towel slung low around his waist. He absently examined the graying hairs on his chest.

"These are new," Lawrence said.

"You're beautiful," Charles said.

Lawrence raised an eyebrow. "Thank you, my dear. You feeling feverish?"

Charles shook his head, his lower lip stuck out. "I'm sorry."

"For what? I'm not the one you punched in the face." Lawrence took off his towel and swung it onto the bed. He opened the drawer with their underwear in it, and took out a clean pair.

"Not that." Charles loved watching Lawrence get dressed. It was always the same — underwear first, then a shirt, then socks, then pants. He pulled his socks all the way

293

up, even in the summertime, though his spindly calves could never keep them there. Lawrence's hair was wet and nearly black, and fell neatly along his part — Charles missed having hair, though it was better that Lawrence did, anyway. That way, Charles always had something lovely to look at. "I just wanted to tell you something. I mean, I want to tell you something."

"Go ahead." Lawrence still wasn't paying much attention. He sat down on the bed next to Charles in order to put on his socks.

"Just, you know, in light of all this new information." Charles stuttered on the word *information*.

The stuttering made Lawrence pay attention. "Mm-hmm."

"Before I say anything, I just want to say how much I love you, and how much I want us to have a family together, or not, whatever the universe decides. But I love you, and you're my husband, my only husband, forever, okay?" Charles shifted in his seat, and pulled Lawrence's damp towel onto his lap, stroking it like a dog.

"You're actually scaring me." Lawrence crossed and uncrossed his legs. "Just spit it out."

"It was a really long time ago," Charles said. "Like, a hundred years. You and I were just starting to get serious."

"Was this before or after we got married?"

"Before, before!"

"Are you about to tell me about that idiot kid, the bohunk art handler from the gallery?"

Charles looked up from the towel, tears in his eyes. He nodded. "I'm so sorry, my love, it was so stupid. I mean, it was the definition of stupid."

Lawrence reached over and clamped his hand on Charles's knee. "I know. You were just getting your ya-yas out. I knew it then, you fool."

"You did?" Charles put one hand on top of Lawrence's, and the other against his chest. "Why didn't you ever say anything?"

"Because it didn't really matter. I knew when it was over. And that was so long before we got married. It was your midlife crisis." He smiled.

"So when's your midlife crisis?" Charles asked.

"Marrying you." Lawrence stood up, bringing Charles with him. "I forgive you. Just don't ever do it again. You're going to be the father to my children."

"I won't," Charles said. "I want to be Daddy, though, is that okay? I think I'm a Daddy. You know, *Can I have a pony, Daddy?*

Want to have secret ice cream cones before Dada comes home, Daddy? Don't you think?"

"I do," Lawrence said, and kissed his husband.

The news about Carmen spread through the house quickly, and when Sylvia set the table for dinner, she put out only six plates, which was better math, anyway. Despite his well-documented mixed feelings about the relationship, Bobby wasn't taking it very well, and he slumped on the bench, in the seat closest to the wall. Jim put his ice pack back in the freezer and sat opposite Bobby. His eye was darker than it had been the day before, a shiny brown circle, like a panda bear. Franny and the boys were making dinner — bacalao on toast, shrimp in a garlicky sauce, wilted greens. Tapas at home.

"I feel like shit," Bobby said, to anyone.

Sylvia slid onto the bench next to Bobby. She didn't feel like talking to her father, and didn't have much interest in her brother, either, but he was too pathetic to ignore.

"I'm sorry about Carmen," she said. "She wasn't as bad as I thought. The fact that she broke up with you like that actually makes me like her more."

Bobby crumpled further, his head only a few inches above the table.

"Sylvia," Charles said, setting down the platter of shrimp. The smell was rich and buttery, and made Sylvia's stomach gurgle. "Take it easy on him."

"No, she's right," Bobby said. He sat up straight and put his elbows on the table. "It's my fault."

Sylvia shrugged, content to have made her point. Franny and Lawrence brought over the rest of the food and sat down, Lawrence as buffer zone between Jim and Charles, though Jim didn't seem angry, and neither did Charles. A détente had been reached.

"I've had my heart broken, too, you know," Sylvia said. "You people do not have the monopoly on this. I want you to know that."

Franny leaned forward so that she could see her daughter. "What? Sweetie! Why didn't you tell me?"

"Right," Sylvia said. "Because that's a normal thing to do, to tell your mother when someone cheats on you with your best friend and then you want to chop up their body into little pieces. I don't think so."

Jim and Franny both scrolled through all of Sylvia's friends in their minds, trying to picture the likeliest candidate for betrayal.

"Katie Saperstein," Sylvia said. "Stupid fucking Katie Saperstein."

"With the horn?" Franny asked, incredulous.

"With the horn," Sylvia said, equally mystified. She could tell everyone about how the reason that Gabe preferred Katie to her had to do with how many blowjobs Katie had given, but decided not to.

"You're so lucky," Bobby said.

"Excuse me?" Sylvia said.

"You're just starting," he said. "In less than two months, you're going to be in a whole new place, surrounded by thousands of new people, people who have no idea who you are, or where you come from, or what your story is. And then you can be whoever you want. This kid, whoever he is, he doesn't matter. You're at the very beginning. It's good." He looked up from his empty plate.

"Want some?" Sylvia said, offering the plate of shrimp to her brother. "It's really fattening."

"I'd love some." Bobby leaned his head against his sister's shoulder for a split second, an affectionate tap.

"Me, too," she said. "This looks good, Mom."

Franny made eye contact with Jim across

298

the table, slightly bewildered but pleased. "Thank you," she said, and then folded her hands in her lap. If she'd been a prayer, she would have prayed for her children, two sweet souls deep down inside, but instead she was a cooker, and passed them the bowl of sea salt. "Here, put this on top."

Franny licked some powdered sugar from her finger. She had been feeling inspired and had tried to bake her own *ensaimadas,* the delicious and flaky pastries that were all over Mallorca. Yeast and shortening and flour and milk, all coiled up like a sugary snail. Islands were such funny creatures, when it came to food. Most of the normal things were imported and therefore up-charged, and so many of the local delights were flown out on airplanes. It felt like a book, maybe — *Tiny Islands.* What people eat in Mallorca, in Puerto Rico, in Cuba, in Corsica, in Taiwan, in Tasmania. There would be a lot of travel, of course, probably several months' worth. All through the lens of life after infidelity — everyone was writing books like that, a woman rediscovering herself after love gone wrong. Maybe she'd ask Gemma if she could come back in the fall, after Sylvia was at school. Mallorca by herself. Franny pictured herself sitting in the exact same spot by the pool a few months down the line, the air just warm enough to swim a few laps and then hustle back into the house. Maybe Antoni would come over and they could practice serving with invisible racquets.

Bobby had limped up to bed right after dinner, and Sylvia was parked in front of the television with Lawrence. One of his movies was on television, miraculously, dubbed into Spanish, but with the push of a button, the actors were speaking English again. It was Toronto made to look like New York, and Sylvia loved to point out the myriad inaccuracies — the subways were wrong, the streetlights, the buildings. Jim was back in Gemma's study, an ice pack pressed against his face, and so it was only Charles and Fran for the nighttime swim.

The lit-up houses on the other side of the valley were like polka dots in the darkness. Every so often, one would turn black, or another would brighten, stars dying and coming back to life. Franny didn't want to get her hair wet, and had on a shower cap over her tiny paintbrush of a ponytail. Even so, the short hairs that had fallen out were already soaked and sticking to her neck. Fran did a few laps with her head held high like a Labrador swimming for a stick, and then gave up, tossing the cap aside and diving under.

"I feel like an otter," she said. "A nocturnal otter."

"Water is very cleansing." Charles was swimming in place at the deep end, waving his arms and legs around under the surface.

"Did you read that on a tea bag?"

"Maybe." He splashed her as she swam by. "Also, remove after five to seven minutes and add honey."

Franny flipped onto her back and winked at him, though she wasn't sure he could see her eyes. In New York, darkness was a relative concept; there were always other people's windows illuminating the night sky, and sweeping headlights. Here, there was nothing except the stars overhead, and the houses across the way, both of which seemed equally magical and far away.

"I always thought that having little kids was supposed to be the hardest part," Franny said. "You know, taking care of someone who was completely dependent on you. Teaching them to speak, to walk, to read. But it's really not true. It doesn't end. My mother never told me that."

"Your mother raised you like a baby manatee — she let you stay close for a year, tops, and then pushed you out into the ocean."

"Is that what manatees do?"

"I don't know, I think so. I read that on a tea bag, too."

Franny opened her mouth and let it fill with water, which she then spat out, in Charles's direction. The water felt like heaven. They would be cold when they got out, she knew, but it didn't matter. She wasn't ever going to leave the pool.

"We're trying, you know." Charles hoisted himself halfway out of the pool, his once muscular arms now a bit softer against his upper body.

"Trying what? Don't talk to me about weird sex stuff, please. I haven't gotten laid in a hundred years and it will make me hate you." Franny rubbed the water out of her eyes. She was facing away from Charles and swiveled her body so that he was directly in front of her. The bottom of the pool was slightly pebbled, like a popcorn ceiling, and she drew her knees to her chest.

"No," Charles said. He let himself fall back into the water with a splash. "We're trying to get a baby."

Franny wasn't sure she'd heard him right. "*Get* a baby?"

Charles swam over and put his hands on

Franny's shoulders. She let her legs straighten out and put her hands on his hips, so they were both standing in the shallow end, in fifth-grade-dance pose.

"Get a baby. I mean, adopt a baby. We're trying to adopt. It's close. I mean, it could be. Someone picked us, and we said yes, and now we're waiting." Charles didn't expect to be nervous telling her this, but then again, he supposed there was a reason he hadn't brought it up until now. The process had been going on for a year! More than a year! And Charles had wavered from the beginning, he'd wavered until the day before, when he saw once again how patient Lawrence was, how loving, how forgiving. How could anyone want more than that in a parent, or a spouse?

Franny didn't flinch. "My love," she said, and closed the gap between them, pressing her wet body against his. She wanted to tell him that he would be a wonderful father, and that having her babies — that's what they were to her still, her babies, no matter how old they got — was the best thing she'd ever done, no matter the stress and complications. She pulled back and saw that Charles's eyes were wet, either with pool water or tears, she wasn't sure, but it didn't matter, because hers were, too. "Yes," she said. "That is a wonderful, wonderful idea."

Day Twelve

Joan arrived promptly at eleven as usual, but instead of coming inside, he stepped back and held the door open for Sylvia to come out. She blinked in the bright sunlight and put on her sunglasses, a pair of Franny's from the 1980s, giant ones that took up half her face and made her look like either a grandmother or a movie star, she wasn't sure which. She'd had trouble deciding what to wear for their day out and about, and had finally chosen a short cotton dress with daisies on it. Joan then opened the car door for her and jogged around to the driver's side. The car was so much bigger than the two rental cars that it felt like a Humvee, but it was probably just a regular-sized sedan. It smelled like Joan's cologne, and she inhaled deeply, wanting to fill her nostrils. Sylvia tucked her hands under her thighs on the leather seat. It was already hot outside, and unless Joan immediately put on the air-conditioning, she was going to sweat and stick to the seat and there would be gross red marks when they got up, like she'd been attacked by a giant octopus who happened to live in his car. Sylvia smiled when Joan sat down, turned the key, and a great big blast of cold air shot out of the vents.

"So, where are we going?" Sylvia asked.

"It's a surprise," Joan said. "But don't worry, I won't make you wear a blindfold. You can swim, yes? You have a bathing suit?"

"Yes," Sylvia said.

"Then we go," Joan said, and they were off.

Once she got over the embarrassment of her tennis lesson, Franny decided that she was a professional journalist, not a lovesick teenager, and called Antoni at the number he'd given her, an extension at the tennis center. She booked the late afternoon — not for tennis, for talking. She could always pitch it to someone later, if she felt like it: *Travel + Leisure, Sports Illustrated, Departures.* Sylvia was out with Joan, the lucky duck, and the boys seemed content to sit by the pool and read, Jim with a hat pulled low over his wounded eye and Bobby with a frown so deep she thought it might leave a scar. Charles and Lawrence were on Bobby duty — making sure he didn't hurt himself or, worse yet, call a taxi and book the first flight back to Florida. Franny wanted him there — miserable or not. It was the same philosophy she'd had about the children drinking alcohol as teenagers: better in her house, where she could keep an eye on it, than in the streets, where they might get arrested. She'd presented her afternoon out as work, but she wasn't sure. Franny patted Jim on the arm and then drove herself back to the tennis center, stalling only once.

Antoni was waiting for her in the office, his arms crossed. Instead of his handsome gym teacher outfit, he was wearing a pair of dark blue jeans and a white button-down shirt that made his skin look as if the sun had kissed each pore individually. His sunglasses hung around his neck on the cord, but when she came in, he pulled them off over his head. Antoni walked toward her, his hand outstretched. When Franny met him in the middle of the room, she was surprised to find herself being pulled even closer, and Antoni quickly kissed her on both cheeks.

"Oh," Franny said. "Isn't that a lovely way to start the day."

The phone rang, and the girl behind the

desk picked it up and started speaking quickly in Spanish. Antoni ushered Franny back in the direction of the parking lot. When they were outside, Franny realized that they hadn't made an actual plan — clearly he didn't expect her to play, but they hadn't talked about what they'd do while they talked. That was her favorite part of interviews: the starlet who scarfs down a plate of french fries in her favorite diner; the chef who walks around his small town with his dogs nipping at the heels of his wellies, a sandwich in his pocket. Franny liked to see what people ate.

"Have you had lunch?"

Antoni looked at his watch. "No, it's early. Are you hungry? I'll take you to the best tapas on Mallorca. Tourists aren't allowed, but for me, they'll make an exception. First we have a tour of the center, then we eat."

"Well, yes," Franny said, though Antoni was already walking through the lot and toward the chain-link fence at the far end. He strapped his sunglasses back on his head, and pulled a baseball cap out of his back pocket. Franny's sandals thwacked against the ground, forcing her to walk with her knees jutting forward like a child playing dress-up.

There were thirty courts in all, in two long

308

rows on either side of the administrative office. They ran camps for children, more serious training for competitively ranked juniors, and lessons for adults who were hopelessly past their prime but still interested in getting a better serve. Antoni looked at Franny when he mentioned the serve. Nando Filani was their most famous export, but Antoni was clearly proud of the center's entire staff. Every time they passed a lesson in progress, or a sweating teenager hitting ball after ball, Antoni would clap twice and then nod or offer a few words of encouragement. Nando's name was on the door, but it was Antoni's clubhouse. Franny took notes that she doubted she'd ever use: *Sound of auto tennis-ball machine. Sneakers sliding on dusty clay courts. Red ankles, white socks. AV/peacock, feathers extended.*

She'd been writing a bit over the last few months, what would ultimately wind up condensed into a first chapter, or a prologue, if she kept it at all. That was where the anger lived, the hurt. The rants about Jim and the sanctity of their union. It was crazy, what young people believed was possible, what so many earnest twenty-three-year-olds took for granted about the rest of their lives. Franny's parents had been married for a hundred years, and she doubted that either of them had ever strayed, but what did she know? What did anyone know about anyone else, including the person they were married to? There were secret parts of every union, locked doors hidden behind dusty heavy drapes. Franny thought she must have them, too, somewhere deep inside, drawers of forgotten indiscretions. She certainly hoped so. It wasn't any fun to be on the other side, to be the wronged party. Franny liked the idea of doing a little bit of wrong. Maybe that's what the book would be, a memoir in the future tense. *A Catalogue of My Future Sins.* A middle-aged woman's post-divorce sexual reawakening. There would be a mirror on the cover.

Antoni was speaking to a student, a young girl, maybe twelve years old. She had the steely gaze of a professional but hit two slightly wobbly backhands in a row. He stood behind her, his back at the fence, and murmured words of correction. Her third shot sliced through the air like a Ginsu knife.

"*Sí,*" he said, and clapped twice. Franny clapped twice in response, and he looked over at her and winked.

The roads were faster on the back of a motorcycle, the turns sharper. Jim hadn't been on the back of a bike since he was in college, and the physical logistics were more challenging. His arms were wrapped around the pediatrician's thick waist, and his helmet kept knocking against Terry's. It seemed unlikely they would end up anywhere but at the very bottom of a very steep cliff, but after only about twenty minutes of silent prayer, Jim felt the vibrations of the motor slow beneath him. He opened his eyes and saw the gate for the Nando Filani International Tennis Centre. Once they'd reached a complete stop, Jim tugged off his helmet.

"This is it," he said. As requested, Terry had stopped outside the entrance, some twenty feet down the road.

Terry tipped the bike over to one side so that Jim could dismount. He swung his left leg over the back of the bike and felt something pop. Riding motorcycles — hell, even just getting off a motorcycle — seemed to be a younger man's game, but Jim didn't want to appear too stodgy. Ignoring the pulled feeling in his groin, Jim walked over to the stone wall and peered into the tennis center. He could see the parking lot, which was all he really needed. That way he could see if Franny and her Don Juan took off. Jim wasn't sure why he'd felt the need to follow his wife, but he had. It wasn't sweet or romantic. It was possessive, and a little bit desperate, and he knew it. That didn't matter. What mattered was that he kept Franny in his sights as long as he could, even if it meant giving Terry a bear hug for the next few hours.

Terry was used to sitting on his bike on the side of the road, taking in the scenery, and didn't object to waiting. He closed his eyes and turned his ruddy face toward the sun. The bike wasn't large enough for Jim to sit on without feeling like things had taken a turn for the truly intimate, and anyway, he couldn't stop pacing. He walked up and down the road beside the entrance. The shoulder wasn't wide enough for a car, but the bike tucked in nicely, allowing the regular traffic to zoom by. Every now and then a car would slow and pull into the parking lot of the tennis center, and every now and then, a car would pull out. When that happened, Jim would duck behind the bike as quickly as possible, or bend over as if he were inspecting the back tire. Terry would peer into the car, and say "Nope" if Franny wasn't in it. This happened three times, until Terry said "Yep." Jim stayed crouched behind the bike, his back facing away from the entrance, until the car turned onto the road, and then he climbed on the back of the bike as quickly as possible, wrapping his arms around Terry with genuine affection.

"Let's go," he said, and Terry revved the engine. Jim had never been a car guy, or a speed guy, but he was starting to understand the appeal of life on the blacktop. If he hadn't cashed in his chips on Madison Vance, he might have splurged on a midlife crisis on wheels. He could see it so easily — he and Franny zipping up I-95, or smaller, prettier roads, taking in the fall foliage al fresco, at a sixty-mile-per-hour clip. He'd get her a helmet in whatever color she wanted, though of course she would want black, or maybe gold. Franny Gold. That was her name when they met, *Franny Gold, Franny Gold, Franny Gold.* He'd always loved her name, even though Franny joked that it was "shtetl chic." How could you do better than gold? Terry turned the bike around slowly, and then they were off, Antoni's BMW directly ahead of them. When he turned, they turned. When he stopped, they stopped. Jim couldn't see what was directly in front of them — that was just the back of Terry's helmet — but he watched the arid countryside turn into the streets of downtown Palma. They were on the ring road by the marina, curving underneath the shadow of the cathedral. Jim wished he knew what they were talking about, how much thicker Antoni's accent had gotten since he left the spotlight. He prayed briefly for some sort of brain injury but then retracted the prayer from the record. Franny had done nothing wrong. If she wanted to sleep with a handsome Mallorcan, he wouldn't stop her.

Joan had four CDs in his car: Tomeu Penya's *Sirena,* Enrique Iglesias's *Euphoria,* Maroon 5's *Hands All Over,* and One Direction's *Take Me Home,* which he claimed belonged to his younger sister. They started with One Direction, at Sylvia's request, and Joan tried not to nod in time with the beat. It was a perfect day — warm and breezy, and once they were driving, they didn't even need the air-conditioning anymore. Both Joan and Sylvia rolled down their windows and let the actual air do the trick. Sylvia's hair whipped around her face like a blond tornado, but she didn't care. When she'd had her fill of pop confection, she ejected the CD and put in the Tomeu Penya, the one person she hadn't heard of. In the photo on the CD cover, Penya (she assumed) looked like a creepy hitchhiker, in the same way that Neil Young looks like a creepy hitchhiker. A song began — Joan hit fast forward to the second track, and Sylvia clapped along.

"This sounds like a lullaby by a guy in a tiny jacket playing in the corner of a Mexican restaurant."

Joan looked at her as if she'd called his mother a whore.

"What? Do you actually like this?"

Joan shook his head, which at first Sylvia took as him agreeing with her, but his face turned red, and that was clearly not the case. "This is *Mallorcan* music," he said, pointing at the stereo. "This is our *national, country music.*"

"Right. And everyone knows that country music sucks, Taylor Swift notwithstanding. Makes perfect sense." She turned the CD case over in her hand. "Wait, we have to listen to the 'Taxi Rap.'" Sylvia hit the forward button a few times and waited for Tomeu to start rapping about taxis, which he did.

"Oh my God," she said. "This is like seeing your grandfather naked."

Joan slammed the stop button, silencing the car. "You are such an American. Some of us have actual pride in our history, you know! You sound so stupid!"

Sylvia wasn't used to being yelled at. She crossed her arms over her chest and stared out the window. "Whatever," she said, until she could think of something more cutting.

"There are five languages in Spain, plus dialects, did you know that? And Franco tried to demolish all of that. And so yes, it is important that we have a Mallorcan singer, who sings Mallorcan songs, even if they are sometimes not the best."

Sylvia sat as far back against the seat as possible, as if she were in the dentist's chair. "You're right," she said. "I'm sorry."

"It's not all about your swimming pool and whether or not your brother is an asshole," Joan said.

"You're right," Sylvia said again, and said good-bye to the idea of Joan ever coming close enough to kiss her again, and to the idea that the rest of the day would be any good whatsoever. She almost told him to turn around and take her home, but she feared it would make her seem too petulant, and so she just kept her mouth shut and stared out the window.

The restaurant was on a pier, and shabby in the way that Franny liked, with tablecloths that were soft from being washed a thousand times, and dusty decorations hanging on the wall. It wasn't for tourists — there was no English menu, no German menu, only

Spanish. The waiter brought them two glasses of wine and a plate of olives and fresh bread. Antoni took his hat off and put it on the empty chair beside him. There was a faint mark across his forehead that Franny thought was from the hat, but quickly realized was a tan line.

"Do you enjoy coaching? It must be exciting to work with Nando." Franny let a piece of bread soak up some olive oil and then dropped it into her mouth.

Antoni took a short sip of wine. "It is good."

She waited for him to elaborate, but Antoni turned his attention to the menu. A moment later, the waiter returned, and he and Antoni had a brisk exchange. Franny thought she understood the word *pulpo* and the word *pollo,* but she couldn't be sure.

"Did you ever think about leaving Mallorca?" she asked. "When you were playing on the tour, you must have gone all over the world. Was there ever another place that spoke to you? You know, somewhere you wanted to stay?" She cupped her hand under her face. "Do you have any kids?"

"You ask a lot of questions," Antoni said. "Or maybe you're still recovering from your brain injury."

Franny laughed and patted herself on the

head, which did indeed still have quite a lump, but Antoni didn't smile. He wasn't kidding.

Joan and Sylvia stopped for a coffee in Valldemossa, a charming little town with pitched cobblestone streets and a robust number of tourists wearing backpacks and Coppertone. They sat outside and drank their coffees out of proper little cups, which made Sylvia feel like she'd been a hobo all her life, carrying disposable paper cups down the street. Mallorcans knew how to slow things down. After their coffees were done, Joan directed them up a small hill to the monastery where George Sand and Frédéric Chopin had spent a miserable winter.

"Seriously, if you were going to move into a monastery with your boyfriend . . ." Sylvia said. "No, even if it was in the summer, that still seems like a bad idea."

Despite scolding her in the car, Joan seemed happy to play tour guide. He pointed out everything — ikat fabric in a shop window that was made on the island; powdery *ensaimadas,* even better-looking than the ones Franny had made; wild olive trees twisted into snarling shapes. He pointed out cats dozing in the sun. When

Sylvia began to fan herself, he produced a bottle of water. Every time she accidentally brushed against his arm, Sylvia felt an electric jolt running the length of her body. It wasn't that he was perfect for her, or even that they had so much in common. Sylvia had more in common with the sullen girl selling the pastries, she was pretty sure, but that didn't matter. Joan was as handsome as a man in a Calvin Klein ad, one of the ones where it looked like clothes had never been invented, and thank God. He could have been steering a sailboat wearing only a skimpy pair of underwear and no one would have complained. Complained! Tourists would have paid money to have their photographs taken with him. Sylvia doubted that she would ever be so close to anyone that naturally good-looking ever again. The odds just weren't good.

It was almost time for lunch, and Joan had a place in mind. They were driving farther north, to the water, but he wouldn't say more. He put on the Maroon 5 CD and sang along.

"You know Maroon 5?"

"They're okay, yeah," Sylvia said. In her normal life, she would have made fun of him, but now she felt like a stupid American who no longer had the right to say if things were good or bad.

Joan took this as encouragement and turned up the volume. He danced in his seat as he drove, mouthing the words. Sylvia couldn't tell if he was being serious or ironic, but decided it didn't matter, some people were beyond reproach. They drove for almost an hour, on roads that made her wish she'd packed a Dramamine, before Joan made a sharp turn and the car started to go down the mountain instead of up. Tall pine trees lined the road on both sides, and the abundant sunlight was quickly gone.

"Are you going to murder me?" Sylvia asked.

"Hmm, no," Joan said, and kept driving, now with both hands on the wheel.

They drove for a few more minutes before coming to a small, empty parking lot. "We walk from here," Joan said. He hopped out and opened the trunk, removing a sizable backpack and cooler.

Sylvia had never been on an actual date before. She'd gone out with bunches of people, some of whom were boys, and Gabe Thrush had shown up on her doorstep a thousand times, but at no point had anyone ever called or texted or passed her a note that asked her out on a real, serious date. Even before Joan had yelled at her, she'd had no indication that this was an actual date. She wasn't sure how to behave.

"So you, like, planned this?" Sylvia said.

"Did you want to eat sand?" Joan shrugged. He was a professional.

"Only if you packed sand sandwiches, I guess," Sylvia said. She sounded like a moron. *Get it together, Sylvia.* The key to being cool was pretending that you'd done everything before; she knew that.

Joan pointed to Sylvia's feet, clad in her dirty slip-on sneakers. "You can walk in those? It's a little hike." She nodded, and then followed him down a narrow path into the trees.

By the second hour, even beatific Terry seemed ready to get on with it. "Oi," he said to Jim. "You sure you want to stick around for this?" They were perched on a bench in a park along the water. Franny and Antoni had been sitting on the restaurant's sunny patio for what seemed like eternity. From his bench, Jim could just make out Franny's arm movements.

"Yes," Jim said. "Please."

Terry acquiesced. "Whatever you want, mate. I'll just shut my eyes for a moment." He lay down on his back along the wooden bench, and let out a satisfied groan. "That's the stuff." His enormous leather boots rested against Jim's thigh.

Franny and Antoni must have had at least four courses — the lunch went on forever, and waiters kept coming back to the table, holding aloft more dishes. Jim's own stomach began to gurgle with hunger. He thought about sneaking into the restaurant and ordering something to go, but he didn't want to take the risk of getting caught. And so he waited. Every few minutes he thought he could hear Franny's laugh carrying over the sound of the water, which was enough motivation to keep him going.

Eventually, Franny and Antoni stood up. Antoni put his hand on Franny's lower back as they walked through the restaurant, and he kept it there all the way until they reached the car. He opened the door for her — Franny always had liked nice cars, even though they thought it was silly to have one in New York. When they got home, if she took him back, Jim vowed he would buy her a car, whatever she wanted. A car and a motorcycle and anything else. He wanted to be the one to drive her wherever she wanted to go. Jim nudged Terry awake.

"Oi," Jim said. "We're back on."

Jim's biggest fear was that Antoni would take another route — have another destina-

322

tion, like a hotel, or maybe his house — but the car went back the way it had come, straight to the tennis center. Terry and Jim stayed enough of a distance behind that they weren't obvious, but close enough to catch up if necessary. They stopped in a different spot from where they had the first time, a little ways farther back, because Franny was a nervous driver and was sure to look both ways several times before attempting to pull out into traffic. It didn't take long — Jim peered over the wall and watched as Franny and Antoni said good-bye. She was facing the courts, and Jim could only barely make out the lower half of her body, the rest hidden by trees. It was clear that Antoni was embracing her, and leaning toward her face, but Jim couldn't see what was actually happening. Then Franny started to clomp away, always unsteady in those shoes, and Jim hurried back to the bike, pulling on his helmet. He hid again behind Terry's leg, accidentally hitting himself in the wounded eye on Terry's knee. "Shit," he said.

"Okay, there she goes," Terry said, and Jim hopped back on. He was starting to feel like he'd lived his whole life wrong — maybe he should have been a motorcycle cop, or a private investigator. He'd spent too much of his allotted hours on earth indoors, staring at a page with words on it. Franny would have cried hallelujah to hear him say it — she'd been telling him that for years, that life was lived outside, on the move, out of one's comfort zone. She'd gone so many places without him, and Jim mourned them all now. Franny was driving slowly, and Terry matched her pace. Jim wanted to move to England and retroactively send his children to see Terry, clearly the world's greatest pediatrician.

Terry shouted something, but Jim couldn't hear him. They were still slowing down. Over Terry's shoulder, Jim saw the tiny rental car swoop over to the shoulder of the road and come to a halt. Jim knocked on Terry's back and then pointed at Franny's car. He held up his palm, STOP in the name of love, and Terry did just that, gracefully exiting traffic and pulling over just in front of Franny's car.

She hadn't gotten out but was squinting through the windshield. Jim took off his helmet and tucked it under his arm like an astronaut. He hoped that he looked handsome and rugged, and not like he'd just removed a scuba mask, but he feared the latter was probably true. Recognizing her husband, Franny shook her head and dropped her chin to her chest, just what she did in dark movie theaters when a serial killer was about to jump out and claim his next victim. Jim walked to the driver's-side window and waited for Franny to press the button to roll it down. She didn't want to laugh — was trying not to laugh — but she couldn't quite keep it in.

"Jim," she said. "Are you following me?"

He crouched down, holding on to the bottom of the car's window. "Maybe."

"Have you been following me all day? On the back of that guy's motorcycle?" Franny gestured with her chin toward Terry, who really did cut an imposing figure when you didn't know him. He was on the phone now, scowling into the middle distance. He saw them looking and waved.

"Maybe."

"Why, if I may ask such a pedestrian question?"

"Because I love you. And I don't want to lose you. Not to some tennis pro, not to anyone." Jim stood up and opened the car door. He reached a hand down for Franny. She paused, put her foot on the clutch, and turned off the car.

"I keep fucking that up," she said, once she'd climbed out. "I think we're going to have to buy it when we return it. I'm pretty sure that I've ruined it completely."

Jim put his hands on Franny's shoulders. She was so much smaller than he was, almost an entire foot. His parents, who'd wanted him to marry some gangly sylph from Greenwich, had never understood. They were worried about the gene pool, about producing generation after generation of tall blonds. But Jim loved her, only Franny, only his wife. "I'm the one who fucked up. Fran, I am so sorry. I will do anything. I can't be without you, I can't."

Franny reached up and traced the outline of Jim's black eye, which had started to turn green. "It's healing," she said, and tilted her head up in the way that meant he could kiss her, and so he did. Behind them, Terry let out a wolf whistle, triumphant.

After walking through a short tunnel cut into the side of the mountain, Sylvia and Joan finally found what they were looking for. The beach was magnificent — a tiny horseshoe of sand, completely empty. Sylvia could see the bottom of the water for fifty feet, bright blue and clear. Joan set down his bag and the cooler, and quickly got them set up. He unrolled a thick blanket, and stacked heavy things in the corner to keep it down, though the beach seemed totally protected from the wind. There were no waves, not even small ripples. Sylvia kicked off her shoes and waded in.

"This is literally the most beautiful place I have ever been in my entire life," she said. "And I'm pretty sure that will always be true."

Joan nodded. "It's the best. No one knows about it. Even local people don't know. My grandparents live right up there," he said pointing up the mountain behind them. "They would bring me here when I was little. Very good for toy boats." He had packed enough food for four: ham and cheese sandwiches, wine, thin butter cookies his mother had made. "Do you want to swim first, or eat?"

Sylvia walked over to the blanket, her wet feet and calves now caked with sand. "Hmm," she said, turning back to face the water. "Normally I would pick the food, but right now, I don't know."

"I have an idea," Joan said. He pulled the corkscrew out of the bag and opened the bottle of wine. He took a slug and then handed the bottle to Sylvia, who followed suit. When she'd passed it back, he recorked the bottle, set it in the cooler, and peeled off his shirt.

Everyone on earth had a body, of course. Young people had bodies and old people had bodies and all bodies were different. Sylvia would never have described herself as someone who cared about muscles; pecs and abs did nothing for her, theoretically. That stuff was for idiots who didn't have better things to think about. That was for girls like Carmen, who didn't know enough to see that their boyfriends treated them like garbage. Working out was a punishment, a gym-class nightmare. Sylvia tried to remember if she could even touch her toes, but couldn't, because she was hypnotized by the sight in front of her. All of her speculation about Joan made the actual physical reality of him without his shirt on seem like a joke. She didn't even know which muscle groups to imagine! They were all there, the little ones and the big ones and the ones like arrows pointing toward his crotch. She truly had had no idea that bodies were actually made like that, with no Photoshop in sight. Joan folded his shirt and laid it on the blanket, and then reached for his fly. Sylvia had to turn around.

"I'll race you," she said, mostly because she wasn't sure her legs could take seeing any more, like they might just give out from under her and then she'd die on the spot. She quickly pulled off her dress, revealing the tank suit underneath. She threw her dress in a ball behind her, not caring where it landed, and then ran into the water. She ran until the water was as high as her hips, and then closed her eyes and dove.

When her head bobbed up a yard later, Sylvia could hear Joan in the water behind her. She turned around, treading water, and watched him swim to her. She felt like a flounder swimming next to a dolphin. When Joan raised his head, his hair still looked perfect, just wet. Sylvia smoothed her own hair back, feeling all the knots from the windy drive.

"You know," she said. "I think Anne Brontë is really underrated. In terms of the Brontë family. Don't you think so?" She kicked her legs, and her right foot made contact with some unseen part of Joan's body. "Sorry."

Joan dipped his chin into the bay, showing no sign that he'd heard her.

"Elizabeth Gaskell, too," Sylvia continued. "I mean, George Eliot gets all the love, and Elizabeth gets nothing, don't you think that's weird?"

Joan swam closer, so that his shoulders were only a foot away from Sylvia's.

"I won't kiss you if you don't want it," he said.

Sylvia wished for a camera, for her telephone, for a reality television crew. Her heart was beating so quickly that she thought the water around her would begin to boil. "That would be okay," she said, and Joan closed the gap between them. She let her eyelids flutter shut, and then she felt his mouth on hers.

Not counting whoever she'd kissed at the party, drunk out of her mind, Sylvia had kissed five people in her life, roughly one a year since she was twelve. Joan was number six, and the difference between him and the previous five was so hilarious that Sylvia couldn't contain herself. Gone were the searching tongues, the cumbersome teeth, the bad breath, the too-soft lips that belonged to every single boy in New York City.

"Are you laughing at me?" Joan said, pulling back. He reached for her waist, unafraid of her answer, and Sylvia felt herself lift her legs so that they wrapped around his torso. Her entire body felt warm and buzzing, like a fluorescent lightbulb. She wanted to kiss Joan until she couldn't breathe, until they needed to call for help because they were both dead by make-out.

"I think we should have sex," Sylvia said. Joan put his hands underneath her thighs to brace her weight, and then walked straight out of the bay, dropping to his knees when they reached the blanket. He deposited Sylvia gently on her back, and then slid one shoulder of her bathing suit off at a time, never taking his mouth off hers. When her bathing suit was off, Joan moved his mouth down her body. When he started going down on her, an experience she'd never particularly liked before, she realized that there were parts of her body she'd never met, and he was introducing her to them, which felt chivalrous and empowering and like she'd been sitting in a dark room for her entire life, and now she was naked on a beach in Mallorca and maybe there was a God after all. There was a condom in the basket, or in his pocket, and when Joan leaned back to put it on, Sylvia got to look at his entire naked body, which was so phenomenally beautiful that she forgot to feel embarrassed about her own.

The actual sex didn't hurt (as Katie Saperstein had years ago told her it would), and she didn't bleed (again, Katie Saperstein). Sylvia couldn't say that it actually felt *good,* either, but her whole body was still humming from whatever Joan had just licked and nudged and paid glorious attention to, and so Sylvia happily went along for the ride. He moved around on top of her, going in and out, and she could hear the bay sloshing around and the birds flying overhead. If anyone had walked down the steep slope and through the tunnel to the beach, they would have seen them, full-on, no question, but no one did. Joan finished with a final push, his beautiful face briefly changing into something complicated and taut, and then relaxing back into its natural state of perfection. Sylvia wrapped her arms around him, because it seemed like the thing to do, and Joan rested his head on her clavicle. He stayed inside her for a moment, and then gently pulled out and rolled onto his back. Their legs were wet and sandy, and when Sylvia sat up, the whole beach seemed to spin. The world was different now that she knew this was a possibility.

"So," she said. "I think it's definitely time for a sandwich."

After a long day of doing absolutely nothing (in pool, out of pool, snack assemblage, snack intake, repeat), Charles and Lawrence had convinced Bobby to play another game of Scrabble with them. Jim and Franny had come home and vanished upstairs, their cheeks red, likely in the middle of another argument. Bobby watched the stairs for a little while like a hopeful puppy, but returned his attention to the game when he realized his mother wasn't coming back anytime soon. It was Lawrence's turn, and he laid down *PITHY,* connecting to Bobby's *PEAR.*

"You guys don't have to take care of me, you know," Bobby said. "I'm not going to jump off the roof."

"No one thinks you're going to jump off the roof," Charles said.

"No," Lawrence said. "Not the roof. Maybe an upper window, but not the roof."

Bobby smiled.

Charles took a moment and rearranged his tiles. In the upper corner of the board, there was an empty double word score, and Charles filled it with *SORRY.* "Sorry," he said.

"No, you're not," Lawrence said, but then kissed him on the cheek.

The front door opened and Sylvia slunk in, her hair wet in spots and dry in others. "Hey, guys," she said. "I'm just going to take a shower." She hurried toward the stairs.

"Whoa, whoa, whoa," Charles said. "You were out with Joan this whole time?"

Sylvia didn't blush, but she also didn't slow down. "Yes. Yes, I was." And with that, she was up the stairs, in the bathroom, and in the shower. It didn't matter how cold the water was, or who could hear her. She sang "Moves Like Jagger" until she didn't know the words, and then she made them up.

"Huh," Lawrence said.

"Huh," said Bobby.

"I think we should focus on the game," Charles said, and they did.

DAY THIRTEEN

Lawrence woke up early to check his e-mail. *Santa Claws* would be the death of him, he was sure. The last e-mail he'd received from Toronto was about the lead actor going on strike because of a heat wave, and the suit, and the fur. It was not Lawrence's problem, except that he had to keep track of every dollar they spent, and the actor's strike meant that they were spending lots of money on craft services and union lighting rigs when nothing was actually being shot. He carried his laptop into the kitchen and stood with his back to the sink.

There were twenty new e-mails in his in-box. He scrolled through quickly — mostly J.Crew and the like pressuring him to buy more summer clothes — but stopped when he got to an e-mail from the adoption agency. He opened it with one finger, pulling the computer closer to his chest. When they'd started, Lawrence thought the whole adoption process would be like the scene in John Waters's *Cry-Baby,* with children performing domestic scenes behind glass, like at a museum. You'd pick the one you wanted, take them home, and love them forever. But it wasn't that simple. Lawrence skimmed the e-mail, reading as fast as he could. The e-mail was short — *Call me. She's made a decision. You're it.*

Lawrence nearly dropped the computer. He didn't realize he was making any noise until Charles rushed out of their bedroom in his pajamas.

"What happened?" he asked, worried. "What's wrong?"

Lawrence shook his head vigorously. "We have to go home right now. We need a phone. Where's the phone?" He spun the computer around so that Charles could read the e-mail. Charles took the reading glasses off Lawrence's face and put them on his own.

"Oh my God," Charles said. "Alphonse."

Lawrence started to cry. "We have a baby boy."

"A baby!" Charles shouted. "A baby!" He put the computer down on the kitchen table and pulled Lawrence into his arms, dipping him, murmuring names into his ear. *Walter. Phillip. Nathaniel.* It didn't matter where Alphonse came from, what the circumstances had been. What mattered was that they were going to take him home.

With all the commotion of booking new flights and helping Charles and Lawrence pack and get out of the house, everyone was awake and alert much earlier than usual. Franny decided that pancakes were in order, as they were a celebratory breakfast food. Jim stayed close to her, cracking eggs when instructed, and searching through cabinets for vanilla extract. Bobby sat at the table alone while Sylvia made the coffee — it had always been her favorite activity, the French press. She timed the brewing on the oven clock, no longer even missing her phone. She could have thrown it down the mountain and watched it crack into a thousand pieces and she wouldn't have cared. Whenever she closed her eyes, she could feel Joan's mouth on her body.

"They're going to be really good, don't you think?" Bobby was starting to look more like himself — he'd been sleeping better and eating like a teenager.

"I do," Franny said. "I really do." She whisked the batter and then slid her finger around the edge of the bowl and stuck it in her mouth, nodding with self-approval. She knifed a small pat of butter and melted it on the hot griddle. "Are you making coffee with your eyes closed for a reason, Syl?"

Sylvia's eyes flew open. "I was just testing myself," she said. "Yep, three minutes." She carried the French press to the table and released the plunger. Bobby held out his cup. "Pour it yourself," she said. "I'm busy." Sylvia slid down the bench toward the wall and closed her eyes again, a half-smile on her face.

"You are a weirdo," Bobby said.

"Oh, yes," Sylvia said, eyes still shut. "I am."

That was exactly what his sister had always been good at — being herself. Bobby thought about the slick suits in his closet that he wore when he showed expensive apartments, the hi-tech fabrics he wore to Total Body Power, the faded jeans he'd had since college that he wore when Carmen wasn't around because she called them "dad pants."

"You know, I don't even like real estate that much," Bobby said. "Or working out. I mean, I like working out because I like to feel healthy, but I don't really care if I have the best body in the world." He paused. "I wonder how hard it is to adopt a baby."

"Let's just deal with one thing at a time,

sweetie, okay?" Franny said, swanning over with a plate stacked high with thick pancakes, some dotted with blueberries.

"Okay," Bobby said, and forked three of the pancakes onto his plate.

"Okay," Sylvia said, finally opening her eyes. "These are the best pancakes I have ever seen." She looked up at her mother. "Thank you, Mom."

Franny wiped her hands on her skirt, slightly flustered. "You're welcome, my love." She turned around to get the syrup, which Jim was already holding.

"I don't know what happened to our children," she said. "But I like it."

Jim kissed Franny on the forehead, which Sylvia and Bobby pretended not to see. All four Posts held their breath simultaneously, each wishing for the moment to last. Families were nothing more than hope cast out in a wide net, everyone wanting only the best. Even the poor souls who had children in an attempt to rescue a dying marriage were doing so out of a misguided hopefulness. Franny and Jim and Bobby and Sylvia did their silent best, and just like that, for a moment, they were all aboard the same ship.

Sylvia had been thinking about Joan every minute since she'd left his company the day before. She wanted to have sex again and again, until she felt like she really knew what she was doing, and Joan seemed like a good partner. He could pick her up, for fuck's sake. He knew about secluded beaches. Who cared if he listened to terrible music and wore shirts with fleurs-de-lis printed on the shoulder when he went out dancing? At home, Sylvia would never in a million years have been interested in anyone who went out dancing, period, but that wasn't the point. The point was that she needed to figure out a totally natural way to sneak Joan upstairs to her bedroom without her parents noticing.

In the few minutes before he rang the bell, Sylvia opened her laptop at the kitchen counter. There was a message from Brown with her rooming situation — Keeney Quad, what she'd been hoping for, where most of the freshmen lived — and contact information about her new roommate (Molly Krumpler-Jones, of Newton, Massachusetts). It was the e-mail that Sylvia had been waiting months for, but she barely even looked at it, because right above it was an e-mail from Joan.

S — Sorry to cancel our second to last session, but I won't be able to come today. I will see you tomorrow at ten to say good-bye. Had fun at the beach. — J

He could easily have sent it in a text message, but if he'd texted, she would have seen it faster and responded. The e-mail was a time bomb, waiting for her to open her computer in order to detonate. Sylvia felt her cheeks go up in flame, but then she heard someone at the door and was instantly relieved. He'd been joking! Obviously, Joan wasn't that much of an asshole — he was just playing with her. Sylvia scrambled to the door. She considered flashing him when she opened the door, but her breasts had never been particularly impressive, and decided against it. She was laughing as she pulled the knob.

A tall woman — taller than Sylvia by several inches, which meant she was close to six feet — was bent in half on the other side of the door, rooting around like an anteater in a gigantic leather purse.

"Can I help you?" Sylvia asked. She put her hands on her hips in hopes that her posture would communicate that she was not the slightest bit interested in doing anything of the sort.

The woman looked up startled. "Oh, Lord. You must be Franny's daughter, are you? I saw the car in the drive and knew that I must have mixed up the dates. Isn't that just like me," she said, as if Sylvia would be able to corroborate. She stood up and gave her long, wavy blond hair a shake. "I'm Gemma," she said. "It's my house!"

"Oh," Sylvia said. "Then I guess you should come in." She gestured toward the foyer, stepped inside, and screamed for her mother before retreating to her bedroom.

Franny hadn't seen Gemma in person in a decade and was horrified to find her remarkably unchanged. Gemma got herself a glass of water — *Oh, you've been using the filter? I just drink straight from the tap like a cat. I think it's what keeps my immune system in such top shape* — and then they went out to sit by the pool. Gemma had just come from her house in London, a limestone in Maida Vale, but before that she'd been in Paris for two weeks, and before that, Berlin.

"It's so exhausting," Gemma said. "I really envy that you have this lifestyle. You can pack up the kids and just go somewhere for two weeks and no one will even bother you." She widened her eyes at the word *bother.* "You can just *get away.* I would pay a million dollars for that. Even when I *do* go on vacation, the gallery is always calling me, or one of my artists, and then I have to get on a plane just to massage someone's fragile ego, and I want to say, you know, I was just about to have a snorkel in the Maldives." Gemma ruffled her hair with both hands, laying it over the back of the chaise longue. "It's a nice house, isn't it? Quaint."

Franny could have described the house using a hundred adjectives, and *quaint* wouldn't have been on the list. "It's incredible," she said, not wanting to contradict Gemma outright.

"Most Brits think Mallorca is for drunken teenagers," she said. "It's sort of like reverse psychology, buying a house here, up in the mountains. It really is the best place to get away. It's like if you and Jim decided to buy a house on the Jersey Shore, everyone would think you'd gone mad, but then there you are at your lovely house, miles away from the puddles of sick and the beaches covered with pale skin and babies in dirty nappies. None of my British friends would ever come here."

Franny stared out at the mountains. If the house had belonged to her, she would have invited everyone she knew, and they all would have oohed and aahed. She could have her whole terrible book club come and read George Sand and laugh about how wrong she'd been about the island, how depressive. Literally any person in the world would love the view, the food, the people. Franny thought she could write a new brochure for the tourist board if someone so much as slipped a pen into her hand.

"Well, we've all had a wonderful time. Eating our way through, really."

"Oh, I never eat anything. Just the ice cream. I come for a week, eat only ice cream, then go home feeling like I've been on a cleanse." Gemma closed her eyes. The sun was beating straight down on them, and Franny felt the warm part of her hair. "So," Gemma asked, eyes still shut, "where's my Charlie?"

He hadn't told her. Of course he hadn't told her! If Charles hadn't said a word to Franny, then he wouldn't have dared say anything to Gemma. Not since she was in the eleventh grade had Franny felt such delight in the knowing and dispensing of news about her friends' lives.

"Oh, you don't know?" Franny feigned surprise. "That's so odd that he wouldn't tell you — I know how close you two are."

Gemma's eyes flew open. She blinked several times in a row, giving the impression of a rodent emerging from months spent in a dark hole underground. The skin around her eyes had begun to crease, and maybe even sag. Franny didn't often revel in other people's flaws, but in this case, she would make an exception. Gemma was waiting for her to speak, with her own lips parted, as if that was where the information would enter her body. She looked like a beautiful, stupid dog. Franny wanted to kiss her on the mouth and then shove her into the pool.

"They went home to get their baby," Franny said. "A boy. They're adopting a baby boy."

"They left? To buy a baby?"

"They're not *buying* a baby, they're *adopting* a baby."

Gemma let out a bark. "On purpose? I thought babies only happened to people by accident. I've had three husbands and have narrowly avoided them half a dozen times! What on earth is he thinking? Really. Oh, Charlie. Now his paintings will all be dewy little portraits of a half-naked Lawrence with a baby asleep on his chest." She paused. "Now I'm doubly sorry to have missed him. The last hurrah!"

Franny tried to smile, but couldn't. "I suppose."

"Are you and Jim in the master, upstairs?" Gemma asked. She slipped her sunglasses out of her purse and put them on. "You wouldn't mind moving to whichever room Charlie and Lawrence were staying in, would you? You know how it is to sleep in your own bed. All the other mattresses are too soft for my back, like sleeping on giant pillows. You'll be fine for one night, I'm sure, won't you? If it's not too much trouble." She stood up and dusted off her spotless blue jeans. "I'll call Tiffany's and send over a spoon."

"How nice," Franny said. "Now, if you'll excuse me, I'll start packing upstairs so that you can have your bedroom back."

The two women walked toward the door side by side, each one trying to reach the handle first, as if to stake claim to the entire property. Franny would have won if her legs had been a few inches longer, but Gemma grabbed it first, her long, thin fingers gripping it like it was a loose diamond floating in the swimming pool. She held the door open for Franny, who walked in with her head held high. She wouldn't tell Charles what a bitch his friend was — that would turn her moral high ground to mush. Instead, she would just be secure in her knowledge that she was the better friend, and that his baby, whoever he was and whoever he would grow to be, would call her his aunty, whereas Gemma would never be more than a terrifying shrew on the other side of the globe.

■ ■ ■ ■

Bobby wanted to swim until he could no longer feel his arms or legs. His personal record in a pool was a mile, mostly because that was six laps at Total Body Power, and doing less than six laps seemed pathetic, but he didn't much like swimming. No one in Florida did. Swimming was for the tourists, splashing around in a way that would never equal the calories in a single Cuban sandwich. Right now, being in the pool was the only way to make sure that no one would speak to him, and so that's where Bobby wanted to be, exhausting his limbs and his lungs and avoiding his entire family.

It was so easy for most people. His high school friends had all gone to college and found women to marry. His college friends, too. They met in the dining hall, or in Psych 100, or at a party after a football game, just like they were supposed to. There were a few holdouts, a guy here or there who'd dumped or been dumped or was too much of an introvert to get a real girlfriend. When those friends came through Miami, they'd always have a good time. Bobby would take them to clubs and they'd drink all night. Girls in Miami wore the tiniest dresses and the highest heels, and his friends were always shocked by how many of them there were, like ants on a picnic table. The married friends didn't visit much, and when they did, it was for dinner and maybe a single drink, and they went to bed. Not even to fuck, but to sleep. Bobby would pretend to leave when they did, but then circle back to the bar by himself. Who went to bed at ten o'clock? He was close to thirty, but he wasn't dead.

Bobby hadn't had a real girlfriend until Carmen. Sure, there had been girls, but never anyone serious. When he lost his virginity his freshman year at Miami, he didn't tell the girl it was his first time, though it was probably pretty obvious. In retrospect he wished he had, because he'd never forget her name — Sarah Jack, *like a lumberjack,* she'd said at the party where they met — and now it felt weird, like he was still keeping a secret, even though it was almost ten years ago. Bobby felt his outstretched fingers brush against the wall of the pool, and did a somersault underwater to go back in the opposite direction. The water wasn't chlorinated, and he could open his eyes without them stinging. There were leaves at the bottom of the pool, and he thought about diving down to get them, but he didn't.

There had been a dozen weddings since college, and he went to all of them — some in New York, some in Florida, but mostly scattered around in the brides' various hometowns, with some destination exceptions. The most expensive wedding had been in Vail, Colorado, at the top of a mountain. He and Carmen went skiing together for the first time that weekend, and she met all of his friends from high school. A few of them pulled Bobby aside afterward, in the lodge and at the house they were sharing and at the reception, and they all wanted to know how old Carmen was. Some of them were impressed and some were clearly weirded out, but none of them expected to get an invite to Bobby and Carmen's wedding, that was for sure. At each subsequent event, they were surprised to find the pair still together. A few even included Carmen's name on their wedding invitations, instead of just a plus-one. But there was always someone sticking his elbow into Bobby's ribs, always someone calling Carmen a cougar.

Twenty-eight was neither young nor old. Obviously it was young in the scope of someone's whole life, but it was already getting late in terms of figuring out what you wanted to do. Bobby's parents got married when they were twenty-three and twenty-five, which seemed normal only in the context of time, as though they were cave people who didn't expect to live to thirty. But that's when his friends had started getting married, too.

Selling real estate was supposed to be steady, but it wasn't. There were reality television shows about guys his age selling ten-million-dollar houses in Malibu, but Bobby was struggling to rent fifteen-hundred-dollar apartments. He and Carmen lived like roommates or, worse yet, family members. He cooked and she cleaned. Carmen reminded him to pick up his dry cleaning and kissed him on the cheek when she felt like it. She had never wanted kids — never. If he was being honest, that was the problem. Not her age, not anything else. Carmen may have wanted to get married, but she never wanted to have children, and he did. It was how he knew it didn't matter that he didn't love her.

Bobby let himself slow down. The muscles in his back were already tired. It was so hard to know when you'd made a mistake. What was it? Staying with Carmen for so long? Cheating on her? Telling himself that it was justifiable, because he knew they weren't going to last, so what did it matter, anyway? Bobby opened his mouth and let it fill with water, and then pulled his face out of the pool and spat the water out. Maybe the problem was Miami. Maybe the problem was the gym, or the debt, or the loneliness. Maybe the problem was him. It all seemed so easy for everyone else, choosing the right person to marry, as if they had some secret sign, a tattoo in invisible ink. How else were you supposed to know? Bobby was looking for certainty. He'd tried to ask some of his friends, in an offhanded way, how they knew their girlfriends were "the one," but the question always sounded hypothetical and got him answers like "I know, right?"

From the middle of the pool, all Bobby could see were the sky and the trees ringing the property. An airplane flew overhead, and Bobby wished he were on it, going somewhere he wanted to go. Instead, he put his face back in the water and kept swimming, back and forth, back and forth, until he was so tired he thought he might have to crawl to the house on his knees. It was time for him to straighten out, and if nothing else, he could start with this, the length of this pool, over and over again.

Jim and Franny took their time packing

their things and bringing their suitcases downstairs to Charles and Lawrence's room. Charles hadn't stripped the bed when they left, being in such a hurry, and so Jim and Franny were changing the sheets, even though it seemed silly, just for one night. Franny was buzzing with irritation. It was Gemma who'd made the error, not them.

"If it was me, I would sleep in the guest room for a night," Franny said, for at least the tenth time. "I would."

"I know, Fran." Jim pulled the sheet over the upper left-hand corner of the mattress, and waited for Franny to do the opposite one.

"I might even go stay somewhere else or, at the very least, offer!" Franny threw her hands up. "It's so rude."

"It's so rude." Jim pointed, gently, at the tangled sheet. Franny nodded and pulled it taut on her side, stretching the elastic over the thin bed. "But it is her house."

"The other beds really aren't as nice as hers, huh?" Franny quickly tucked in the last corner, and they moved together toward the pile of pillows, throwing them back on the bed. "What a cow."

"What a cow," Jim repeated, and softly pushed Franny onto the bed.

"What," she said, not unkindly, as he

moved on top of her, his knees on either side of her waist. Jim lowered himself as gracefully as he could and kissed her on the forehead. His eye socket was still green, but she was getting used to it.

"I was just remembering how it felt to bring Bobby home," Jim said. "How terrifying it was — driving those fifteen blocks from Roosevelt felt like driving to Timbuktu. The world was so loud. All those honking taxis. Do you remember?"

"You drove so slowly," Franny said. "I loved it. I wish you'd always driven that way, like the car was made out of glass."

"I don't think Charles and Lawrence have any idea what they're getting themselves into," Jim said. "But neither did we." He rolled onto his side, tucking his long legs against Franny's body.

"They'll be good," she said.

"We were good, too, weren't we?"

Franny could remember those first few days as a complete haze, as if shot in soft focus. Her nipples had hurt more than she'd thought they would, but really, what had she thought at all? It was almost impossible to imagine an actual baby existing where there wasn't one before, even when you could feel it kicking away inside you. It was easier with Sylvia, of course. Poor Sylvia.

The second child never did get the same kind of attention. They'd leave her wailing in her crib, they'd set her down on the kitchen floor with nothing more than a wooden spoon to entertain her. Every time Bobby screeched, they ran. Maybe that was the answer to good parenting — pretending the first child was the second. Maybe that was where they'd gone wrong, by always giving in.

She rolled onto her side, too, her nose level with Jim's. A swath of her dark hair fell out from behind her ear, covering her eyes. "Should we worry about him?"

Jim reached out and brushed Franny's hair out of her face. "Yes. What choice do we have?"

"I love you as much as I hate Gemma," Franny said. "Which, right now, is a lot."

"I'll take it," Jim said. "And you know, I kind of like being down here. It's more private. Doesn't it feel like we're in a hotel? Or, at the very least, a bed-and-breakfast?"

"Oh, God, bed-and-breakfasts," Franny said. "Where you're forced to eat subpar blueberry muffins with strangers."

"Yes, and have sex with your wife." Jim put a hand on Franny's lower back and pulled her toward him, pressing her against his body hard enough that she would be able to feel his erection.

"Is the door locked?"

"I locked it as soon as we got in here," Jim said. "I was a Boy Scout, remember?"

"Ooh," Franny said. "Tell me again about those tiny little shorts."

Jim let the joke go, wanting to move on, wanting to take her clothes off while she'd still let him. That was part of the appeal of Madison Vance, not knowing when and if she would stop him. He thought he knew Franny well enough to know that she was ready, but it had been a long time, and it seemed possible that the signals had changed. He kissed her neck the way she liked, up next to where her jaw met her earlobe, and then climbed backward to pull her dress off over her head.

Franny pushed herself up on her elbows, creasing her stomach at the waist. Jim quickly undressed next to the bed, his hard-on springing upward joyously when he pulled down his boxer shorts. Franny's body knew just what to do, her hands and her mouth and her legs, and she was ready to do it all.

"Take them off," she said to Jim, and he obediently pulled down her underwear, one side at a time, inch by inch, until they were wrapped only around her left ankle. "Now come here," she said, and he moved back on top of her, filling her mouth with his. They didn't speak again until it was over and they were lying on their backs, glistening with a job well done.

Day Fourteen

The flight to Madrid left at noon, which meant that they had to leave for the airport by ten-thirty a.m. at the very, very latest. Everyone was packed and ready to go, even Franny, who was notoriously bad at such things. Sylvia had begun to pace.

"He said he'd be here by now," she said. "I don't know what to do."

Sylvia had already texted Joan three times: The first was a friendly *Hey, what's up?* The second was a slightly more aggressive *You're still coming over, right?* And the third was a toe-tapping *Where are you??? We're waiting to go to the airport until you come. So come.* He hadn't responded to any of them.

They were all standing by the car — Bobby and Jim had arranged and rearranged the suitcases in the tiny trunk, with one squishy bag left over that had to ride on laps in the back. Gemma poked her head out from time to time, as if to check if the

Posts were gone. Every time her lollipop head disappeared back inside, Franny made a horsey noise with her lips, big and wet.

A minute later, a car honked and then pulled into the drive. Joan's BMW. Sylvia rushed over to the driver's side of the car, unable to keep herself from grinning. He shut off the engine and swooped his hair back, making eye contact with Sylvia through the closed car window before opening the door.

"Hola," he said, and kissed her quickly on both cheeks. Joan put a hand on Sylvia's waist for a split second, patted her like an ineffectual airport security guard, and then walked around the car to greet the rest of the family.

"Oh, good! I thought Sylvia was going to have a heart attack," Franny said. She pulled Joan close for a hug. "Ugh, you smell so *good.* Let me find your check, it's in my purse."

Joan shook Bobby's hand, then Jim's. Sylvia stood off to the side, still hovering by Joan's car door. "Hey," she said, and he reluctantly returned to her side. Lowering her voice and turning her body away from her parents, Sylvia said, "You're not taking the check, are you?"

Joan shrugged. "You're right — I should

358

charge extra." He ran a hand through his hair, so casual.

Sylvia laughed. "Is that supposed to be a joke?"

Franny hurried over, waving a check in the air. "Here you go, here you go!"

"Thank you, Franny," Joan said, rolling out her name because he knew she'd enjoy it. He folded the check in half without looking at it and then slipped it into his back pocket. Sylvia was torn between feeling like stabbing him in the genitals and just wanting to stuff cotton in her ears so that she'd never have to hear him speak ever again. Which, of course, she wouldn't.

"Hey, Mom, wait," Sylvia said. Franny and Joan both stopped and looked at her. "Take our picture, okay?"

Sylvia had thought about taking a picture of Joan every day for the last two weeks, but hadn't ever worked up the courage to do it. To take someone's photo, you were acknowledging their importance, saying that you wanted to remember them, that you wanted to look at their face again. She couldn't have asked to take his picture — or just fucking *done* it — without tacitly admitting that she liked him. He knew it, of course — Joan had known from the second he walked into the house, from the second he saw her in those tiny little towels. How could she not? She was a heterosexual human being, and he was made out of Mallorcan clouds and dreams. But it was too late. If she didn't take his picture now, Joan would vanish into the ether, like some made-up Canadian summer-camp boyfriend, whether he'd been sweet and doting or a complete asshole or somewhere in between. No one would believe her. She wished she had taken a picture of him on the beach, his wet bathing suit slung low around his hips, but she hadn't. This would have to do.

"Of course!" Franny said, and started patting herself down, as if she were going to find a camera around her neck. Sylvia thrust her phone at her mother. Franny squinted at the screen, and Sylvia's stomach dropped, but what could she do? She looked plaintively at her brother, who somehow, magically, understood.

"Here, Mom, let me," Bobby said. He aimed the phone at Joan and Sylvia and waited for them to move into position.

"Okay," Sylvia said. She turned her body so that she was facing Joan and gave the phone her profile. Without giving herself a moment to chicken out, she reached up and grabbed Joan's chin and turned his mouth toward her, planting one on him. She kissed him for a moment and then let go, hoping that her brother had thought to take more than one picture. "Okay," she said again. Joan looked slightly stunned, and demurely swiped at his lower lip with his thumb and pointer finger.

"Have a safe flight," he said. He opened his arms to Sylvia, but she just slapped his hand instead.

"Will do." Sylvia crossed her arms over her chest, nodding. She waited for Joan to get into his car and back out of the driveway, which he did.

"Well," Franny said, and then left it at that.

"I'll drive," Bobby said. Jim started to protest, but Franny tugged him with her into the backseat, and he acquiesced. Bobby handed them his duffel bag, which wouldn't fit in the trunk, and they laid it across their laps. Sylvia sat in front. Sometimes love was one-sided. Sometimes love wasn't love at all, but a moment shared on a beach. It stung, sure, but Joan had done her a favor. Sylvia was going home a changed woman. Fuck Katie Saperstein, fuck Gabe Thrush. Fuck everyone. She had gotten exactly what she wanted. Sylvia put on her sunglasses and turned on the radio.

"Rock and roll," she said, apropos of nothing but her own beating heart.

Bobby had to decide at the airport — his flight was booked to Miami, but there was nothing for him there. Franny and Jim thought he should come home to New York for a little while, until he could figure out what to do about the money, what to do about Carmen, where he'd live. Iberia was able to get him a standby ticket to JFK, but the gate area seemed crowded, and Bobby was nervous that there wouldn't be room on the plane. There was nothing to eat in the enormous terminal except ham sandwiches, so they all ate some of those.

"This is actually not bad," Franny said with amazement. Bobby had two.

Sylvia and her parents were all sitting together, their carry-on bags slumped around their calves and on their laps. Sylvia had her nose in a book, and Franny and Jim were sitting quietly, not doing anything but staring into space. Every now and then, Jim would put his arm around Franny and hug her close, and then he'd let go again. Bobby wished he'd brought a book or something. He had movies on his iPad but didn't want to watch them. Carmen had left her self-help bullshit behind, no doubt on purpose, but Bobby had left it at the house.

"I'm going to go look at the magazines," Bobby said, and set off. The terminal was endless, one long hallway of gates with a ceiling several stories tall and a moving sidewalk to get people from one end to the other. He walked into one of the small shops and stood in front of the magazine rack. Most things were in Spanish, but there was a stack of *The New York Times,* and a few magazines, including the British edition of *Gallant,* which he loyally ignored.

Bobby picked up the newspaper, a copy of *Time,* and a mystery novel that he'd heard about. He'd checked his e-mail before they left the house, and he thought that if Carmen had written, then he'd go back to Miami, but she hadn't. And what was the point of going back, if he already knew it was the wrong thing? She'd made it easier on both of them, really. Or at least easier on him. Bobby paid for his stack of stuff, throwing in a pack of gum at the last minute. His bank account was so close to empty that every purchase was paid for with crossed fingers, but this one went through without a delay. New York would be okay for a little while — just until he was back on his feet. He could meet his friends for dinner — maybe just dinner. A few of them would try to set him up, and this time, he wouldn't resist. In New York, twenty-eight was younger than it was in Florida. Only one of his friends had a kid. Bobby looked down at his free hand and realized that it was shaking. He waited for it to stop before rejoining his family. When he sat down, Sylvia looked up from her book and smiled, her face relaxed and content. He was making the right decision, he just knew it.

"Gimme some gum," she said, and so he held out the pack.

Before the plane boarded, Jim took one last walk to stretch his legs. In all of the recent excitement, he'd forgotten to feel nervous about going home. Despite the fact that Franny seemed to be tolerating — even responding to — his touch, his job would still be gone when they got home. He was only sixty. Only sixty! Jim made himself laugh. He remembered when sixty was as old as eighty. His parents had been sixty. Hell, his grandparents had been sixty. And now he was, too, just like that.

Jim did not want to go on cruises, or learn to play golf. He did not want to wake to find that his pants were too short and his neckties were too thin, or too wide. Jim walked as far as he could without having to show his ticket and pass through security again, and turned back. He passed Spanish families with their belongings strewn around them as though they were sitting in cafés, not a care in the world. None of the children were on leashes. The airport was longer than a football field, and Jim had to quicken his pace to make sure he made it back in time to board. Franny was so nervous about small things — her seat would still be there, but if a crowd had formed, bottle-necking the jet bridge, she would be up and fanning herself with her ticket, scanning the masses for his face. That was what Jim wanted — to never make Franny nervous ever again. He walked faster, so that he was almost jogging. The Spaniards around him, a slow-paced people, watched with interest.

Their gate was twenty yards ahead. There was a fairly orderly line already in place, which meant that he had somehow missed the announcement over the loudspeaker. Franny and the kids weren't in the spot where he'd left them, and he craned his neck to see where they'd gone. He walked halfway down the line, as if he needed to get within six inches to recognize his family, when he finally noticed Franny standing by herself off to the side.

"I'm so sorry," Jim said. He swiveled his

body around. "Where are the kids?"

"They're on the plane," she said, and put her hand on his arm.

"Shit, I didn't realize we were boarding so soon." Jim was flustered, doubly so by Franny's unusual calm.

"It's okay," she said. "They won't leave without us."

The line was getting longer, and Franny looped her elbow through Jim's, guiding him gently to the back of the line. His heart was still beating at a rapid pace, and his underarms felt warm and damp. His forehead was slick with sweat. They waited for the line to move, which it did. One by one, the travelers in front of them boarded the plane, tucking their suitcases into the large compartments above their seats. Jim and Franny were among the last to board, but their seats were still there, empty and waiting. Franny settled into her seat and shoved her purse under the seat in front of her. She held her hands in her lap primly while she waited for Jim to sit.

Despite the circumstances, she was delighted to have Bobby coming back to New York with them, her two little ducklings under her roof together for a little while longer. She would have to remember to not baby her son, to treat him like an adult, and to expect adult behavior from him, just like she would have to not ask Sylvia too many questions about what happened with Joan. The human heart was a complex organ at any age. Teenagers were no less impervious to true heartbreak and lust than they were to getting hit by buses. If anything, the odds were dramatically higher.

Bobby's problem was that he'd never had anything he wanted to fight for — Carmen was a comfort to him, a kickstand. Now that she was gone, he was going to have to use his own legs. Franny thought that it was true of all of them, to some extent. Jim would need to find a way to fill his days; Sylvia would have to reinvent herself as a college girl. Bobby would have to learn to be a responsible adult; Franny herself would have to find her own tiny islands and populate them with food and love and words. She would have to forgive her husband without forgetting what he'd done. No — she didn't have to, but she wanted to.

Jim was arranging himself for the long flight — his reading glasses were already on, and he had one book in his lap and another in the seat pocket in front of them. There would be a folded-up crossword puzzle somewhere, and a pen. The skin around his eye was now a pale shade of green, the color of a peridot, his birthstone. It got lighter every day, and soon would be gone entirely.

The engines rumbled and the plane began to glide forward on the runway. The people with the orange vests and pointers had all backed safely away, on to their next departure. Franny wove her fingers through Jim's, and held the entire knot in her lap. He leaned forward to stare out the window at the receding airport and the well-tended expanse of the runway. There were mountains on their left, and he pointed to them. The airplane turned onto the straightaway, and the noise from its body increased. As they began to pick up speed, Franny closed her eyes and rested her cheek on Jim's shoulder. She felt it in her stomach when the wheels left the ground, the sudden suspension of disbelief that this, too, would work just as it should. She lifted her chin so that it was closer to her husband's ear, and over the roaring of the plane, Franny said, "We made it, Jim." There was nothing in life harder or more important than agreeing every morning to stay the course, to go back to your forgotten self of so many years ago, and to make the same decision. Marriages, like ships, needed steering, and steady hands at the wheel. Franny wrapped both of her arms around Jim's right one, her grip firm and ready for any turbulence ahead.

ACKNOWLEDGMENTS

Thank you to Valli Shaio Kohon and Gregorio Kohon for their Mallorcan generosity, and to Olga Ortiz for her Mallorcan brain. Thank you to the Hotel Gran Son Net in Puigpunyent for heating their bathroom floors.

Thank you to Rumaan Alam, Maggie Delgado, Ben Turley, Lorrie Moore, Meg Wolitzer, and Stephin Merritt for their help with language and logistics. Thank you to Christine Onorati and WORD, Mary Gannett and BookCourt, Julia Fierro and the Sackett Street Writers' Workshop, Noreen Tomassi and the Center for Fiction, the 92nd Street Y, Vanderbilt University, and *Rookie* for their love and employment.

Thank you to Jenni Ferrari-Adler, Stuart Nadler, and my darling husband for being such smart readers. Thank you to my family: the Straubs, the Royals, and the small but mighty Fusco-Straubs.

Thank you, as always, to everyone at Riverhead Books, especially the indomitable Megan Lynch, Geoff Kloske, Claire McGinnis, Ali Cardia, and Jynne Martin.

And thank you most of all to my son, the patient traveler, for waiting until I was done to be born.